Revenge

Revenge

A Tale of Old Jamaica

H.G. de Lisser

MINT EDITIONS

Revenge: A Tale of Old Jamaica was first published in 1919.

This edition published by Mint Editions 2021.

ISBN 9781513297057 | E-ISBN 9781513298559

Published by Mint Editions®

MINT
EDITIONS

minteditionbooks.com

Publishing Director: Jennifer Newens
Design & Production: Rachel Lopez Metzger
Project Manager: Micaela Clark
Typesetting: Westchester Publishing Services

This tale of the most stirring, poignant
period of our Island's Story,
I dedicate to my most Candid Critic,

My Wife

Contents

BOOK I

I

The Mountain Fire

Seated on a low verandah which ran completely round the large single-storey house of brick and wood, four persons were gazing in silence towards a range of mountains some eight or ten miles away.

Two of them, Mr. Carlton and his wife, were elderly; the others were Mr. Carlton's son and niece. The young man was about twenty-seven years of age, tall, well-set-up, with a frank, humorous, sunburnt face and kindly eyes. He featured his father, but his face showed a stronger, more determined character. The girl who sat beside him was of slender figure and moderate height; a blonde with delicate, aquiline features, sparkling light-blue eyes, and a proudly-held little head crowned with a glory of pale golden hair. These two had been talking of "home" a little while before, meaning England thereby, though Dick Carlton was Jamaica-born. Then the conversation had lulled, the attention of the group being attracted to the mountains beyond.

Black but distinct the huge piles loomed, their summits silhouetted against a sky all sable and quivering gold. And on the crests and slopes of some of these mountains fierce fires were blazing, each one a glaring tongue of flame that licked viciously upwards as if hungry for destruction.

It was about eight o'clock. The day bad faded swiftly into night, the darkness having fallen immediately after the setting of the sun. By seven the sky was blazing with innumerable stars and the Milky Way was a shining track of light. It was a typical West Indian night, serene and still and beautiful exceedingly; a night when the darkness of the earth seemed designed as a setting to the wonderful brilliance above.

"This is the worst drought I have ever known," said Mr. Carlton at length, breaking the silence. "Those fires show how severe it has been." There was a note of sadness in his voice, which his niece's quick ear detected.

"Are the fires very dangerous?" she asked: "all the mountains seem to be burning."

"Not very," her cousin answered lightly; "they are farther from one another than they appear to be from here, and I don't think there are any villages or houses near them."

"We have been expecting you every winter for the last three years," he continued after a brief pause; "you were always coming, yet only now you have come."

"I would have come two years ago," the girl replied, "but mother—"

"God bless my soul!" exclaimed Mr. Carlton.

They turned towards him quickly: he was bending forward and looking with a puzzled expression at the distant fires. "What is it?" asked his wife.

"I may be mistaken;" he said slowly, "but, do you know, I fancy some of those fires have started since we came out on the verandah."

"I am sure you are right," said Mrs. Carlton. "That blaze to the left was not there half an hour ago."

Dick was now staring at the fires as earnestly as his father. Joyce observed his anxious attitude. "What is the matter?" she asked softly. "Is the wind blowing the sparks about?"

"That is not it," replied Dick slowly; "the wind would not be strong enough to carry embers so far."

"Then if it is not the wind—"

"Look!" cried Mrs. Carlton, and pointed north-eastward as she spoke. Their eyes followed the direction of her uplifted hand.

A tiny point of light, looking no bigger than one of the great stars that shone serenely overhead, glimmered on the summit of a mountain which had up to then been shrouded in darkness.

"It almost looks like a star," Joyce murmured; "they seem in this country to rest upon the hills."

"But this particular star is growing bigger," said Dick, and even as he spoke a tiny tongue of flame flickered upwards.

"Dick," said his father positively, "some of those fires are being set. It can't be anybody clearing land in this dry weather?"

"No, dad, they wouldn't clear land in a drought." Dick hesitated a moment, then made up his mind to speak:

"I believe those fires are a call to righteousness."

"What?" asked his mother astonished.

Dick turned to his cousin.

"You must expect to hear some queer things in this queer country of ours," he said to her apologetically. "Similar fires have been seen elsewhere of late. Only this morning, before I left Aspley for Kingston, my overseer told me that the people in St. Thomas were talking about a great religious revival. They believe that the drought is a sign of God's displeasure, and that they are called upon to purge the wickedness out of the land. Some of those fires are lighted as a warning to the unrepentant."

Mr. Carlton laughed, but his wife did not seem to see anything humorous in her son's explanation. "Those fires are not only warnings," she said bitterly; "they are signals. And we are the 'wickedness' to be purged out of the land. Haven't you noticed the change that has come over the people of late?—I have spoken of it before. But only now have they begun to set fires and plan revivals, making the drought an excuse."

"Nonsense, mother, you mustn't let yourself be worried by idle rumours," said Dick quickly. "If we are 'the wickedness' we'll take a lot of purging." He turned to his cousin: "too tired to take a walk in the garden, Joyce?"

"No," she said, "I should like it," and throwing a light shawl over her head and shoulders she went down the steps and into the garden with him.

On either side of the path that led to the main entrance of the penn grew crotons and coliases and elder-flower, which in the daytime made a brave show of varigated colour. Beyond the limits of this carefully tended plot of earth the long guinea grass grew, and huge, heavy-foliaged, wide-spreading trees which created oases of shade even when the day was at its hottest. Fruit trees abounded in this property; mangoes and limes and grapefruit; shaddock, guavas, starapple and orange; and tonight the perfume of orange blossoms filled the air and was carried far away by the cool breezes which came stealing gently downwards from the hills.

"Let me give you a hint," said Dick, as they strolled out of hearing. "Our people are just now passing through one of their periodical fits of depression, and you will probably hear them expressing fears of negro uprisings and all that sort of thing—you heard mother tonight. I am quite used to it, but you are not, and you may be frightened. Don't allow yourself to be. The danger is purely imaginary."

"I have heard a lot of such talk before," said Joyce. "I was saying that I would have come out to Jamaica two years ago, but mother changed her mind almost at the last moment."

"Yes?"

"That was because she became afraid; she has never quite recovered from her experience here as a girl. She insists that she and Aunt Charlotte were very nearly murdered by the negroes."

"She does not exaggerate," said Dick grimly; "but that was thirty-five years ago."

"Mother really did not want me to come But I had so often promised Aunt Charlotte to come out that I simply had to. Father said my visit could no longer be postponed."

"And that is the only reason why you came?"

"Well," she replied coquetishly, "there is Aspley, our estate, you know."

"And what about your promise, that some day you would come to Jamaica, and that when next we met you would answer my question? That had nothing to do with your coming?"

"I was a mere chit of a girl when I said that," she laughed, "and you were only a boy."

"I was twenty-two. In the intervening five years I have not changed. Have you?"

"Perhaps I am as uncertain as ever," she said gently. "I don't know. But I am here, with you. Dick." She paused for a moment. "I cannot answer now," she pleaded, "don't press me."

The orange blossoms filled the air with their delicate perfume, and the stars filled the heavens with light. Beyond them the darkness wrapped the earth as with a shroud, and hung a veil of mystery between them and the world. Far away, like giant sentinels, towered the solemn mountains, and through the tropical night the lurid fires blazed. But they saw nothing save one another just then, were conscious of themselves alone. He made no comment on her last words; indefinite as they were. She was with him, as she said, and that for the present was enough.

Suddenly, shrilly piercing the silence, came the measured beat of a chant. It intensified the brooding silence, added a touch of weirdness to the wonder of the night.

"A revival meeting in the neighbourhood." Dick explained. "It begins at ten o'clock precisely and sometimes lasts all through the night. It is growing late. I suppose we must go in now."

They returned to the verandah. Mrs. Carlton, thinking that Joyce must be tired, offered to accompany her to her room.

"When are you going to Aspley, mother?" asked Dick, as he bade them goodnight. "I shall have to set off early tomorrow morning, I regret to say."

"Saturday," replied Mrs. Carlton; "we can hardly leave Denbigh sooner."

"Good-bye until Saturday, then," said Dick, and joined his father for a talk and a cigar.

JOYCE'S BEDROOM WAS ON THE left wing of the house, and, like the drawing room, faced towards the north. It contained a huge mahogany bed, large enough to accommodate four persons at a pinch, and enveloped by a fine mosquito net that hung from a hook screwed into the ceiling. The rest of the furniture was in keeping with the bed; it was all of solid make and exquisitely polished. The room itself was large and airy; straw mats were spread upon the floor, and on the dressing table two lovely bunches of flowers set in China vases gave forth a pleasant odour.

Joyce was tired, but too excited to sleep. Only that morning she had arrived. For three weeks she had been on the sea, cramped in a narrow cabin at nights, and almost as confined during the weary days of the tedious passage. That had been an awful time; but she was here at last, and Dick was here. . . She walked to an open window; once again her eyes rested on the mountains. Swiftly the current of her thoughts altered. Were those really signals, as her aunt believed, beacons set up by negro fanatics as a call to their own people to purge something out of the land, and that thing her own race and class? She listened to the singing: now it was louder, shriller than before, and rose and fell, and rose again, with intervals of intense silence and crescendoes of weird, ear-piercing screams. In spite of her cousin's warning, she wondered: was there a threat in it?

She turned from the window and called the maid who stood patiently waiting by the door.

"What is your name?" she asked the girl kindly.

"Maria, ma'am. Gwine to bed now, ma'am?" the girl enquired.

"Yes, I think so; I won't keep you long, Maria."

She undressed quickly and got into bed, Maria searching diligently to see if any mosquito had hidden itself within the net. Finding none, she closed the net, pulled down the sashes of the windows, leaving the upper parts open, then put the candles out.

"Good night, Miss Joyce," she softly called out as she was shutting the heavy door.

"Good night, Maria," Joyce answered.

It was long before she slept. She was thinking: thinking of Dick, of how he looked, of what he had said that night. He had made love to her when he was last in England: she was hardly more than a schoolgirl then. She had listened to him half-frightened, wholly delighted. They were five years older now, and he still cared; his voice told her so; more, her heart told her so. So she lay there, thinking of him, painting in her mind, half-consciously, an idyllic picture of her stay in this beautiful tropical land. . .

And rising and falling in monotonous cadence the distant singing came to her, swelling at long and measured intervals into a shrill, menacing scream.

II

SOME NEW ACQUAINTANCES

A negro lad, holding by the bridle a saddled horse, stood at the foot of a broad flight of stone steps which led up to a flagstone platform upon which opened a pair of heavy mahogany doors.

The building in front of which the horse and lad were waiting was of a type common to the larger West Indian properties at that time; it was two storeys high, oblong in form, with solid stone walls and plentifully supplied with windows. The windows of the lower storey were barred with iron and secured by heavy wooden shutters, those on the upper storey were of glass. But these too were protected by wooden shutters, so that the house, when closed, was not unlike a barracks erected for strictly utilitarian purposes.

But if Aspley Great House had no architectural pretensions, the view it commanded was pleasing, and even beautiful. Built upon rising ground, it commanded an extensive range of country. From any of the upper windows of its facade you saw, to your left, at some distance down below, the estate's boiling house where the canes of the estate were turned into golden grains of sugar, the trash house where the refuse of the expressed cane was stored, the rum distillery, the cane mill, and the long range of buildings where the sugar and rum were kept. On the opposite hand, a few hundred yards away, was a settlement of neat little structures where some of the estate workers lived. These cottages were of wood, thatched with straw and palm, and stood amidst clusters of banana and breadfruit trees.

A sparkling river flowed through the property, and this supplied the power by which the mill was driven. You saw it distinctly from the house as it flashed back the rays of the sun, you saw it as it gleamed dark at night under a starry sky or glimmered in the soft radiance of the moonlight. Between low banks it ran, and except in flood weather it could easily be forded on foot. Farther on it joined and was lost in a larger river which went rolling to the sea.

The ground upon which Aspley Estate stood undulated upwards to north, east, and west, then gradually swelled into low hills behind which rose range after range of towering mountains. To the south it sloped gently downwards. In that direction was the nearest town, called Morant Bay, which looked out upon the sea.

The whole landscape was shining now in the light of the ascending sun. The pale clouds of the dawn had melted away; the blue of the sky was deepening as the great golden orb grew more fiercely bright and seemed to throb and quiver with its own excessive heat. The young groom waiting at the foot of the steps threw an impatient glance upwards, then looked at the sun. "Missis is late," he muttered, but at that moment a slender girlish figure appeared on the platform above, and ran lightly down the steps.

"De sun is up already, Miss Joyce." he said in a semi-reproachful tone. He was Joyce's groom and special male attendant, and, with the freedom of West Indian servants, he had already elected himself to the position of guardian angel of his mistress.

"Yes, that's a pity, Charles," she answered, "but it doesn't much matter."

He held the stirrup for her to mount and she sprang into the saddle. He was hurrying off for his own horse when she dashed his hopes with—

"I think I'll ride alone this morning, Charles," and cantered off.

Merrily she rode down the long path leading from the Great House to the gate, and then out upon the open road. Joyce loved these rides. At first her cousin had accompanied her; then, because his duties on the estate began early in the morning, she had insisted that Charles would serve very well to show her the way about. She thought she knew the countryside sufficiently now to dispense with an attendant. Charles, it must be confessed, was an extremely locquacious guide. And there were times when she revelled in the long silences of the Jamaica landscape, which were marred and profaned by the jabbering of her groom. This morning she had decided to ride alone.

She was enchanted with the country. She loved to watch the sun rise over the eastern hills and to hear the cries of the birds and the hum and buzzing of insects as they rejoiced in the dawning of the day. The sense as of a new beginning of all things, a reawakening of life—this never failed to delight her: it was one of the charms of this strange land. But how evanescent! A hour ago this charm was there, now it was already fading away, was almost gone, and already the languorous spirit of the tropical day was insidiously spreading its influence over earth and sky. The birds were falling to silence; only the black vultures soared overhead in ever widening circles and with scarcely perceptible motion of their

H.G. DE LISSER

huge wings. Her horse slowed down to a walk, and she let him go at that pace. She also was affected by the dreamy langour which seemed to be nature's own mood in these regions.

How still it was. A whispering sound went sometimes through the trees that bordered the road, but it only intensified the silence. No human voice was heard, no living creature seen; the fields when she passed them looked burnt, withered, deserted; the sky was brilliant, but distant, hard, inscrutable; the sky of a drought-stricken country. The earth seemed asleep, lazily, torpidly asleep. One felt inclined to muse, to dream, to drift placidly, taking no thought as to whither one went. . .

She pulled up suddenly. Deep in reverie, she had taken a bye-path which she thought must be the one pointed out to her a couple of days before as leading to a village whose queer name had caused her to express a desire to see it. She had been riding slowly along this path for some ten minutes; now she heard a clamour of voices, a sound as of angrily protesting people. Was she close to the village? A motion of her arm, and the horse walked on.

The path ended abruptly on a large open space of land, part of an estate as she saw at a glance. There was a low range of wooden buildings a little farther on; before this stood a crowd of peasants, with one white man in their midst browbeating them. As she caught sight of the group, the white man's voice rang out threateningly—

"Come now! Stop that damned noise at once, you worthless nigger, or out you go!"

A woman's voice answered: "If John Roberts is a damn nigger, you is a bumptious white man," and there was a shout of approbation from the crowd.

The man thus addressed wheeled suddenly to single out the speaker; at that moment he caught sight of Joyce, who had sharply checked her horse, surprised. He waved the crowd contemptuously aside and approached her. The peasants drew nearer, following him, and whispering among themselves.

"I am sorry," Joyce began quickly. "I must have missed my way. Pray don't let me disturb you."

"You are welcome, Miss Graham"—he knew her at sight, though she was certain she had never seen him before. "This is Cranebrook. My name is Solway; Mr. Burton is my uncle. You have heard of him, perhaps?"

"Yes; but you are busy, Mr. Solway; I mustn't interrupt you. I was going to a village about here; Jigger-foot Market is the name, I believe. I can find it if you will tell me the way," she replied quickly.

"You are not likely to find it by yourself; I must send one of these niggers with you. Here, Roberts," he called out peremptorily to an angry-looking man in the crowd. "You live at Jigger-foot Market. Take this lady there!"

"Take the lady you'self," replied the man defiantly, encouraged by the sympathetic crowd surrounding him. Then he modified his attitude, as Solway opened his eyes at him in speechless astonishment. "I will go wid the lady when you pay me my money," he muttered.

"Oh, will you?" snarled Mr. Solway, and Joyce was startled by the anger in his face and voice.

"No, please," she protested hurriedly; "I really need no guide. Perhaps I wont go today. It's all right, thanks, I'll—"

"But you shall go, for you want to go," cried Mr. Solway, cutting her short. "And if that man doesn't obey, he need never hope for work on this estate again. A good whipping is what he wants badly." Joyce noticed that Mr. Solway held a heavy riding whip in his hand.

Roberts hesitated, knowing well the nature of the man he had to deal with. The crowd murmured and looked ugly: one or two women laughed rudely, with an insolent stare at the girl on the horse. The peasants numbered some thirty persons; they appeared, in Joyce's eyes, distinctly dangerous. But the white man glared at them with contempt, and Joyce felt that only her presence saved John Roberts from a thrashing on the spot. She was again about to urge that she needed no one's service when a girl among the people spoke.

"I will show you the way, Miss Graham," said this girl pleasantly. "I am going to Jigger-foot Market meself, so it's no trouble," she added, seeing that Joyce was about to refuse her offer.

"I am goin' that way too," said a short, thickset, black man with a bloodhound cast of countenance, who had been standing a little apart from the people, listening to their complaints with an amused look on his face. "I will walk along with you, Rachael."

"It don't necessary, Mr. Raines," the young woman answered curtly. "I prefer to go my own way, an' I offer to show the lady the way first."

"I am supposed to show the lady," replied the man quickly; "I am a Maroon."

"Whatever you are makes no difference to me;" replied the other tartly; "I am Rachael Bogle, an' I can find me own way. However, the lady can say which one of us she prefer to show her Jigger-foot Market, for if you going, I am not."

"Thanks very much," said Joyce to the man, "but I will not trouble you."

She held out her hand to Solway, who was now standing by her horse. "I am sorry I mistook my way," she said, "But I wont interrupt any longer."

"You are always welcome to Crane-brook," he answered heartily. "Indeed, I should like to ride with you to Jigger-foot Market myself: you can never trust a nigger. If you will allow me?—"

"I couldn't hear of it." She spoke firmly: Mr. Solway was looking up into her face; his manner was a trifle overbold. "Good morning," she said.

"We shall meet again, shortly," he answered. "We—my uncle and I—would have called at Aspley days ago, but he went off on business to Kingston the day after you arrived."

"I shall be very glad to see you both," she said, and turned her horse's head towards the path.

Mr. Burton she had heard of from her mother; he was an old friend of her family. He had been spoken of more than once by Mrs. Carlton since they had come to Aspley. But Solway's name had not been mentioned: Joyce remembered that now.

The young woman who was to guide her to Jigger-foot Market had already started down the path. When they came out upon the high road she slackened her pace till she was abreast of Joyce. The latter glanced down at her, observing her now more closely than before.

She seemed about twenty-two years of age, and, for all her dark complexion, was comely enough, Joyce thought.

Her nose, though slightly platerine, was not badly formed, her large black eyes danced merrily as she walked along. She looked a strong young woman physically, and healthy; her voice, when she was protesting against Raines' decision to go with her to Jigger-foot Market, had taken on a ring of determination that showed she was strong in character also. Joyce noticed, further, that Rachael's chin did not retreat, and that her lips, though full, had no unpleasant thickness about them.

Her head was wrapped in a gaudy turban, she wore shoes—which none of the labouring women did—and her clothes were neat and clean.

"She isn't an ordinary peasant girl," thought Joyce, "I wonder what she can be."

She noticed that the girl was closely observing her, and began to think of saying something to her. She asked, after riding on for some time in silence, during which they had taken another bye-path: "Is Jigger-foot Market very far from here?"

"That is Jigger-foot Market, Miss Graham," Rachael replied, pointing to a collection of huts not far from where they were.

"Already! And do you live there?"

"No; I live at Stony Gut with me father. He send me here with a message this morning, an' I only call at Cranebrook to see somebody I know there. I see you riding about very frequent, Miss Graham, these two weeks now."

"My name seems to be known very well in this neighbourhood," Joyce responded, smiling.

"Oh; my father know whoever come here," said Rachael proudly: "he is Paul Bogle. It will be hot for you to ride back, Miss Graham."

They were now on the outskirts of the village, and already some curious persons, idlers evidently, had come out of their huts to stare at the strange young white lady whose name they guessed, for they had heard of her coming to Aspley. "You going into the village, Miss Graham?" Rachael asked.

"No," said Joyce, "I don't think I can remain out any longer this morning; I must come back another day. I should like to see your village too, Rachael, and if you ever come to Aspley you must remember to ask for me."

"I come to Aspley frequently," the girl replied, showing two even rows of strong white teeth as she smiled.

"Very good; I am certain to see you, then. Now don't forget to ask for me, and goodbye for the present."

Joyce glanced at the people who were staring at her, then, turning her back on the village, rode briskly away. Rachael gazed at her until the graceful figure in the grey riding habit was out of sight. A wistful look came into the girl's eyes when Joyce was finally lost from view.

"I wish I was white like her," she murmured; "if I was only white like her!"

III

RACHAEL AND RAINES

Rachael turned after Joyce had disappeared, and walked rapidly on towards a hut which was situated at the farther side of the village. Arrived at her goal, she entered the hut without rapping, and was greeted by an old woman, black, wrinkled, hideously ugly, who peered at her with bleared eyes, and, recognising her, bade her sit down upon a box that was placed before a table. The hut was a scene of squalor, and its occupant apparently miserably poor. Clothed in rags, evil eyed, her grey locks plaited into little carrot-shaped tufts that stuck out at different angles, her hands restless and bony and reminding one of the talons of some wild bird, the woman looked like the witch of popular imagination.

She blinked up at Rachael, offering the girl a claw-like hand.

"What bring you here today, me daughter?" she asked briefly. Rachael explained.

Her father intended holding a great religious meeting at his village some weeks hence; the date was not yet fixed. He wished the old woman to be present; she had the Spirit of the Lord, Who would probably speak through her mouth. She and Paul Bogle were old friends, and he was depending on her. He would send for her when he was ready.

"A big revival?" muttered the crone, peering into Rachael's face. "But you don't believe in de Spirit, me daughter?"

"I don't know, Mother Bicknell," answered Rachael hesitatingly.

"You doan't know; you go to school and you believe everybody who can't read and write is foolish. But you will live and learn! 'Tell you' father him can send for me when him ready."

"You will dance and prophesy?" Rachael asked her, remembering her father's insistence on this point.

"Yes," answered the old woman, "I know what Paul Bogle want to hear!"

Rachael, glad to escape out of the presence of the woman, hastened into the sunlight once more. She sauntered towards a cluster of huts, where some peasants stood waiting to receive her. They welcomed her with demonstrations of pleasure.

The miserable huts which constituted Jigger-foot Market were counterparts of those to be seen in hundreds of other negro villages all over the country. Poverty stood confessed, the trees were dry, the children were wretched and meager, and men and women loafed about in every attitude of sloth and indifference, as though hope and ambition were strangers to their hearts.

"What make you come up here, Miss Rachael?" asked a young woman of Rachael as she neared the group.

"Some business. Me father is having a big meeting, and he want Mother Bicknell to come. He says that I to tell everybody up here, so that them can all come if they want. It is going to last all night. How is George?"

"Come inside an' see how him is," said the young woman, leading the way as she spoke. She entered one of the huts, and there, on a mat spread upon the bare ground, a young man lay in the last stages of consumption. His emaciated frame was covered with an old sugar bag ripped open, his eyes shone large in their sunken sockets; even the inexperienced could see that death could not now be long delayed.

The hut contained two tiny rooms; it had no other furniture besides a table, an old chair and a bench. Mats rolled up in a corner showed how the family slept at nights. The windows of the hut were closed; but little fresh air found its way into the germ-laden sty occupied by five persons besides the dying-man. These breathed the breath he exhaled and pigged it along with him as a simple matter of course.

Rachael had known George a long time, had heard he was dying, and wished to see him once again. He was too weak to talk: she glanced at him, then went outside after lingering a moment or two.

"You don't get a doctor for him?" she asked the dying lad's sister.

"No. De doctor wouldn't come up so far widout we pay him a couple o' pounds, an' we don't have a shillin'. If you doan't have no money, you must dead when you sick; it can't be helped." The young woman dismissed the subject as having been exhausted. "Who was de lady you come wid?" she asked; "Miss Graham?"

"Yes."

"I wouldn't show any white people de way" was the comment, "for them not putting themself out of them way to do anyt'ing for black people. Them only take advantage of us, as you father always say. If I was you, I wouldn't do anyt'ing for them.

"I would make her lost her way," said a man with a loud laugh; "no one is better than anoder. If we live or we dead them doan't care. All them do when we sick is to rejice."

"Not all," answered Rachael quickly. "Young Mr. Carlton is very kind; everybody say so."

A slight frown knitted her brows as she made this remark. Rapidly approaching was the man whose company to the village she had refused not two hours before. She tossed her head and turned her back upon him as he came up. He did not appear disconcerted.

"You wouldn't let me walk up with you, Rachael, but you see I find me way up by meself," he said, when near enough. "I don't know what is the matter with you, why you going on like this. Don't I am your father's friend?"

"Not all me father's friend is my friend," Rachael answered him over her shoulder; "an' I tell you all times not to follow me up, for I don't like it. I am not havin' anything to do with you, for I don't want to be friendly with no Maroon."

"Hi! she proud!" exclaimed some of the women, regarding Rachael with astonishment and the man Raines with respect. "Hear how she talk!"

"I talk like that all the time," Rachael volleyed back, tossing her head. "An' since Mr. Raines come, I am going. Goodbye all. Remember the meeting."

They bade her good-bye as she moved off; Raines watched her for a few seconds, then leisurely followed. She knew he was behind her, but took no notice of him. When they had passed out of the village and were upon the road, he quickened his pace and came up with her.

They walked along in silence for some time, and then he spoke.

"I don't understand why you going on like this; I am not rude to you; I talk straight to you, an' yet you insult me. You don't 'fraid that some day I lose me temper?"

Rachael's eyes flashed.

"Who 'fraid for temper?' she called out to him. "You think I afraid of you? Let me tell you, me good man, that, Maroon or no Maroon, the day you ever do me anything I will take you to the court house. You needn't threaten me, for you can't frighten me. This is not Maroon country, it is Queen Victoria country, an' it is the white people that have the law, not you."

"An' you think white people care for you more than for me?" he asked her scoffingly. "They know I am a Maroon, an' they bound to treat me well. Who are you? Paul Bogle's daughter? What them care about him an' you?"

She laughed scornfully as she replied.

"The day you ever do me anyt'ing, I will tell Mr. Carlton at Aspley, an' I know him won't let you take an advantage of me. Him is not a Maroon; he is better. He is a white man."

"Ho, ho!" growled Raines. "I see how it is. That is why I hear you always goin' to Aspley now. You want a white man, an' think you can talk to a Maroon as you like, because I am black? Well, let me tell you that the day I ever hear you have anything to do with Carlton, that day will be a bad day for you and him. Mark my word, for I am not a man making fun."

His voice rang high and threatening, the whites of his eyeballs had become bloodshot with rage. Rachael merely laughed.

"An' what can Carlton do for you?" he asked her. "What you think him can do for you?"

"What you want to do for me?" she demanded in return. "You want me to come to you, and that is all. You don't say you want to married me, an' if you did say it I wouldn't believe you, an' if I did believe you I would have nothing to do wid you all the same. You want to make a fool of me for a time, an' when you tired you would send me back to me father. You must be mad! An' who you calling 'Carlton'? If him was here, you think you could call him by his name as you please? You would be so frighten that the word wouldn't come out of you' mouth. You have courage now because you is behind his back, but you not better than everybody else, an' you wouldn't forget you'self to talk impertinence before him."

"Say that again if you dare!" Raines howled at her. She guessed the thought in his mind.

"If you attempt to knock me I will bawl out," she threatened, "an' you know there is plenty of people to hear. I not afraid of you, me good man; just understand that.

"And if I choose to talk to Mr. Carlton," she continued defiantly, "I will talk to him, an' you can't prevent me. Me father is the only man that can say anything to me about what I do, an' even him can't go too far, for I can work for me self. I am a big woman now, an' I can read and write; nobody can do what they like with me. I will go to Aspley when I choose; I tell you that at once."

Breathing hard, she marched swiftly along, and Raines kept pace with her. He was fiercely angry, but even in his anger he realized that

H.G. DE LISSER

there was nothing to be gained by continuing the quarrel. The girl had said enough to put him on a track which he might be able to follow with advantage. At the next bye-path they reached, he halted and said:

"All right, Rachael; I hear what you say, an' you hear what I say, an' I mean it. I give you fair warning."

He plunged into the track as he spoke, and she, already some distance ahead, deigned no reply. Under the burning sun, but walking as if not affected by or feeling the heat, she trudged on to Stony Gut.

IV

Mr. Solway Calls

Visitors, Joyce," said Mrs. Carlton. From a window looking towards the path to Aspley's gate she had caught sight of two horsemen riding up to the house. "Mr. Burton and his nephew," she continued, recognizing them. "I suppose they will stay to dinner."

The two gentlemen were met by Dick, who conducted them to the drawing-room where his mother and Joyce were waiting. Mr. Burton, a bluff, good-natured-looking man, with a round bewhiskered face and hearty voice, did not wait to be introduced to Joyce. He rushed up to her, shook hands enthusiastically, and declared that she was the very image of her mother. "Whom I knew well in the old days," he cried; "did she ever tell you about me?"

Joyce took to the old man at once, assured him that often and often she had heard of him. Solway claimed a previous acquaintanceship; he explained that his uncle had returned to Cranebrook only that morning, and that both of them had hurried to pay their respects at Aspley. He spoke with some restraint, Joyce noticing at once that though he had been greeted politely there was no such cordiality evinced towards him as was shown to his uncle. She guessed shrewdly that Solway would not have come to Aspley unaccompanied by Mr. Burton.

Yet he was rather a striking-looking man. About thirty years of age, he was as tall as Dick, more sunburnt, and with distinctly strong, handsome, prominent features. He possessed keen, staring, insolent eyes; the mouth hard and conveying a suggestion of coarseness. His manner was quick and direct; passionate. You gathered from it that he was more in the habit of commanding labourers than of conversing with ladies.

Dinner was almost immediately announced; at Aspley they dined at seven, and Mr. Burton, with planter freedom, mentioned at once that he had ridden over to dine with his friends. "It is very rarely that we see you at Aspley," remarked Mrs. Carlton as they sat down to dinner. She addressed Mr. Solway, Dick being engaged in bestowing his attention on the other guest. (Dick, Joyce remarked, seemed only to speak to Mr. Solway when politeness compelled him to do so.)

"I couldn't let the opportunity pass without riding over to see your niece," said Solway bluntly. "Inadvertently she she paid us a call the other day."

"It wasn't a call," laughed Joyce; "it was a trespass."

"It was not a trespass," said Mr. Burton heartily, "it was a misfortune. I mean, it was a misfortune that I wasn't at Crane brook, and that John could not take you to Jigger-foot Market himself. You met with a rather inhospitable reception at our estate."

"I wanted to ride with Miss Graham to the village," said his nephew, "but she wouldn't hear of it. I did not press her; she was quite determined. Weren't you?" he asked, addressing Joyce.

"Quite," she answered. "You would have had to leave your business for my idle pleasure."

"Was that your only objection?" he laughed. "You spoke so decisively at the moment that I thought you did not want poor me to accompany you. In future, Miss Graham, let me assure you that I shall be delighted to make your pleasure my business." He saw her flush suddenly and at once perceived that he had spoken too boldly. "Any planter in St. Thomas will gladly say the same thing," he added quickly; "and we'll all mean it."

Mr. Solway observed that Dick's face was clouded. A twitch of his mouth expressed something not unlike contempt for his host. He still addressed himself directly to Joyce.

"You may be interested to know that I had that nigger, Roberts, kicked out of the property soon after you left. That's the man who refused to show you the way to Jigger-foot Market."

"You discharged him?" asked Joyce with a faint note of displeasure in her voice. She was not pleased to learn that she had been the cause of a man's dismissal.

"Naturally; what else could he expect? Thirty years ago he might have been flogged within an inch of his life."

"Thirty years ago is not today," Dick broke in quietly. "Thirty years ago we owned these people, and lived in dread of our throats being cut."

"They would like to cut our throats now," returned Solway, "but that pleasant desire of theirs causes me no dread I know how to handle niggers."

"You don't believe in being kind to them?" enquired Joyce. Her glance, as she spoke, was cold.

"Kindness is too often merely a mistake" Solway answered. "This Roberts is an impudent fellow; he was quarrelling about his pay before you rode in; I had stopped his money for a misdemeanour. Then he was distinctly rude to you. Now I shall take good care that he does not get another situation in this district."

"It is a pity the fellow behaved badly," said Mr. Burton apologetically; "I believe he has a son ill at his village; dying most probably, for these people never take proper care of themselves. He asked me the other day to lend him some money to get a doctor."

"Yes," said his nephew grimly, "and had it not been for me you would have lent it. It is like this, Miss Graham: when a nigger borrows money he has made up his mind to decamp. It is his way of giving legal notice. My uncle knows it, but is soft-hearted; so he is often imposed upon. Roberts would probably have left us, even if I had not sent him about his business."

"But it is quite true that his son in ill at Jigger-foot Market," said Dick.

"Is it?" asked Solway indifferently. His manner showed that the matter did not interest him.

"Yes," continued Dick, "and I am thinking that it might be wise for those of us who are planters to show some sympathy now and then with these negroes. They are no longer slaves. Harm might come of our forgetting that."

"Harm? What harm? You are not afraid of them, are you?"

The question sounded commonplace enough; but the stare of Solway's eyes indicated contempt for the courage of the other man. Dick understood. Between him and Solway there had always existed a deep-rooted dislike based upon a fundamental antagonism of character. Wherever these two men might have happened to meet there would have been something not unlike hatred between them. They might honestly have tried to be friendly; the result would have been the same. If there are natural affinities there are also natural repulsions.

Dick ignored Mr. Solway's question. He was not going to protest his courage. Joyce who had not noticed anything between the two men, spoke again.

"What troubles me," she said, "is that I am the cause of this man's losing his situation. . . there's his sick son."

"One dead nigger more or less will not make much difference in this country," said Solway frankly. "You must forgive me if I say now what you will say a year hence if, as I hope, you are still amongst us then. But I'll tell you what I'll do. It isn't customary here for us to take back a nigger after we have dismissed him; it makes him cheeky. But if you'd like me to take him back; just say the word. I'll gladly do it—if it will please you."

Joyce was pleased. The compliment was not delicately put, but Mr. Solway did not pretend to delicacy. On the other hand he was offering to break what was evidently a sort of planter's unwritten law, merely because she had expressed sympathy for Roberts and his son. She was about to thank him when Dick spoke: spoke smoothly and calmly, but quite deliberately.

"It would be a pity, wouldn't it be, for you to break your rule in this instance?" he asked Solway. "If you restored the man on the ground of justice, that would be only fair. But why as a favour? Roberts refused to do something that was distinctly not his duty. It seems that his case has a right to be considered on its merits."

"I did not say anything about a favour," returned Solway a trifle sharply. "If I take back the man to please Miss Graham the obligation will be entirely on my part. And I can hardly think that a nigger's refusal to show your cousin the way to his own village is a good reason for my considering that I ought not to have punished him, or that I ought to reinstate him on grounds of abstract justice. I am afraid I fall below your high standard of conduct in such matters."

There was a jarring note in his voice. Mr. Burton looked troubled. Mrs. Carlton, who knew that the two young men had never yet met but to disagree, thought hastily of some uncontroversial topic. Joyce understood that Dick did not like Solway, but perceived in a flash of insight that it was not merely any old dislike of Solway that was urging him to thwart that gentleman's evident wish to do something to please her. A mischievous twinkle crept into her eyes. She would let them decide the question of John Roberts between themselves, if that were possible.

But Solway turned to her. "Shall I take back Roberts, Miss Graham?"

"I was about to say," Dick remarked suavely, "that perhaps I could help you out of this dilemma by employing Roberts at Aspley. You will then be able to keep your rule about dismissed labourers, and Miss Graham will feel no remorse at the thought of having caused the man to lose his livelihood. You will have maintained your—discipline. And Roberts will have lost—nothing at all. Don't you think that will help?"

"I am waiting for Miss Graham to answer."

"May I venture to suggest, Joyce, that we might give Roberts a chance to choose between Aspley and Cranebrook?" Dick was smiling; at least his face was, but his eyes were hard. "Mr. Solway is on the side of mercy. I am on the side of what I think to be justice. We will make you the arbiter. We can offer Roberts his choice, if you decide that we should do so."

"That sounds only reasonable, doesn't it?" said Joyce to Mr. Solway with a smile.

"Mr. Carlton can have the services of John Roberts," answered Solway quietly, though there was an angry gleam in his eyes. He knew quite well that Roberts would not elect to go back to Cranebrook, and in his heart he cursed Dick for an ill-bred cad. Then Mrs. Carlton saw her opportunity and turned the conversation into a new channel.

About an hour after dinner the gentlemen took their leave, Mr. Solway promising to give himself the pleasure of riding into Aspley sometimes. He was taking advantage of the hospitality of the planting fraternity, which made the visitor, and especially the neighbour, welcome at any time and as often as he pleased to call. He had even mastered his feeling of annoyance to talk cordially to Dick; he laughingly wished him joy of John Roberts as he bade good-night. But as he and his uncle got out of hearing he scowled heavily. "Did you see how that cad deliberately prevented my taking back Roberts?" he asked Mr. Burton.

"I do wish you two could be friends, John," replied the old man pacifically. "Dick isn't such a bad fellow."

"He is a damned prig, that's what he is," the other man retorted with sudden violence. "This property belongs to him and his cousin, but I am sure he is trying to get it all by taking her along with it—he is quite capable of it."

"Well, she's pretty enough to tempt him," said Mr. Burton good-humouredly.

"But he would pretend that he loved her for herself alone, and all the rest of that sort of nonsense. He is a prig, and no better than anybody else, in spite of all his pretence. The confounded sneak! He makes people think he is a Simon Pure, while all the time he is carrying on with a nigger girl about here—Paul Bogle's daughter. What do you think of that?"

Mr. Burton, knowing his class, thought the assertion very likely to be true, and was not disposed to think any the less of Dick if it was true. He said nothing.

"I wonder what the pretty cousin would think of him if she knew of his intimacy with a nigger gal? Maybe he would come down an inch or two in her estimation; at any rate, she would know him for just what he is."

There was the whisper of a threat in Mr. Solway's voice: Mr. Burton detected it. But he held his peace. He knew that nothing he could say would influence his nephew.

V

Mr. Solway is Angered

Mr. Solway was not a frequent visitor at the houses of the neighbouring gentry. He had accompanied his uncle to Aspley; it was the first time for three years that he had set foot in the Great House there; yet here he was, but three days after that visit, preparing to ride to Aspley again, this time by himself.

He had no doubt whatever that his visit would be remarked, its motive known. No one would be foolish enough to think that he called to see Mrs. Carlton. His antipathy to Dick he had hardly ever sought to disguise. Had Dick's father been at Aspley, Solway might have pretended that he wanted to see him on matters affecting estate management; but the old man was far away, in St. Andrew, and that excuse was therefore out of the question. Not even from himself could Mr. Solway hide the truth: he was going to Aspley because Joyce Graham was there, and this was the first time in his life that any white woman had given him a moment's thought, or had caused in his mind a struggle between two powerful impulses.

For if the wish to go to Aspley was compelling, the inclination to shun the very neighbourhood of the place was also strong. He had not been blind to the sort of welcome extended to him three evenings before; he was well aware that his name was unfavourably commented upon even by the members of a dissolute plantocracy. He was perhaps no worse than many; he had been rather more open, more shameless, not paying to virtue that tribute which hypocrisy is supposed to be. It was not in his nature to be mindful of public opinion; he had never thought he would have reason to care about it. He knew that Dick Carlton's way of life was considered the reverse of his; he had merely sneered at Dick in consequence, holding him to be a milksop and a fool. But now he was beginning to take a more than usual interest in what was said of young Carlton. There was that tale about him and Rachael Bogle, the gossip of the estates. He was prepared to believe it true. He wanted it to be true.

He had no excuse for riding over to Aspley that day. The most he could do was to ask Miss Graham to fix a day for visiting Cranebrook;

he would pretend that he wished to be there to show her the estate, to take her about the neighbourhood. She would not be deceived by this sort of talk, he did not want her to be. It was her people, not herself, that he must find specious reasons for. He was certain that the Carltons, friends of his uncle though they were, would not hesitate to influence Joyce against him; they would show him quite plainly that they did not desire his frequent visits at Aspley. He set his teeth at the thought of this; his blood grew hot at the mere possibility of an affront. Then he remembered that Aspley was as much the property of Joyce as of Dick, and the girl was of age. Why should he, in every respect her equal in birth and position, not call to see her if he so desired?

He mounted his horse and set out upon the ride, choosing the afternoon in the hope that Dick Carlton would not be in the house when he arrived. He communed with himself as he rode along: this wish to see the girl was a weakness on his part; he would never have thought himself capable of yielding to it; why was he yielding to it? He had no answer to this question; he had merely an unpleasant feeling that, by going to Aspley, he was giving people who did not like him an advantage over him. And to a man of his disposition the thought was wormwood. He had been obliged to be polite to Dick on the last occasion he was at Aspley; he should be obliged to be even more polite today. And he confessed to himself that he was willing enough to be so. . . because he wished to be able to see Joyce Graham often. His life of semi-barbarous independence he must sacrifice to the conventionalities of polite society—for a girl.

He had calculated well. Dick was not in the Great House when he got there. It was Joyce who received him, telling him that Mrs. Carlton would be out in a little while. Her greeting was so unaffectedly cordial that at once he knew that her mind had not been prejudiced against him.

He told her that he and his uncle wanted her to see Cranebrook as soon as possible; "and I have not waited till you should call," he explained; "I came to ask you to pay us a visit as soon as you can. We are savages here; you must excuse our rough-and-ready methods and manners. For me especially you will have to make any number of allowances."

"I rather like your Jamaica ways," she answered pleasantly; "they are free and easy, and genuine. Of course I'll go to Cranebrook as soon as I can."

"About when?" he asked her eagerly. "This week?"

"It depends on my aunt's convenience: but I hardly think we'll be able to go this week; next week, perhaps."

"It cannot be too soon," he said; and looked full into her eyes. He cast restraint aside: "Do you know that I have paid more visits to Aspley within the last four days than during the previous four years?"

He hoped she would ask him why; instead she merely remarked, "indeed?"

"Yes; I never wanted to come before; I am rather a solitary man; too much so, maybe. But now—"

Joyce looked at him with a quick sidelong glance. She liked admiration, but Solway was decidedly precipitate. She did not in the least desire that he should make love to her in blunt, downright fashion, and he evidently had not the art of turning compliments neatly. She began to wish that her aunt would come into the room.

"Now," he went on, "I want to come to Aspley as often as I can, if you will allow me."

"You are always welcome," she returned prettily; "my aunt and I shall always be glad to see you, I am sure."

His face fell a little. He wished she had left her aunt out of her speech.

She was sitting by an open window. What next he might have said she stopped with a sharp wave of her hand and a little exclamation. "'Look! There's your man, John Roberts. He is working at Aspley now." Looking at Roberts was a good reason for not meeting Mr. Solway's tell-tale eyes.

"He might have been at Cranebrook if you had wished it," he replied, without bestowing a glance on the labourer outside. "I wanted you to give me the chance to break a rule I had never broken before. I would have done so gladly on this occasion, but you gave your cousin the preference."

"No, I was willing to leave it to Roberts to decide, and he did decide." The last words slipped out unintentionally.

Mr. Solway was quick to hear them. "Oh, so you asked Roberts whom he would choose?" he queried with just a suspicion of bitterness in his voice.

"Not exactly that. The morning after you were here, we—Dick and I—rode over to Jigger-foot Market. Dick told Roberts that he could go back to you if he wished, or come here: he told the man I had interceded for him, though that was scarcely so. Roberts said he would come to Aspley. His son is really dying, you know: poor fellow."

"Roberts said hard things about me, didn't he?"

"Oh, no. I would not have listened to him if he had begun complaining."

"You would not have listened? Will you promise me something now?"

She began to feel uncomfortable, apprehensive. Mr. Solway had warned her that he was a sort of savage; he had said it in jest. But his ardent manner, his earnestness, his apparent determination to establish a sort of intimacy between them, strangers though they were, forced her to realize that he would not long refrain from saying anything that he wished to say, that he would go directly to the point, brushing aside every shred of conventionality. He had little restraint. There was something strong, overbearing about him; something that appealed to her feminine nature. Here was a very determined man, and the look of admiration in his eyes he made no effort to conceal. She gazed at him in question. "What is it?" she asked, in a manner which she intended to be, and which appeared to be, one of polite indifference.

"I want you to promise me that you wont believe anything you hear about me. I am not loved in this parish; that is because I walk by a path of my own and pay but little regard to my good neighbours. And when one is not liked, harsh things—things untrue—are said about one. I have no defence against that sort of attack. I have never cared what may be said. But I do care that you should not believe anything against me. Will you promise?"

He was looking hungrily at her dainty figure, her fresh delicate complexion, the beauty and alluring attractiveness of her. He spoke earnestly. He wanted her to promise, was pleading that she should do so. She could not but note his eagerness, the energy of his appeal.

"I do not usually believe what is said in disparagement of others," she answered, somewhat coldly, "and I do not see why you should fancy that you will be spoken badly of to me. I don't quite understand. . ."

"No; you do not understand. But suppose disparagement is attempted? Wont you promise me not to believe it until I have had a chance of explaining?"

"What I believe could hardly be of much interest to you," she fenced. "What could it matter?"

"What you believe will mean everything to me, will make all the difference in the world to me; I do not want you to think badly of me."

Her eyelids fluttered and fell before his burning gaze. She was about to give the promise he asked her for, glad of anything to put an end to this scene; she was confused, flustered, puzzled too. She opened her lips to speak, when Mrs. Carlton entered.

Mrs. Carlton brought with her into the drawing-room the atmosphere of an iceberg. She had overheard at the door—she could not but overhear—Mr. Solway's last words. Unconsciously he had spoken with particular distinctness, throwing the feeling that possessed him into his voice and the words, "I do not want you to think badly of me." And the good lady knew that if Joyce but guessed one half of what known about this man she, with her ideas formed in an English home, and with her natural purity of feeling, could not but think badly of him, however much she might strive to do otherwise.

She was frightened. That Solway, Solway of all men, should be imploring Joyce to think well of him, was enough to startle her. He had come to see Joyce, his intention lay on the surface. He would seek every possible opportunity to make love to her if he wished to do that, and he was a man such as many women would look kindly upon. Many a simple and decent girl of the neighbourhood had done so to her cost.

The chill of her manner affected the younger people. She was icily courteous. Mr. Solway asked her if she would fix a day for going to Cranebrook; she was firm in her refusal; they would go some day; she could not say when. Under her influence conversation languished. Ten minutes after she had entered he bade them good afternoon, not having been able to obtain a word alone with Joyce.

He cantered towards the gate with a disquieted spirit. What he had been fearing was already coming to pass. There would be no welcome for him at Aspley; if he went there again he must at the best expect a cold greeting, except, possibly, from Joyce. And she would wonder why he was not welcome. Well, he must bear all this for a while; he was not to be turned from his purpose by a young man's impudence and an old woman's hauteur and distrust. His purpose? What was his purpose? He would be frank with himself. He, who had hitherto sneered at all the softer sentiments, wanted Joyce Graham, wanted her to think well of him, would put up with much if only—

He was out of Aspley, just beyond the great gate, and before him, on his horse, was Dick. Dick had been inspecting the fences; he looked at Solway, surprised. The latter checked his horse and spoke cordially enough.

"I have been on a visit to Aspley, Dick," he smiled, reverting to the form of address he had used when Dick and he were boys.

"You wanted to see me?"

The question was pointed. It implied a belief that Mr. Solway could have wanted to see no one else.

"Well, no. I called on the ladies." Mr. Solway made an effort to be pleasantly at ease.

"I did not know that you paid much attention to ladies." The words, the accent, were deliberately provocative. Dick was glad that Solway was on neutral ground. He was going to put a stop to this man's visits; he had made up his mind to do so at the moment he caught sight of Solway. And when Dick made up his mind he acted with a promptness that could not be bettered by Mr. Solway himself.

The patience of the latter was exhausted. His anger suddenly boiled over. "What do you mean?" he demanded sharply.

"My remark was plain enough, I think. I have always understood that the women you preferred to mix with were not ladies. You have made no secret of it. You do not object to my alluding to it now, do you?"

"I object to your damned impertinence," shouted Solway. "I have the right to call to see your cousin, so long as she is living in a house that is as much her own as it is yours. If you were a gentleman you would not insult me, a guest. But I suppose you have your private reasons."

"We will leave the question of my gentility alone for the present," retorted Dick "As for my reasons for speaking to you as I do, you ought to know them better than anyone else. They are my mother's reasons. They would also be my cousin's if she knew them. Do you want her to know them?"

"You are quite capable of lying," sneered Solway.

"Be careful. I have not the slightest desire to speak of you to my cousin; I avoid mentioning you."

"Jealous? Is that it?"

"I have my riding whip in my hand, Solway!"

"And, by God, I have mine also! Don't forget that. I suppose you have deliberately picked a quarrel with me to prevent my coming to Aspley again. That is your game, is it?"

"Believe what you like."

Very well. But I will get even with you yet, Mr. Dick Carlton. You cur!"

With a bitter curse Mr. Solway spurred his horse and rode at a gallop to Crane brook.

VI

RAINES OUTLINES A PLAN

A passionate man, proud in his own way, resenting opposition, and unforgiving by nature, Mr. John Solway felt as he rode away from Aspley that he had drunk to the dregs the bitter cup of humiliation. He was not one whom people insulted lightly; they preferred to avoid him. Yet he had been deliberately insulted by Dick Carlton; and what almost sent him mad with anger was the thought that he had put it in the power of Dick to show him plainly, without restraint, without any regard for his feelings whatever, that he was not welcome at Aspley, that he was not the sort of man with whom the ladies there would care to associate. He would gladly have murdered Dick at that moment. He saw blood-red as he galloped home. "No nigger could have been treated more contemptuously," he thought, in an agony of wounded pride, in the misery of a self-esteem brutally trampled upon and soiled. "Insulted like a dog, insulted like a dog!" The words sang in his ears to torment him. He could find no salve for his hurt. One thing alone was impressed upon his mind, his soul, his whole being, set and sealed in him as it was by the spirit of hate. Dick Carlton must be punished for this, must pay for it bitterly with a worse humiliation, with a suffering more intense. He would see to that. God! he would be the dog like which he had been treated if he did not make Dick Carlton pay with terrible interest.

Arrived at Cranebrook, he waited till it was dark. Then he set out on foot for a walk of about half a mile, which brought him to a little house more commodious and of better appearance than the usual peasant's hut. The door opened as he placed his hand upon it; evidently his step had been heard and his entrance anticipated. The inmates of the house were a young woman, dark brown in colour, and two very young children of much lighter hue. The woman smiled a welcome, the children toddled towards Mr. Solway, who turned his back impatiently upon them. Whereupon they made a detour in order to get in front of him once more. Noticing his impatient movement, the woman's face became serious and a trifle apprehensive.

"You were telling me something about Rachael Bogle and Mr. Carlton the other day," said Mr. Solway abruptly, still standing. "He is carrying on with her, isn't he?"

"So I hear," murmured the woman timidly, "but," she added hastily, "I don't know if it is true."

"I want you to find out if it is true, and get as many people as you know to find out also. Talk about it as much as you please. Don't be afraid of anything; no one can harm you. You understand?"

"Yes," she answered eagerly, satisfied now that Mr. Solway was not angry with her for repeating scandal about a brother planter. "In fact it must be true, or Rachael wouldn't want to go so often to Aspley. She have no young man of her own colour, an' she always saying what a nice man, an' what a kind man, Mr. Carlton is."

"I don't doubt that she is his sweetheart," said Mr. Solway brutally. "Find out all you can about it for me." Here the elder of the two children threw its arms round his leg, making infantile noises to attract his attention. He draw back with a snarl, the woman hastily snatching the child away, and being rewarded by the latter with a prolonged howl of annoyance. The mother frowned. "You might have knocked her down," she cried angrily, trying to soothe the little one.

Solway had not intended to hurt the child; his movement had been an involuntary one of bitter disgust, the quick expression of a sudden surge of self-contempt experienced probably for the first time in his life. As the child's arms touched him it had flashed through his mind that they, and other little arms like them, might prove steel-strong barriers separating him from Joyce Graham, barriers of his own creating which enemies like Dick Carlton might ruthlessly employ. He sickened on the instant. The look he flashed at mother and infant was one of dislike. If Joyce were Jamaican, knowing the customs and habits of the country—well, she would know how to make allowances. But a stranger, with self-interested mentors like Dick Carlton and his mother, could easily be induced to think the worst of a man who was, after all (so Mr. Solway felt), rather better than worse than his fellows, since at least he had always despised hypocrisy.

With an expression of something like shame on his face he turned towards the door. "Don't forget what I have said," he muttered, and was gone. The woman, still hushing her child, uttered a curse on Rachael Bogle in a flash of suspicion and jealousy.

Meanwhile Solway walked rapidly back to Cranebrook, with more bitterness in him than was good for any man. He had an uneasy feeling that he had done a mean thing by setting this woman to spy upon and gossip about a girl and a gentleman. He still felt the child's clasp about his knee, and he could picture Joyce looking at such a scene—no, she would never look; her back would be turned upon it with horror and disgust, with a scorn which no words could utter forth. All this made him hate Dick Carlton all the more. But for Dick, he argued, he could set every thing right; he could so arrange that his past should be relegated to a decent obscurity, never to trouble his future: a little money, a decent arrangement, could do that. But Dick Carlton was clearly determined that it should not be done. Well, there was Rachael Bogle, and Dick would see that two could play at the same game.

"Squire!"

Mr. Solway turned sharply in the direction of the voice. "Well, what is it, Raines?" he answered, recognising the man.

"Nothing particular, Squire; but I have something to tell you."

"Very good. Come into my office."

They were in Cranebrook, and within a stone's throw of the little building wherein Mr. Solway transacted the business of the estate. He opened the door, lighted a lamp, and threw himself into the one chair the room contained. The rest of the furniture consisted of a dealboard table, and a cupboard in which some account books were kept.

"What have you got to say?" he demanded of Raines.

The man hesitated. His narrow, sinister eyes rested anxiously on Mr. Solway. He had a cruel mouth; sometimes his voice took on a threatening intonation not pleasant to hear. Even as he stood there before the planter whom he addressed respectfully, it was noticeable that he carried himself with an air of independence such as was lacking in the peasants who worked on the estates.

"Why can't you go on with your tale, if you have any?" cried Mr. Solway irritably, as the man continued to look at him without speaking. "You don't suppose I am at your disposal all night, do you?"

"You mustn't say anything about what I am going to tell you," replied Raines slowly. "You promise, Squire?"

"No."

This answer disconcerted Raines. But he knew Mr. Solway well enough to hope that he would secure his promise of silence afterwards. "Squire," he said confidently, lowering his voice. "Paul Bogle really mean trouble."

"I have heard that before—ever since those infernal mountain fires."

"Yes; but now he going to have a big revival meeting at Stony Gut, an' the whole parish is going to it, and Mr. Gordon is coming to this parish to see him."

"Hum! Gordon is a damned madman who will set this island in a blaze some day. How do you know all this?"

"Because I am Bogle's friend, and he want me to get the Maroons to join him if it come to a fight."

"Oh, indeed. So there is revolution in the air, is there? The brutes!"

Raines laughed scornfully. "What can they do, Squire? There is plenty of soldier, an' the Maroons alone could finish Bogle and his plantation niggers."

"Yes; but we want to prevent trouble, Mr. Raines. That will be better than giving your brother Maroons a chance to indulge their savage instincts."

"But Bogle don't do nothing yet, Squire, so you can't interfere with him."

"No, but he can be watched."

"I am watching him; in de meantime. . ."

"Well?"

"He is talkin' about stopping labourers from working on the estates."

"The devil is he!" cried Mr. Solway, springing up. "I am glad you warned me. This explains the trouble we are now having with the plantation hands. I must find a way of stopping Mr. Paul Bogle before he proceeds to ruin me!"

"He won't do that, Squire; he wont interfere with Cranebrook, if I talk to him. But there is Mr. Carlton's estate. . ."

"By all that is holy, who put that idea into your head?" demanded Mr. Solway, staring, astonished, into the sinister face of the Maroon.

"Mr. Carlton interfere wid me," growled Raines threateningly, "an' there is only one way to prevent him going on."

Brusquely he told of his grievance against Dick, expressing his conviction that there was already an understanding between Mr. Carlton and Rachael Bogle. Raines had no doubt that Paul Bogle, when he heard of the scandal affecting his daughter, would not only forcibly prevent her from having anything more to do with Mr. Carlton but would instantly wreck his vengeance upon him. The one way of doing this just now was to forbid the labourers to continue working at Aspley, and so great was Bogle's influence with the neighbouring peasantry that at least the major portion of them were certain to obey him. Bogle would enjoy this visible proof of his power, and would for the present refrain from carrying out any of his threats against the other planters of the parish.

"An' if he want to go any further," added Raines, "I will tell him that the Maroons will fight against him. They are the only people Bogle is afraid of."

The Maroons, to whom Raines boasted he belonged, were tribes of negroes, black Highlanders, who had for nearly two hundred years lived in wild freedom in the mountain recesses of the colony. They were the descendants of slaves freed by the old Spanish colonists and of runaway slaves who had taken to the inaccessible mountains long ago, from which fastnesses they had periodically descended to harry the lowlands and carry off the cattle from the sparsely scattered estates. A treaty with the Government, after a long Maroon War, had established their independence; they elected their own chiefs and held their lands free of all taxes; in return they were pledged to assist the Government to quell all local uprisings, the Government's policy being to keep these Maroons apart from the rest of the population. They were a bold, hardy lot of men, regarding with contempt the servile peasant population of the island. They knew every inch of the hills and the forests, and every man amongst them was a hunter.

Raines himself was one of the hardiest and most skilful hunters of the wild hog in the parish of St. Thomas. It was as a hunter that he had attracted Mr. Solway's favourable attention some years before. His patience and skill were remarkable. He had become a sort of confidential, though unattached, assistant of Mr. Solway, whom he had always served faithfully enough. Mr. Solway's recklessness and courage when hunting boars had won such admiration as Raines had to bestow on any one.

"And why do you tell me all this, Raines?" asked Solway slowly, seeing in the man's plot the very means he required of striking at Dick.

"Well, Squire, you know I am a Maroon," the man answered, "an' if the Government or my own people know I have anything to do with these common niggers, an' was helping them in any way, it would go hard with me."

"It would."

"But if you know the truth, Squire, you won't be surprised at anything you hear; and you can always defend me. You are powerful, an' a word from you will go a long way."

"So you are asking me to help you to carry out a plot against a planter?"

"You don't like Mr. Carlton you'self. Squire."

"That's true enough."

"An' he don't like you."

"How do you know that?"

"He was up at Jigger-foot Market the other day, offering John Roberts a job. And he told John Roberts he could go back to Cranebrook if he like, or go to Aspley. An' Roberts say he would rather dead than come back here, and Mr. Carlton laugh. Miss Graham was with him, an' she hear him. An' that's not the only time he laugh at you, Squire; he always doing it."

"I don't want to hear what he does," cried Mr. Solway fiercely. "So Mr. Gordon is coming to this parish, is he?"

"Yes, Squire."

"He wants more watching than Bogle. I must see the man when he comes."

"But you wont mention what I just tell you?" asked Raines anxiously. "They wont interfere wid you."

"Mention it? Oh, no. I don't see it is any of my business. I presume that you are the virtuous lover and Bogle the vigilant father! I have no right to come between you and your efforts to rescue an erring damsel." He laughed. "Good night Raines," he concluded, with a chuckle.

"Good night, Squire," but the man lingered.

Mr. Solway tossed him a few shillings. Raines always waited for this. Mr. Solway was liberal.

After Raines had gone, the young man sat thinking with a smile on his lips. The whole parish, would shortly be hearing about this liason between Bogle's daughter and Mr. Dick Carlton who was sometimes held up as an excellent though perfectly futile example to youthful members of the plantocracy. How St. Thomas would laugh! It would be the first time that a strike would have taken place in the interests of peasant virtue. And after Mr. Paul Bogle had acted a father's part and brought about a parish-wide exposure, it would hardly matter much what Dick might say about anyone. Thus would hypocrisy meet with its due reward.

VII

A Meeting of Conspirators

In a one-roomed furnished hut situated on the out-skirts of the town of Morant Bay, partly sheltered by the trees that grew around, and yet within sight of the stretch of sea that rolled unrestingly shorewards from the far-off eastern horizon, sat a tall, loosely-built, middle-aged man. His yellowish complexion and grizzled hair showed that he was a man of mixed blood, an offspring of the black and white races that had inhabited the colony now for some two hundred years. His semi-clerical attire might have led a stranger to think that he was a minister of religion.

His face was clean-shaven, save for a narrow band of hair running under the chin from temple to temple; it was a long face, obstinate in every line, with square chin, salient pugnacious lips, and sullen untrustful eyes which glowed behind a pair of gold-rimmed eye-glasses.

This man was Mr. George William Gordon, planter and merchant; bankrupt now, it was being whispered; an orator whose impassioned denunciations of Government and gentry had stirred the country from one end to the other, who was worshipped by the common people as their heaven-sent leader, and cursed by the upper classes as one who was rapidly leading the island down the slippery path of revolution.

With Mr. Gordon sat a big burly black man who had come with him from Kingston to St. Thomas. This man was decently dressed, an urban dweller obviously; he carried himself with an air of supreme importance. He was known as Mr. Robson, and once had been a sergeant in the Police Force, from which he had been dismissed some time before.

These two men had arrived at the hut but a couple of minutes when three others entered, the last one closing the door behind him. The first of these newcomers was Raines the Maroon; the second was a small, somewhat elderly fellow, with a pert, cunning, malicious cast of countenance, as black as it was possible for a human being to be. But it was the last of the three men upon whom Mr. Gordon and his companion fixed their eyes, and whom they rose to welcome.

Paul Bogle was a stalwart, determined-looking negro, with a pock-pitted face and fierce eyes. He carried himself with a more independent mien than even Raines; his voice was deep and far-reaching. The heavy nose and long, heavy chin denoted much more strength of character than one usually found amongst persons of his class.

After shaking hands with Bogle, Mr. Gordon glanced enquiringly at Raines.

"This is Mr. Raines," explained the man with the cunning face, who rejoiced in the name of Bowie; "he is with us heart an' soul."

"Very good," said Mr. Gordon, as they all sat down, "and now, Bogle, how goes the good work?"

"You are to tell us that, Mr. Gordon," replied Paul Bogle in his deep bass. "You come from all over the country; we can only wait for you to say what we should do. That is why I write to ask you to come here."

"Yes," chimed in Mr. Bowie, "we not idle here; we are making a move."

"Ah," cried Mr. Gordon, looking at him keenly, "that is good news. It is cheering to hear that the people are stirring at last. I have had the whole burden of the fight up to now, you know."

"That is the fact," boomed his satelite, Robson. "From rise of sun to going down you have fought the good fight, and your abundant reward must come. In de meantime we depending upon you to go on giving the Governor an' all the white people fits."

"You may trust me to do that," said Mr. Gordon bitterly. "What I have done up to now is only a beginning. But you, Bogle, you have not told me yet what you propose to do. And I have come here at your invitation especially to hear it."

"First of all," said Paul Bogle deliberately, "we want to awaken the people to a sense of the wickedness in the land."

"Quite right, Bogle, we must be of a humble and contrite heart before we can expect the Lord's assistance."

"And I am marshalling the people to stand up against the oppressors."

"Yes, my friend; but how?"

"How?" thundered Bogle, with an intensity of passion that caused Mr. Robson to start with fright. "You can ask how, Mr. Gordon? There is only one way! The people of Hayti are black, like me, yet they drive the white man from out of their country; and if Hayti can do that, why can't we? Hayti is only next-door to Jamaica. Black men there are generals and colonel and president. What is a black man in Jamaica? We want land, an' we can't get it. We want freedom, an' we can't get it. We want justice, an' we can't get it—not a black man can win a case in a court-house here against a white man. There is only one way to get justice in Jamaica—wid fire an' cutlass! You know that you'self. I tell you—" here Bogle raised his voice—"there would have been blood an' fire long ago in this parish, if it wasn't that I was waiting on you. But we getting tired of waiting now, for the oppression is too hard, and' the cry of the people is going up to God! It must be soon or never!"

As he listened to Paul Bogle's declamatory oration a look of terror swept over Mr. Gordon's face. As for Robson, he glanced, terrified, towards the single window of the hut, wondering with beating heart if Bogle's words could have been overheard by anyone upon the road. But Mr. Bowie crowed approval, while Raines, with non-committal expression, watched the other men keenly and waited to hear what Mr. Gordon had to say.

With nervous fingers tapping the little table in front of him, Mr. Gordon brooded for the space of a minute. While they waited for him to speak, Paul Bogle's face twitched fiercely, and Mr. Robson seemed as if affected by a slight ague fit. The swish and hiss of the waves breaking on the beach outside was the only sound that broke the stillness.

Mr. Gordon spoke at last.

"What you say is true enough, Bogle; I agree with every word of it. But we must be careful about making a premature move. You mention Hayti. In Hayti the people were united; here they are not—not yet. I am working to unite them, and you are helping me; but they have still to be awakened to a sense of the bitter wrongs from which they suffer. That is why I say to you, hold your hand; wait!"

"Yes," agreed Mr. Robson hastily. "Hold you' hand! We not strong enough yet. Rouse de people! Stir them up! But don't do nothing for the white men to arrest us for; I been a Policeman meself, an' I can tell you it is no fun when the cell-door close upon you. In de meantime, though, we must talk strong. Them can't do us anything for talking."

"There will be more than enough of strong talking soon," agreed Gordon with a bitter smile. "Through the whole island I am going, Bogle, and my voice will be heard denouncing oppression. There will be such a cry in this country that it will be heard all over the world. Those who, like the Governor, are purposely deaf, will nevertheless hear. I am learning their vile secrets every day. I will cry them out from the housetops. I will shake down the tyrants like rotten fruit from the branch of a tree. I know the people want land and cannot get it; justice, and it is denied to them. But they must move as one, and it is to that end that I shall speak to them."

"There is hot times coming!" chuckled Robson gleefully, taking care, however, not to raise his voice. "Well, I am behind you, Mr. Gordon, I are behind you all de time. When it come to talking strong, I am there—no man can beat me. You are a brown man. Mr. Gordon, but you are not like the rest of your colour. You support the black man, an' as black people is the most numerous in this country, they should rule."

"They shall rule!" exclaimed Gordon glad of the pacific support of Robson. "The pity is that they are divided. There are the Maroons—"

"Them will join us," interrupted Mr. Bowie proudly. "Mr. Raines is a Maroon."

Mr. Gordon darted a glance, full of suspicion, at Raines. He was not at all pleased to hear that a Maroon had been listening to his remarks. Mr. Robson started violently and tried to look anything but a conspirator. Raines perceived that he had to say something reassuring.

"The white people don't trouble the Maroons," he observed, "for them afraid of us. But we don't trust them."

"You hear?" cried Bowie triumphantly. "When Raines get all his people to join him, we can sweep de country from east to west."

"But, in the meantime, patience," counselled Mr. Gordon.

"Yes, patience," fervently echoed Robson.

"You must give me time to do my work," continued Gordon. "You look disapointed, Bogle, but what is a few months more or less in the sight of the Lord? Continue your activities. Keep the people near to religion. Tell them that I pray for them unceasingly. Tell them to look to heaven for help in their terrible distress, and to have faith in me, and stand ready to support me. They must all be registered as voters; I must again be returned to the House of Assembly as a member for this parish if I am to serve them well. See that every qualified man is properly registered. Deliverance must come to the people, for the oppression increases; as you have said, Bogle, their cry has gone up to God, and the axe is laid to the root of the tree."

He was once more the lay evangelistic preacher. As this, even more than as politician, he had won the adoration of the multitude. His fervour impressed Paul Bogle.

He raised his voice. "I am working and praying, praying and waiting for a sign from heaven. It will come, Bogle, it will come, Bowie, never doubt. The white men and the Government beat down the people and tread them underfoot. But the juice of the wine-press will be bitter, and Almighty God will show His all-powerful hand."

He had risen while speaking, his eyes flashing as it was wont to do when he addressed some religious meeting by the wayside or in some church, his arm gesticulating, his voice ringing loudly out. He paused, and the stamp of a horse's hoof on the limestone road warned the little audience that a listener was outside. Mr. Robson started up apprehensively and darted to the window. Raines smiled slightly, while Paul Bogle, with a fine air of unconcern, moved to the door, and, opening it, perceived Mr. Solway waiting on his horse a little distance away from the hut.

VIII

"I am Sorry—Very Sorry"

Through the open door the other men also caught sight of Mr. Solway, and with one accord, preceded by Paul Bogle, they filed out of the hut.

The emotions of each were different, corresponding to the character of the individual. Robson was plainly and visibly agitated. As he himself had expressed it, when it came to strong talking, he was "there"; but when action was demanded or danger of any kind had to be faced, then Mr. Robson invariably wished that he could immediately be somewhere else. Mr. Gordon was suspicious, recognising in the man on the horse a planter and a white man, and wondering whether he had come there as a spy. Bowie knew Solway and was prepared to be impudent; Bogle, burning with a desire to bring about a crisis as shortly as possible, did not care whether he had been overheard or not. As for Raines, he was quite at his ease; he lifted his hat with a "good evening, Squire," and a malicious grin at Robson's fright. Raines was not surprised to see Mr. Solway; he had told that gentleman of the intended meeting, and Mr. Solway had expressed a desire to see the conspirators. Solway now glanced from one to the other of them with a smile.

"Mr. Paul Bogle, eh?" he said pleasantly; "and Bowie. I think you know me, Bowie?"

Mr. Bowie was flattered to be recognised in this friendly fashion, and Paul Bogle noted with secret satisfaction that he had been addressed as Mister.

"I don't know these other gentlemen," continued Mr. Solway; "friends of yours, Raines?"

"This is Mr. Gordon," said Raines, "and this is Mr. Robson from Kingston."

"Ah, the great Mr. Gordon!" cried Solway; "everybody has heard of him. I am glad to meet you, Mr. Gordon, though you are always attacking the planters."

"I attack them collectively, but there are individual exceptions," said Gordon, who was susceptible to flattery. "Your name, sir?"

"Solway. I am only a planter's nephew though, and will own no estate till my uncle shuffles off this mortal coil, which I hope he wont do for a long time yet."

"Well, I trust that when you are a property-owner you will not forget the claims of the people, Mr. Solway," returned Mr. Gordon earnestly. "Quite so," said Robson, making an effort to attract attention, now that Mr. Solway appeared to be friendly.

"I shall certainly not forget them," Solway replied. "I get on pretty well with them as it is. We quarrel now and then, but they like me. I think Bowie knows that."

Mr. Bowie, knowing that Raines was on good terms with Mr. Solway, was willing enough to vouch for the people's attachment to that gentleman, though he had often heard differently. Mr. Gordon was pleased. It was evident to him that Solway was endeavouring to gain his good opinion.

"I sympathise with your aims generally," Solway went on, noting the favourable impression he had created. "I know, Mr. Gordon, that you mean no harm to anyone who is a friend of the people. As for Mr. Bogle, he has a lot of influence up here, and I am sure that when he uses it he will do so in a proper cause. It is sometimes necessary to show the big men that the smaller men have rights, and that they and their children are not to be treated as if worth nothing. Isn't that your view, Mr. Bogle?"

Bogle, without understanding what Solway meant exactly, replied that it was.

"I am glad you agree with me," said Solway. "I am going home now, but if I can do anything to serve any of you, I shall always be glad to hear of it. Raines can tell you where to find me. By-the-bye, Raines, I shall want to see you tonight."

With that, he bade them good-bye, and rode away.

"How he come to be here?" asked Paul Bogle a trifle suspiciously, directing his question to Raines.

Raines answered without hesitation. "I told him I was going to be here dis afternoon, if him should want me. Don't be afraid. He couldn't hear anything."

"Does he know anything?" asked Mr. Gordon, who was thinking of Paul Bogle's allusion to Hayti.

"Who is to tell him? An' suppose he did know? He an' the other white people don't get on too well. I don't think he like them a bit better than you."

"Yes, there are some white men in this country who are not liked by their class," said Mr. Gordon, reassured. "Some are my friends. I know that."

"I always hear Mr. Solway speak well of you, Mr. Gordon," lied Raines unblushingly.

The men were apparently satisfied. But the conference, having been interrupted, was not resumed; probably because Paul Bogle and Mr. Gordon had said all that they had to say. Bogle had been persuaded to wait a little longer before striking the blow he evidently was planning and preparing; Mr. Gordon was satisfied to have gained some time. For Gordon, playing always for position and power, hungry for applause and hating every opponent with a bitter hate, had never clearly set before his mental vision the possible consequences of his agitation. He was deliberately stirring up the passions of an emotional people in the hope of intimidating the Government; he trusted that he would always be able to control men like Paul Bogle. Which proved that he really did not know Paul Bogle.

He proposed that they should go on to the town of Morant Bay. All of them agreed save Raines, who intimated that he would follow Mr. Solway to Cranebrook. So he parted with them at the hut, expecting, as Mr. Solway was on horseback and he on foot, to arrive at Cranebrook some two hours after that gentleman.

In the meantime Mr. Solway was riding homeward in a grimly satisfied frame of mind. He had made a point of meeting Gordon and Bogle; this was a precaution against labour troubles on his estate. He realised that if Paul Bogle ordered the labourers to desert Aspley and was obeyed, the man would become so puffed up with vanity that he might extend the order to Cranebrook. So far as ordinary inclination was concerned, Mr. Solway would gladly have elected to fight Bogle and Gordon and the whole nest of potential rebels; his feeling for them was one of contempt. But he had his own purposes to serve, and these could only be satisfactorily served by his making indirect use of Bogle. It did not occur to him that he was allying himself with dangerous elements, that he was entering into a silent if not explicit partnership with men whom he would naturally regard as the enemies of his race and class. A week before he would have stood disdainfully aloof from an understanding with women who whispered away one's character; he would have wished to bring a heavy hand down upon conspirators who plotted disorder and social upheavals.

Now he had definitely entered upon a path the end of which he did not see. He saw no farther before him than Gordon did; he looked to the immediate result alone. He must humble his enemies and win the prize; and since to do this he must influence and propitiate men like Bogle, he did not hesitate.

A bend in the road and Mr. Solway caught sight of a slight and graceful figure on a horse some hundred yards in front. He recognised Joyce at once, and guessed that she must have come out for a ride on the highway which ran by the gate of Aspley. He slackened his speed to a quick walk, wondering if he should approach her then. It was not probable that Dick had been back-biting him to her yet, he reflected, but he could not be sure. Dick's mother might have been busy in the interests of her son; it would be safer to wait until Paul Bogle had publicly chastised Dick; then the latter would be too much occupied about his own character to spare much time to besmirch that of other persons. But even while Mr. Solway thought thus, his horse, walking more quickly than that of Joyce, had diminished the distance between them. She glanced over her shoulder and saw who it was. Her pace slackened, and that determined him.

He was by her side in a moment, sweeping off his hat in a gallant salutation.

"My star is in the ascendant today," he cried. "I never thought I should meet you on the road."

"I ride here sometimes," she answered, "in the cool of the afternoon. It's very pleasant."

"If I had known that, I should have been here every afternoon. I would not have missed meeting you for anything," Solway blurted out boldly.

"But I take these rides because the road is usually deserted. That is one of their advantages."

"Which means that you would not be pleased if I too rode here?"

She would not reply. He waited a moment or two, then continued.

"It is not a week since I was last at Aspley, and yet it seems a month; six months. You have never come to Cranebrook. Why?"

"My aunt has not been able to make it convenient. She and your uncle are such good friends that they do not stand on ceremony with one another. I suppose we'll call some day."

"And in the meantime, unless I meet you on this road sometimes, I shall not see you again."

"There's no pressing reason why you should see me, surely," she laughed; "and if we do not stand on ceremony, why should you?"

"Ah, but I cannot come to Aspley. I would not be welcome there."

"Indeed?"

"No; Dick and I have never been friends. His manner has shown me plainly that he does not relish my visits, just now particularly. Even your aunt was not cordial to me the other day, was she?"

"I didn't notice."

"I did; for I was the one affected. Dick's attitude is quite natural; I understand it. But he is with you so much that he need hardly grudge me a visit now and then. I dwell in darkness while he has all the light."

"I did not think Jamaica planters were so given to flowery compliments," she smiled. "And I am sure you are only imagining things."

"No; I know what I am saying: I cannot come to Aspley."

"Well, if you think you are not welcome at Aspley—"

"Yes?"

"The matter rests there, I think."

"But I want to see you ever so much. I must see you."

"You forget that we are only acquaintances; comparative strangers."

"What does that matter?" he burst forth. "Surely you know what I mean. I care for you, love you. I have never loved anyone else in my life. I did not want to never believed I could love. But you came here, and yours was the only influence that could have led me to Aspley. I went there because I must, in spite of the dislike entertained for me by your people. You know the truth now. I love you. And I want to see you sometimes, to meet you. Is that too much to ask?"

As she listened to his passionate outburst her manner changed from flippancy to one of gentle gravity. She would have tried to laugh his words away had he not been so terribly in earnest. One swift sidelong glance at his face showed it set with passionate feeling. His voice was vibrant with emotion. She would not look at him again, but when she spoke it was softly and gently, as if to soothe him for the refusal she had to give.

"I am sorry—very sorry," she murmured "You—you pay me a great compliment; but. . ." And she wished that he would take the rest for granted and say no more.

"I am not asking you to care for me in return," he urged. "You say we are comparative strangers. That is true. I have said that I love you; spoken sooner than I intended, but that I could not help. All that I beg now is that we shall be friends. You will not refuse that, will you? I know I cannot call to see you; I promise that if I do meet you here it shall be rarely, but I want to meet you sometimes. I am tired of this life of mine; it is emptier, more sordid, than you can ever guess. I ask you to have some sort of faith in me, stranger though I am. Then if, in the future—"

"There is no future," interrupted Joyce gently.

"Very well. Even if there is no future, we can be frineds, can we not?"

"If you wish it. But this dislike which you say my people have for you. . . I do not understand. . . you see, it is so difficult for me. . ."

"I know. But don't let that affect you. Your friendship and sympathy may help me to overcome even that. And I need your friendship."

He hoped she would say nothing to Dick or to her aunt of this talk between them, and somehow he felt that she would not. He had appealed to her sympathy, told her that Aspley's doors were closed to him, that she alone had caused him to enter that house. His secret was in her hands, and surely she would keep it. He must trust her for that.

They were very near to Aspley now.

"We'll meet again," he said, as he brought his horse to a standstill.

"I suppose so; when I return."

"You are going away?"

"Yes; to visit some of my relatives on the northside. I have never seen them."

"And your aunt and Dick?"

"My aunt goes back to Denbigh. Dick usually goes about this time of the year to Westmoreland, I believe. His father has a property there."

"Yes, I know; may I ask when you go?"

"About a week hence; before the rains."

"And can I not see you even once before you go. . . out here?"

She shook her head firmly. "You must not wait for me out here; if you do, I shall be obliged to give up my rides."

She held out her hand; he took it in silence.

"Good-bye," she murmured kindly.

IX

RAINES MAKES HIS MOVE

The sun flamed down on Stony Gut, and the fierce light revealed the village in all its squalor. It revealed also Stony Gut's strong and isolated situation. Imagine a ravine formed ages ago by earthquakes and floods. To the north, on both sides of the ravine, the land sloped gradually, rising into high ground; on these slopes were built the huts of the peasants, and the soil here was cultivated with some care. Farther on, the hills became precipitous, so that to approach the village from the north was a task of some difficulty, unless one knew the narrow paths or "short-cuts" which the peasants habitually preferred. To the south of Stony Gut were towering cliffs which formed the walls of the Gut or ravine; these cliffs were so close that but a narrow twisting path was left open between them, a path that might easily be blocked by boulders hurled down from the heights on either side, or held by a handful of determined men against a regiment of soldiers. In times of flood the water rushing through the ravine became a torrent.

On emerging out of this tortuous and difficult way you came upon a fairly wide and level space. Here was built a sort of church, a large thatched hut in which the chief man of the village preached to the people according to his conception of the Christian religion. This man was Paul Bogle, and not far from his tabernacle was his house, immediately behind and almost surrounding which were the canefield and provision ground that he owned.

Trees grew everywhere, huge of trunk and limb, and the tropical forest stretched away on either side, thick and umbrageous Under one great tree that sheltered Bogle's hut now sat a band of men engaged in earnest conversation. Bogle was enthroned amongst them; next to him sat Raines and Bowie, and the consideration shown to Raines was only less than that which was paid to Paul Bogle.

The door of the hut stood open, and within the darkened interior could be seen crouching on a box the crone whom Rachael Bogle had been commissioned by her father to invite to Stony Gut on the morning that Joyce had ridden by accident into Cranebrook. This woman had arrived the night before, and the men's conversation had reference to her; they called her name often and glanced in her direction with awe and respect.

It was the great revival meeting they discussed, the meeting which had been the talk of the parish for weeks and which was to be the equal of any of those which, four years before, had sent a wave of frenzy rolling through the island and had resulted in a strange reversion to primitive African superstitions and rites. This was Saturday, and within a week the people of the distant districts were to be summoned to Stony Gut for the purging of their sins, and other purposes less publicly proclaimed. The high-priest of the ceremony was to be Paul Bogle himself, and one of the chief hierophants was the old woman in the hut.

The conversation was a mixture of religious phrases and fierce denunciation of the Government. In this the Maroon took no part. His eyes wandered ever and again along the farther slope of the Gut as if he expected to see something or someone there. His friend Bowie, who now acted as his agent and mouthpiece, being inordinately proud of his friendship with a Maroon, sometimes followed with his eyes the searching gaze of Raines. And every now and then Bowie brought the conversation round to the necessity of the peasants cultivating the goodwill of the Maroons by every means in their power. This was now the theme he dwelt continually upon at Stony Gut.

One of the men happening to remark that the Maroons had all the land they wanted. Bowie seized the opportunity to descant upon his favourite topic. "We ought to make friends wid all the Maroons," he urged; "we can't win if them turn out against us. An' if we don't come to an understanding with them, they will join the white people an' fight us."

He paused suddenly. Coming towards the group was a girl who, a few moments before, Raines had seen scrambling down the side of the slope which he and Bowie had been watching. It was Rachael. As she approached the men three pairs of eyes were fixed intently upon her, and Rachael had an instinctive feeling that this conference concerned her closely. Her eyes hardened as she caught the gaze of Raines.

She was Bogle's only child, illegitimate; from her mother, a brown woman long since dead, she had inherited the strain of white blood which showed itself in her form and features, Bogle was immensely proud of her; he understood quite well that she was the price which Raines demanded for any help he might give in a rising of the people. He himself secretly disliked the Maroon, but he wanted his assistance.

And that morning Bowie had not only stimulated his ambition but had poured a poisonous tale into his ears.

"Where you come from?" he questioned Rachael, as she was about to pass into the hut.

"Aspley. Don't you know I always go there on Saturdays?"

"Yes; an' I don't like you to go there, as I tell you before. I say that no disgrace must be brought upon my name. You hear, Rachael?"

Rachael might not have replied, but it did not suit Mr. Bowie's plan that the matter should end thus. He intervened, after a swift glance had been flashed to him by Raines.

"Him is not only a proud man, General Bogle," said Bowie, "but he don't care who him offend. He insult me one day because I go to Aspley to talk to some of his labourers. But I am waiting for him. Some day him will kneel down an' beg me to have mercy 'pon him, an' that is the day when I will make him bawl!"

This provocative speech had immediately its intended effect.

"That day don't likely to come, Mr. Bowie," volleyed back Rachael scornfully: "Mr. Carlton wouldn't kneel down to such as you!"

"You seem to know a lot about him," answered Bowie wrathfully; "perhaps it is him you goin' to Aspley for."

She turned towards Bowie with flashing eyes.

"If it was even him I go there to see, it would be my affair," she retorted. "I do what I like."

She had fallen into the snare! Bowie looked at Paul Bogle meaningly; the other men glanced at one another as though wondering at this open defiance of Bogle by his own daughter. From the hut came the cackling laughter of the old woman, who had seen and heard what had passed.

Then Paul Bogle slowly rose from his seat and faced Rachael, and Raines knew that the plot had worked well. "You will do what you like?" the angered man thundered. "You will disobey me for a white man who only want to treat you like dirt, if him not doing it already? This is de curse upon we black people, that our own children turn against us for a white man, an' betray their own colour—'Colour for colour, blood for blood'—that is what I believe in. Now listen, Rachael. I say you not to go back to Aspley any more. An' to teach Carlton that no white man will interfere wid Paul Bogle's daughter. I will warn every labourer on Aspley to treat him like dirt—as he want to treat you an' me. Not a labourer will work for him after Monday, and the whole parish shall know the cause. Him is the first one I strike!"

He had faithfully followed the lesson so insidiously taught by Bowie at the instigation of the Maroon. He would now strike as he had been prompted to strike. Rachael's eyes found those of Raines, and for a few silent seconds they glared at one another, for Rachael knew who had urged Bowie on to inflame her father's mind against her and Mr. Carlton. Then a dogged defiant look crept over her face, and she silently passed into the hut.

X

The End of the Plot

Rachael realised that her father meant to keep his word. He would seek to injure Mr. Carlton, and she would be held by Mr. Carlton to have been the cause. She must try to prevent that. Her father would not act before Monday. If Mr. Carlton were warned, he might be able to speak to his labourers before they were tampered with by Paul Bogle and his agents.

Rachael knew that the Aspley labourers were not discontented, as were so many of the negroes on the other estates. And now John Roberts worked at Aspley, and was never tired of telling what Miss Graham and her cousin had done for him. Her father's influence was great, but something might be attempted against it. In a few minutes she had made up her mind what to do.

She lingered in the hut a little while, then left it and sauntered away carelessly, as though she were merely going to some house in the village. The course she took soon hid her from her father's sight; she knew all the bye-paths leading from Stony Gut, and soon she was hurrying along one of them on her way to Aspley. An hour's hard walking brought her to the estate, and now for the first time she felt nervous. Hitherto she had come upon Mr. Carlton casually, as it had seemed, though the lynx-eyed people about knew that it was no accident that so often brought Rachael across the path of the young master. She had already been there that morning, and had failed to see him. Now she was going to seek him out to do him a service, and he would surely know the reason that prompted her to this.

A labourer told her where he would be found. He was on his horse looking at some calves; there was no one very near him, and of this she was glad.

She had walked so quickly that she was panting when she came up to him. "I want to see you, Mr. Carlton," she said hurriedly: "it is something particular."

"Then why didn't you tell me this morning?" he asked her. "I heard that you were at Aspley."

"I didn't know it at de time; I hear it only a little while ago, and come right back to tell you."

"It must be something very important, then," he answered, smiling. "What is it?"

"Them trying at Stony Gut to put me father up against you. Me father don't hate you, but them tell him a lot of lies, an' I hear him say he will stop your labourers from coming to work on Monday."

Dick was now all attention. He realised at once the value of Rachael's warning. Joyce he thought, had done wisely in showing some kindness to the girl.

"You have done me a very great service, Rachael, which I am grateful for," he said. "I will tell Miss Graham. Shall I say that you did it especially for her sake?"

"It is not only for her sake, Mr. Carlton," Rachael replied quickly: "don't I know you long before I know her?"

"So it is for my sake also. Well, I am grateful to you, though I can't understand why your father should select me to vent his anger on!"

"I tell you it is not me father who dislike you. Bowie put him up to injure you, an' Raines get Bowie to do it, because Raines want to make mischief on you—and me."

Dick stared curiously at the girl standing beside his horse. He thought he began to understand now. He remembered that Raines was Solway's henchman, and had served Solway, as common report had it, in some not very reputable transactions.

"So it is Raines, the Maroon, eh? I know the man: a bad character, I expect."

"Yes, Mr. Carlton." (She spoke very rapidly). "Raines don't want me to come here, an' him threaten me that if I come here he will injure me—an' you. I like to come here, an' I don't trouble nobody when I come. Don't that is so, Mr. Carlton?"

"I am sure it is," he answered promptly. "But don't get yourself into trouble on my account. You mustn't quarrel with your father, for that will do no good. If he tells you not to come here—well, perhaps you had better not, Rachael."

"But if it is Raines?"

"If he interferes with you, you can let me know, and I will teach him that, Maroon, or no Maroon, he is not above the law."

"If me father join wid him, what am I to do?" she asked appealingly, and he was troubled by the look in her eyes.

He felt the awkwardness of the situation. Bogle and Raines would certainly know that the girl had come to Aspley to warn him, and they might illtreat her as a result. This he could not allow, and he was certain that his mother and Joyce would urge him not to allow it.

"Try not to anger your father," he said; "but if they attempt to harm you at Stony Gut you can come here. My mother and Miss Graham will do all they can for you. You understand?"

Her face lighted up as she nodded swiftly and turned to go. It did not matter now what they did at Stony Gut; indeed, she hoped that they would give her some excuse for fleeing from the village. Mr. Carlton had promised to protect her.

For the second time that day she set out on the return to Stony Gut.

And while she wondered if her father's wrath would burst upon her when she returned to the village (and hoped that it would), Raines and Bowie were working insidiously to inflame Paul Bogle's mind. The meeting was over, and Bogle had asked for Rachael. His wife did not know where she was: it was Raines who suggested that she had probably hurried to Aspley to tell Mr. Carlton of her father's intention.

"I know she wasn't going to obey you. General," said Bowie with a laugh, and left his chief to digest that unpleasant remark. But Raines lingered. He wanted to see what would be Bogle's attitude when the girl returned, for on Bogle's attitude that night the success of his plot would depend.

Bogle was mortified, and in this mood might be violent. Raines was inspired by desire and hate. Rachael had wounded him with her tongue and galled him with the preference she so openly showed for the master of Aspley. He would like to witness her humiliation at her father's hands; it would tame her spirit a little. So he sat in the hut and waited with Bogle, who nursed his anger; and thus an hour went by.

The village had fallen silent after the conference in the heat of the sweltering afternoon. It was about this time of the day that heavy clouds began to gather over the hills, clouds black with rain which the parched and gaping ground would drink up thirstily when it fell. Every day brought the rainy season nearer, every day the approaching end of the drought was heralded by that silent cloud-gathering which grew and grew, became blacker and blacker and denser, a harbinger of blessings in portentous form. And when the hilltops were draped in an inky hue the heat would seem to concentrate and grow, and men sweated and dozed and endured as best they could till the cooler hours of the afternoon should come. Thus Stony Gut lay passive and somnolent, even while rebellion was being plotted in its midst.

The sharp sound of barking suddenly broke the stillness, and the noise of a horse's hoofs was heard. Then welcoming cries ran through the village, one or two at first, then a chorus. Bogle leaped up, surprised: some stranger had arrived. He walked to the door of the hut, looked out and uttered an exclamation of pleasure. Raines, thinking only of Rachael's return, started with anger at the interruption, and wondered whom the visitor might be. But Bogle left the hut without waiting to inform him.

He peeped out of the door and a curse escaped him. There, dismounted now, was Mr. George William Gordon, and the awakened people were pouring forth to meet him with shouts of joy. Bogle stood by his side proudly. It was fully five minutes before Gordon could escape from the crowd into Bogle's hut.

He cordially shook hands with Raines, who fervently hoped that he would leave before Rachael returned. But Mr. Gordon seemed in no hurry.

"A bit of a surprise this visit, isn't it,' Bogle?" he remarked. "I doubt if I can come to your great meeting, so I rode up to see you before going back to Kingston. I shall have a meeting there myself."

"Business?" asked Bogle, significantly.

"No doubt about that, my friend. I am starting the campaign I told you of a couple days ago. Men from all parts of the country are going to Kingston to meet me and to make arrangemnts with me. When is your gathering?"

"Next week Wednesday night."

"Very good. I shall have my meeting in Kingston on that same night, so that, though separated, our spirits shall be together in the work; and each shall be doing his share at the same time."

The suggestion captivated Paul Bogle. "We going to begin the real work from Wednesday night, then, Mr. Gordon?" he asked eagerly.

"We are; and now that we have settled that, can you lend me a boy to take a letter from me to Mr. Carlton at Aspley?"

Raines pricked up his ears. Bogle looked astonished.

"Mr. Carlton at Aspley?" he repeated. "But him—him is one of the men—"

"No, no. Bogle," Mr. Gordon interrupted hastily. "From all that I have heard, he is a very decent young man. Not all of his class are alike, you know; I wouldn't want to do business with him if I thought badly of him. Can I get my letter sent?"

"I will call a boy, for you," said Bogle dubiously, and suited the action to the word.

Bogle was thunderstruck to hear Dick Carlton spoken of so kindly by Mr. Gordon. The truth was that Mr. Gordon wanted to buy, on credit, some sugar boilers which he had heard Dick had for sale, and so was prepared to think well of Dick. Gordon's letter was to ask if it would be convenient for him to call at Aspley on Monday morning. The boy was to wait for an answer, and bring it to Stony Gut. Mr. Gordon explained that he was leaving the parish for Kingston on Monday evening.

Like a card-house touched roughly by the finger of a child, Raines saw his nicely constructed plot falling all to pieces. Bogle would not carry out his threat against Dick Carlton, now that Mr. Gordon was there to prevent it. Gordon had spoken as if he were a friend of Mr. Carlton's, and that would weigh more with Bogle than all that Bowie had said: even Rachael's disobedience would no longer be accounted a heinous crime.

Raines glared at Gordon malevolently, and silently wished that he should be present at his hanging. He would not be drawn into conversation. But, though he did not guess it, he was not the only one disappointed at the turn which events had taken: Rachael, when she entered the hut defiantly a little later on, was not a little surprised to be greeted by her father with no trace of anger (Bogle, indeed, was secretly pleased that he was no longer called upon to deal with his daughter harshly). Mr. Gordon made much of Rachael, and when, in answer to a question from him, she boldly replied that she had been to Aspley, he told her that he had a very good opinion of the people there.

After that, Raines waited no longer. He knew that his plot had failed.

XI

"The Voice of the People"

The city of Kingston lay dark under a darkling sky. It was not yet seven o'clock, but all the light had faded out of the west, and the moon had not yet risen.

In the east the stars were rising: as one looked upwards they seemed to spring out clear and distinct against their velvet background of vast unfathomable space. But the few pedestrians who picked their way about the narrow streets gave little thought to stars or sky, being constrained by sheer necessity to confine their whole attention to piloting their feet through unlighted thoroughfares where locomotion was difficult even when the sun shone high.

"Well! the Government ought to be ashamed of itself!" exclaimed a voice, which those who had heard it before would at once have recognised as Mr. Robson's. He had just blundered into a heap of old bottles and broken crockery which some thoughtful householder had deposited in the street but half an hour since, and the contact was the reverse of pleasant, especially as he was not quite certain what next he should do in order to avoid the possibility of being injured.

"Not a light in the city, and yet them take so much taxes from the people! Mr. Mace, you happen to have a match on you?"

His companion had not: he explained that he did not smoke.

"Well, I better step back carefully then," said Mr. Robson, suiting the action to the words by making a slight movement. As he did so, some of the bottles in the heap came tumbling down about his feet, which brought him to a standstill immediately.

"Lord! Just look what I have got meself into dis blessed night! You ever see my trial! There is about a hundred glass-bottle here, an' I am in de middle of them. I don't know which side to take. Brother Mace, lend me you' hand for a moment."

The gentleman thus addressed apparently sympathised with his companion, if mutterings expressive of regret were to be taken as a true indication of his feelings. But he did not seem very anxious to go nearer to the bottles among which Robson stood. He and the latter had been walking together, going slowly and carefully, as prudence dictated, when Robson, stirred by his own eloquence in proclaiming the grievances of the people, had suddenly quickened his steps and marched in front of his friend. With one stride he had landed amidst the refuse of a bibulous house, creating a crash and a clatter which had brought Mr. Mace to a precipitate halt.

Mr. Mace advanced hesitatingly towards the spot where Robson stood, afraid to move.

"I will bring the conditions appertaining to the metropolis forcibly before the attention of the authorities in my next issue," he protested wrathfully, thus at once proclaiming himself a journalist. "I will denounce them in the strongest language. Just fancy: gentlemen cannot walk about the streets without the obnoxious concurrence of accidents such—" his right foot encountering a bottle, Mr. Mace at once paused in his speech to take thought as to what he next should do. A considerable experience of the streets of Kingston after nightfall had taught him much wisdom, and caution was the result.

"Yes, Mace, I hope you will give it to them properly," groaned Robson; "but in de meantime I can't stay here all night, me friend, an' if you don't help me I don't see what I am goin' to do. Give me you' hand."

Thus implored, there was nothing for Mr. Mace to do but to extend his hand to his friend, who grasped it firmly.

"Mind now," warned Robson, "I am goin' to jump."

"Take care you don't land upon me," cried Mace, who reflected anxiously upon the size and weight of Robson.

The latter steadied himself, then made a leap, coming heavily to the ground and almost throwing Mace off his balance. Had he but stepped out boldly in any direction, he would as effectually have accomplished his escape; but the darkness and a certain timorousness of disposition had caused Mr. Robson to believe that he was in a dangerous position, and his imagination had pictured his feet as lacerated and bleeding even while his shoes were still intact.

They continued on their way, their rate of progress now being painfully slow; and sometimes they stepped upon soft malodorous objects, to one or two of which Mr. Robson alluded as "dead puss."

"You will have to come out wid a strong article about this in the paper," said he, as they went on. "I might have come by me death a little while ago if it wasn't that God was watchin'. We pay the Governor a big pay, an' what he do for it? If this isn't oppression, I want to know what it is!"

H.G. DE LISSER

"The Governor isn't directly responsible for the streets," explained Mr. Mace, just then endeavouring to see if it were a pool of water or another pile of bottles which he thought he perceived almost directly in front of him. "It is the town council. Let us go to the side, Mr. Robson, I think there is some water there, an' it's sure to smell bad. Don't walk too quick, or you wont know where you are next. That's all right now. It's the town council. We elect these white men and these fair coloured men, an' they neglect our interest. If the people would only elect men of their own colour, we would have an improvement. Mind yourself!" Mr. Robson, whom misfortune seemed to dog this night, had slipped upon a piece of banana skin, and had only been saved from falling by the timely clutch of his companion's hand.

"If it wasn't that I promise Mr. Gordon to come to de Tabernacle tonight. I would turn right back home," he exclaimed wrathfully. "It seems like de devil is on me track tonight, an' if I am not careful I will broke me neck before I get back."

Then suddenly, without a word, Mr. Robson halted in his tracks. With the dangers of the darkness ever in his mind, Mr. Mace promptly halted also. But this time Mr. Robson was not thinking about bottles or banana skins.

The thought that perhaps, after all, a malignant power was pursuing him, made him wonder whether he should continue on his way. Another thought occurred. What if the misfortunes he had experienced were warnings? Robson was superstitious at heart, and though fiery-worded when addressing a public meeting in the midst of sympathetic friends, and wordily courageous when discussing public matters in the daytime, he was always on the look-out for signs and omens. Also, he knew enough about the nature of the gathering at the Tabernacle tonight to be afraid that a somewhat perilous course was about to be embarked upon by Mr. Gordon and his friends.

"I doan't think I will go on. Brother Mace," he said, after thinking a moment or two. "Something tell me, 'Robson, be careful.' I hear the voice when I was in the midst of the bottle, I hear it again when I nearly broke my back a little while ago. I think I am goin' straight back home; prevention is better than cure, me friend. Mr. Gordon have money, but I don't have a tup (penny-ha'-penny), and if the white people ever hold Robson, goodbye to him! Them don't love me already, an' if them ever catch me—whoy!"

Mr. Mace, to whom no voice had been whispering warnings, presumably because he had not blundered into heaps of bottles or slipped on banana skin, did not approve of Mr. Robson's determination. This backing out on the part of the latter he considered shameful, especially as he himself was one of those who gathered courage from numbers and was not disposed to face any ordeal alone. He remonstrated.

"You could not with expediency leave Mr. Gordon to bear the burden of the political travail upon his single shoulders, surely," he said, bringing all the resources of an ornate vocabulary to bear upon the matter in hand. "We are friends and brothers in arms against wrong and oppression. Let justice be done though the heavens fall. If we are weak, who shall be strong; if we put our hands to the plough and turn back, how will the piladium of public liberty be exalted and the enfranchisement of the people be brought about by constitutional agitation? We are engaged in a righteous cause, and with tongue and pen we must lift up our voices against the strong. If we find Mr. Gordon going too far, we can quietly draw back, for I myself am not going to get myself in trouble like a fool."

He became colloquial. "Look here, Brother R., you come with me an listen quietly to what them saying. We can take our own time if them want to go too fast. But if we dosn't go tonight—an' I am not goin' without you—them will say we are lukewarm. Besides, Dr. Bruce is goin' to be there, an' he is a white man. If the Government touch us, they will have to touch him too, an' they not goin' to want to interfere with a white man like themself."

Hearing that a white man, and a Scotch man too, was to be present at the meeting, Mr. Robson plucked up courage once more. The presence of Dr. Bruce was an assurance of safety for the time being at least. He stopped out boldly, then immediately moderated his pace for fear more dragons in the form of bottles might be in the path.

"I didn't mean to say I wasn't goin', Mace," he explained, "but only that I had a sort of predestination that perhaps I better not go. But I vanish it from my mind, for I am not goin' to desert you and Mr. Gordon, whatever happen."

So saying, they turned up the street which led direct to the Tabernacle, as Mr. Gordon's meeting house was called, and in a little while arrived at that well-known building.

Through the panes of the closed sash-windows a dull light gleamed. The two men entered without rapping, and found themselves among some seventy other persons who had evidently come in but a little while before, for they were still greeting one another. The jealousie blinds were half open, thus at once admitting air and baffling curious eyes. Had Mr. Gordon followed his own mind he would have thrown every window wide, rejoicing in the publicity of the little meeting. But Mr. Robson had suggested to him earlier in the day the propriety of doing everything under the seal of semi-secrecy, Robson's training as a policeman having taught him the value of situations which could confuse witnesses intent only upon telling the truth.

In the dim light of the swinging lamps, Mr. Mace stood revealed as a man not black; that is to say, in the colour categories of the country he was classed as a "fair sambo," this term designating a person who has about one third of white blood in his veins. The habitual expression on his face was at once cunning and consequential. It may here be remarked also that Mr. Mace usually described himself as a journalist, politician and taxpayer, and much regretted that he was compelled to be the last.

"Glad to see you," said Mr. Gordon as he came up to the two friends and shook hands cordially. "I don't think we expect any more people. Gentlemen, I am going to introduce you to Dr. Bruce."

He led them forward to where a tall thin man with a short beard and serious face was standing, and to him they spoke with unaffected deference. With the exception of Mr. Gordon, all the people in the room regarded Dr. Bruce with something approaching reverence. It was known that he was the avowed enemy of the planters and a champion of the common people. And as a Scotchman and a man with the designation of doctor, it was generally admitted that he lent dignity to the cause of political freedom.

Mr. Mace burned with desire to make a speech that should impress the doctor, something that should prove that he, Mr. Mace, was a man of supereminent intellect and character. Mr. Robson assumed his most impressive air, stared at the lamps, stared round the room, coughed loudly more than once, then asked Mr. Gordon how "those fellows" were behaving now. By "those fellows" he meant the Governor and his advisers.

"They are going on as usual, Robson," answered Mr. Gordon. "They are too steeped in their evil ways to change. Only a moral earthquake can awaken them to a sense of the calamity in the land."

He had seated himself with Dr. Bruce upon a platform at the farther end of the room. He now leaned forward in a confidential manner with some papers in his hand, the other men being grouped on the benches and chairs before him.

"Gentlemen," he said, "I suppose you have seen the letter which appeared two days ago in the papers? It was written by a friend of ours in England, and points out clearly the miserable condition of this country."

He held up a newspaper as he spoke. They nodded assent.

"Well, I wont read it to you, for you know what it says already. The Governor is trying to find out how it got into the papers, but he hasn't found out yet, and I don't think he ever will. I knew all about it before it was published, as Mr. Robson can tell you, for I spoke to him about it. But I waited before I said anything, for I knew that with all their trying to keep it secret it would have to come out. Now I can tell you something more. The Governor has sent copies of this same letter to all the clergymen and custodes asking them to answer it, and we know what sort of answers they are going to give. Every one of them will lie, because they are dependent upon him. He wouldn't make a man like Dr. Bruce a custos, for he knows that Dr. Bruce would tell the truth. He took away my commission as a magistrate, because I wouldn't shut my eyes to all the wrong that was being done. But that will not prevent Dr. Bruce and myself from denouncing the evildoers, and we are not going to let the Governor and his satellites have everything their own way."

He paused, and a hum of approval greeted his speech. "That's what I call talkin'," said Mr. Robson, and glanced at Dr. Bruce to see how that gentleman took this exhibition of public spirit on his part.

"But there is more to tell you," Mr. Gordon continued. "Do you know that the Governor has sent a reply to this letter already?"

"Impossible!" exclaimed Mr. Mace; "it has not yet been discussed by the independent press. The deviation of such conduct from the path of strict official correctitude would lead to a constitutional agitation which would know no bounds. I refuse to believe it." Lest they should think that he did believe it (which was indeed the case), Mr. Mace repeated with emphasis: "I refuse to believe it."

"It is the truth," said Mr. Gordon gravely. "They wonder how I hear these things, but I hear them. Yes; the Governor has replied even before his clergymen and his custodes have all answered him. He has sent to tell the Queen that the people out here are worthless and lazy. What do you think of a Governor like that?"

Murmurs of anger arose as he asked the question. He patiently waited till they subsided. Gordon had the actor's instinct and knew how to stimulate the passions of a crowd.

"I am not asking you to believe what I say," he cried, as they waited upon him to continue. "I am not asking you to take my word for anything."

"We believe you, sir," cried his hearers.

"You believe me?" he asked triumphantly; "very well; now believe your own eyes and ears!"

From among the papers in his hand he swiftly drew forth a document, and held it towards them; it was a copy of a letter addressed by the Governor to the English Colonial Office, and though it had not the Governor's signature it was accepted by everyone present as a true copy of a despatch of his.

Mr. Robson was positive regarding the authorship of the document. "The way this letter begin," he declared, examining it at close quarters, "show it was the Governor who write it. Them can't deceive me," he added confidently, the implication being that he had again triumphed over a base endeavour on the part of the authorities to puzzle his acute intelligence.

"Listen, then," said Mr. Gordon, after the writing had been sufficiently passed round, handled, looked at, and returned to him; "listen, and you will hear what the Governor says about you, the abuse he has showered upon you."

Slowly and with bitter emphasis he read the letter out. Fairly judged, it was not merely an indictment of the people, though some of the sentences were biting and severe.

"'The young and the strong of both sexes.'" Mr. Gordon read, "'those who are well able to work, fill the goals of the colony.'" (A howl of execration burst from the lips of Mr. Robson, and was echoed by the other men). "'It is undeniable that wages are lower and necessaries dearer than in former years, therefore—'"

"Well, that is the first true thing that man ever said," interrupted Mr. Mace, his tone indicating regret that the Governor should have admitted the truth. Mr. Mace felt that if the Governor were going to indulge in frank admissions of that kind, the occupation of opposition journalists would soon be gone.

"Yes," said Mr. Gordon, "but listen to this: 'therefore the mere labourer for hire is necessarily poorer.' What does he mean by 'necessarily poorer?' Why necessarily? If the people were paid properly, if they were treated better, if they had the Government on their side, would they be so poor? Don't you see that he is defending the planters, the oppressors of this land? He can't say that the people are not poor, but he says that those who are able to work and who are young and strong are filling up the prisons. That is the character he gives our people to the Queen; but the multiplication of wrongs is the storing up of future trouble."

At this point Mr. Robson rose to make "a few remarks;" but Mr. Gordon, fearing that these remarks might occupy a full hour in the making, hastily waved Robson back into his seat and proceeded with his reading. He selected one sentence for special emphasis: "'Deterioration, decadence and decay are everywhere visible, and the elements which ought to sustain and improve the national character, and promote the welfare and progress of the country, are gradually disappearing.'"

He had ended, and now he stood up, holding the letter away from him as though it were some unholy thing.

"You have heard it!" he cried, "heard what the Governor has said about this country! It may all be true, but who is to blame for it? And what are they doing to improve the conditions they complain of? When I have said things not half so strong, they have cursed me and reviled me and humiliated me; but now that the Almighty has raised up friends for us in England they are bound to admit that what I said was true." He laughed aloud, a hard, bitter laugh. "But they still must put the blame upon the poor people. These are all going to prison. They are all bad. They can all work, but will not. Surely the Lord heareth, and the axe is laid to the root of the tree!"

"Some reply should be sent to that letter," said Dr. Bruce, "it suggests no remedies."

"It shall be dealt with in my paper!" exclaimed Mr. Mace. "I will lash the letter. I will hold the writer up to public scorn as a man without humanitarian principles and devoid of all sense of human understanding. Never shall it be said that I failed in my duty to my country. Tyranny and oppression are stalking abroad in the land, and we must strangle the monster with constitutional agitation."

"You must not mention this letter in print. Mace," said Mr. Gordon warningly, "or they may suspect whom I got it from, and that may prevent me from getting any more of their secrets in the future. That wont do."

Mr. Robson rose.

"Let us call public meetings," he suggested, "meetings to discuss the letter from England that has appeared in the papers. Let us answer that letter ourselves. Why should we allow de Governor, who is only a old cripple, to talk what him like about us? Look at me! Is a man like me fulling up gaols? Am I deteriorating? Look how I been treated. If my skin was fairer I would have a good job today, for there is plenty of jobs going, but as I am black they keep me out of everything an' take no notice of me. I move that we should have public meetings all about to denounce the Governor. The time to talk has arrive, an' I am goin' to be the first to lift up my voice. The voice of the people is the voice of God."

"Hear, hear!" shouted Mr. Mace and there was tumultuous applause.

Mr. Robson mopped his face with a red handkerchief and wondered if he had impressed the doctor as an eloquent speaker. An animated conversation now began, each man offering suggestions as to what might be the best thing to do at what they called "this crisis."

But Mr. Gordon himself said nothing. When the murmur of talk had subsided a little he turned to Dr. Bruce. "What is your suggestion, doctor?" he asked.

Dr. Bruce drew himself up in his chair and looked the quintessence of wisdom. It was obvious that the audience breathlessly awaited his words. Mr. Mace felt that, through the doctor, he was in some way in direct communication with all the Scottish heroes of the past. He whispered to Robson that Dr. Bruce was probably a descendant of King Robert Bruce, and bore a strong resemblance to a picture of that monarch which he possessed.

"I would say, Mr. Gordon, that you should hold public meetings all over the island, as you yourself have thought of doing. The voice of the people must be heard," said Dr. Bruce.

"Your advice is good, doctor, as it always is," agreed Mr. Gordon, highly gratified.

"What a piece of advice, though, eh?" asked Mr. Mace aloud, addressing himself to no one in particular. Admiration thrilled in his voice. "If you try and don't succeed, try, try, try again," he recited: "that is what King Robert the Bruce said when he saw the spider who couldn't get into his web, an' that is what the doctor tells us tonight. I second his resolution!"

"Very good," said Mr. Gordon, "that is decided, and now I will make my arrangements."

There were men there from every parish of the colony, and to everyone Mr. Gordon gave his instructions. They were to arrange for public meetings which he should attend. They were to gather the people in large numbers and impart to them what they had learnt that night about the Governor's letter. Every man was to be an active agent in the work to be done. They had nothing to fear, urged Gordon, for they themselves saw that there were white men who sympathised with their cause. The doctor was the first amongst these men.

"And the greatest," added Mr. Mace enthusiastically. The presence of Dr. Bruce was a great comfort to him.

"And now, gentlemen," said Mr. Gordon, "we have started on a course of action from which they must be no turning back."

"But of course it will be all constitutional agitation?" Mr. Mace broke in anxiously. "It is to be understood by everybody that we are only making use of the rights of free British subjects to indulge in free speech."

"Yes," agreed Mr. Robson emphatically. "Everybody here understand that. Mind, gentlemen: nobody can go away from here and say dat Robson ever say a word that was not constitutional agistation. I remember every word I say, an' anybody that try to put word in me mouth that didn't come out there, I will put him before a magistrate. I suggest, Mr. Gordon, that we sing the National Anthem before we disperse. That will hinder everybody from tellin' lies about us."

"Don't be alarmed, Robson," said Mr. Gordon reassuringly. "We are all friends here. Before you go, gentlemen, I have only one other thing to say to you, but it is important. At this moment, even while we are speaking, a great event is taking place in St. Thomas-in-the-East. At this moment, thousands of people are assembled with Paul Bogle to ask God's guidance at this difficult time. Bogle is a man amongst men, a true leader of the people, one of the humble whom God has called to be great. We are in unison with him in spirit tonight. He is doing his work while we are doing ours."

Again there was applause. Then the men departed, jubilant, talking of the work they had to do.

"And what do you think of tonight's meeting, doctor," asked Gordon, when he and Dr. Bruce were left alone.

"You have been making history," said the doctor, and spoke more truly than he knew.

XII

The Sign from Heaven

Tomorrow Joyce was to leave Aspley for that visit to her relatives in the north of the colony, of which she had spoken to Mr. Solway. She was restless. For the last three days she had not left Aspley, had foregone her usual afternoon ride; this because she more than half suspected that Mr. Solway, who had made no promise, might find some reason for being on the road, especially as he knew that soon she would be many miles away from this neighbourhood.

She had been thinking much about Solway in the intervening days, more than she cared to admit to herself. She had said nothing to her aunt or Dick of her meeting with him; she knew he would have hated that. Not once had she heard his name mentioned by her people. They were leaving Aspley without returning Mr. Burton's call; under different circumstances she herself would have proposed that they should go to Cranebrook, but now she acquiesced in the general silence on this subject, pretending not to notice it. She wondered why Solway was disliked; she had recognised the strain of coarseness in him, the domineering nature of the man; and yet she thought that beneath it all there was something better: she was prepared to make allowances for a man who had told her with every show of sincerity that he loved her, and had pleaded with her for only an occasional meeting.

But still she had refrained from going out upon the highroad: she would not meet him clandestinely, had no reason to do so. And now Dick was gone to the town of Morant Bay; night had fallen, and a fit of restlessness possessed her. Something in the atmosphere affected her; she was filled with a vague discontent, a desire for movement, excitement.

She rose suddenly from her seat by the window, where she had been looking out upon the melancholy shadows of the now silent estate.

"I think I'll go for a ride. Aunt Gertrude," she said; "it is a beautiful evening, and our last here for some time."

"Alone?" asked Mrs. Carlton, a little disturbed.

"No; I'll take Charles with me. There is nothing to fear on the road, is there?"

"Nothing except the rain; but that may come at any moment now."

"It is quite clear above," said Joyce, glancing out of the window; "I'll go and get ready," and she hurried off before Mrs. Carlton could interpose any further remark.

Ten minutes later, attended by Charles, she was galloping along the open road, exhilarated by the cool wind that blew sharply in her face. She judged it had been raining higher up, the air was moisture-laden and delightful; among the trees and bushes on either hand the fire-flies were flitting: a shower of glowing embers. The moon, now nearly at its full, was rapidly rising; it lighted up the wide landscape, threw trees and hills into silvery relief, and paled the brightness of the scattered, distant stars.

To the east, near the glowing orb above, a great mass of dense black cloud was moving slowly across the sky. A vast expanse it covered, the edge of it sharply defined against the pale blue of that part of the heavens which the lamp of night illuminated brightly. It seemed as though the inky mass were gaining inch by inch on the shining space, were menacing it with an inexorable doom of obliteration; it was like a huge formless monster advancing slowly but with pitiless tread towards a thing of beauty which it had doomed to extinction; and as it moved it darted forth tongues of lightning, and growled and muttered with thunderous voice.

"The spirit of darkness and the spirit of light," thought Joyce as she galloped on. "How typical of this land!" A wave of excitement flowed through her; the weird, wild beauty of the night had thrown its spell upon her; she was in the throes of its fascination. It might rain; she knew that, but little recked of it. She would not yet turn back. On and on she went, her attendant keeping within easy distance of her. Then she came to a path which plunged into a wood on her left hand and seemed to lead into its innermost recesses. She pulled in her horse and waited until Charles came up.

"I don't remember having noticed that road before, Charles; where does it lead to?" she questioned.

"To Stony Gut, missis; this is one of the short-cut road to dat place."

"Rachael Bogle lives there?"

"Yes, missis."

"I should like to see this village; is it far from here, Charles?"

"No, ma'am; not more than 'bout half a mile. Dis road take you to it quick."

"I think I will ride there."

"But suppose it rain, Miss Joyce? De cloud is very heavy, an' you may ketch cold."

"I don't think it will rain just yet; shall I ride straight on?"

"Stony Gut is a funny place, you know, ma'am; some bad people live there. An' them have a meeting tonight that them doan't want no white people to see. You may not like it, ma'am."

"Nonsense; they are not murderers or thieves, are they?"

"Oh no, ma'am; but them is very tough, an'—"

Charles hesitated for the right word of dissuasion to employ at this particular moment.

"Are you afraid, Charles?" Joyce asked; "do you really think any of them will trouble me?"

"Them couldn't trouble you, Miss Joyce, as long as I am here," Charles replied stoutly. "I doan't 'fraid for no nagur people like meself; and them must be afraid of you. But I t'ought as you mightn't like to see dem, so I tell you first before you go. Ride straight on till I tell you stop, ma'am."

Joyce rode into the semi-obscurity of the trail, the branches of the trees on each side uniting overhead to form a canopy through which the moonlight struggled in quivering, fitful gleams. Not far in front of her could she see, but the horse went steadily on at a fast walk, and the fireflies danced before her, sometimes brushing across her face. She looked upwards; only tiny spaces of the sky were visible, and it seemed to her that the light was waning. She wondered if the rain would fall before she came to the end of the journey; but curiosity held her and she continued on the way.

Presently she heard a faint sound, a cry that came stabbing through the gloom; it was followed by another and another.

"What is that, Charles?" she asked. He was directly behind her, keeping as close to her as he could.

"De people singin', missis."

The singing grew louder and louder as she went on; surely she had heard something like that before? Where was it—ah, she remembered now; it was on her first night in Jamaica that she had heard it. So this was a meeting like those which were held opposite to Denbigh. A revival meeting. Her heart began to beat faster, her pulses quickened. Was it wise to have come? she asked herself.

But there was really nothing to fear, she reflected; these people did no harm; even cautious Charles had said so.

The singing became clear and distinct; it rose in a mighty volume, accompanied above by the heavy boom and rumble of the thunder.

"Stop, missis!" cried Charles when they had gone a little farther, "if you doan't want them to see you, you musn't go on in dis road."

"You lead the way, Charles."

The lad passed her, peering in front of him; she followed. He turned a little to the left into a still narower path which was hardly more than a foot trail. After proceeding for another couple of minutes he halted and sprang off his horse, leading it out of the way among the trees. He returned and led Joyce's horse almost up to the edge of a steep decline down the side of which went the narrow path. No horse could go that way, but a human being, used to such places, could scramble up and down it with no great difficulty. "You can see from dis spot, missis," Charles whispered to Joyce, "an' them can't see you."

It was a strange wild sight that met her eyes. The ground sloped downwards for some sixty feet, and on the other side rose steeply up again, thus forming a gorge or canon through which, in long-past times, a mighty river may have flowed. The bottom of the gorge, at this point, was wide; farther to the north was the village, but this Joyce could not distinctly see from where she stood. Trees grew on both sides of the Gut, but sparsely, so that though, with the aid of distance, and the now dimming light of the moon, they hid Joyce from the sight of the people, they did not prevent her from seeing what passed in the lighted space below.

The great mass of cloud overhead had encroached still further on the shining blue of the moon-illuminated sky; the edge of it, clear-cut and regular but half an hour before, had now broken into jagged projections and indents; the lightning flickered more sharply and incessantly than before, the growl of the thunder was now continuous. A peninsula of cloud, clinging to the main body by but an inky arm, reached out towards the moon, and to a watcher from the earth seemed but a yard or two away from it. A thin dark veil of vapour had already crept over the face of the earth's satellite, which now shone with a faint and sickly gleam. No longer stood the beauty and the splendour of the scenery revealed. Vague shadows loomed in a ghostly crepuscle, the wind had grown bleak and chill, and was moaning through the trees. And still, from the assembled crowd below, the awful chanting rose steadily toward the cloud-hung sky.

The air to which the people sang was strange to Joyce. It thundered denunciation at times, shrieked agony, sobbed contrition, and surged upwards in frenzied supplication. So may the priests of Baal have sung to their god in olden times, and the fanatics of all ages have implored a sign from heaven. Joyce shuddered. There was something heartbreaking in the sound that filled the gorge and went rolling over wide spaces of country. Most of the people below were clothed in white. Those who wore clothes of an ordinary description yet had their heads swathed in white turbans, save only a few men here and there who wore fantastic turbans of red.

They crouched, these singers, forming a circle, in the centre of which fierce fires blazed. Occasionally armfuls of wood were thrown upon these fires by a woman who moved about with a slow circular motion, like one in a semi-trance. Standing erect within the circle, clothed in white, with a great turban of flaming scarlet on his head, was a man, inclined to stoutness, slightly above middle height, his face deeply pitted with smallpox, his eyes rolling and shining wildly. In his right hand he bore a slender wand, and this he sometimes moved from side to side with a quick nervous jerk. The singers followed the motion of the rod, rocking their bodies to and fro. And now and again he led the singing, thundering forth the chant in a deep far-reaching bass.

Suddenly the chanting ceased. A death-like silence descended on the scene. Only the moaning of the wind was heard, and the rumble of the thunder overhead. Another veil of darkness floated over the face of the moon.

"Listen, oh, listen; for the Spirit will speak to us tonight. Give ear, for the Lord Himself will come amongst us!"

The man had spoken and a groan burst from those who heard him. He turned his face upwards, and Joyce could see the whites of his eyeballs staring at the blackness above. Charles shivered as he looked, and crept a little closer to his mistress.

"The wrongs of the people have not escaped the glance of the Most High. We are oppressed, and we bear it; we are ill-treated, an' we answer not a word. But how long. O Lord, how long! Speak, an' tell Thy servant. Speak through the mouth of de ancient ones, send down Thy Spirit an' communicate wid us, for the burden is more than we can bear. Speak tonight. O Lord, tonight!"

A low wail greeted his words, and swelled into a chant, subdued this time and slow, sounding as though it came from far away, or from singers who sang in their sleep.

Then, one by one, six women rose and stepped inside the circle, moving round and round to the sound of the singing and gently swaying their bodies as they moved. Last of all came an ancient crone, a woman who, even from where she gazed, Joyce could perceive was withered and ugly; she too was draped in white, and in her hand she held a bundle of rods. She joined in the dance, the others forming a ring around her. The man stood still with folded arms and watched her; every eye was fixed upon her as slowly she swept round and round.

Charles was trembling with excitement. His superstitious fears and beliefs were fully aroused; he dreaded lest the woman and the man below should smell him out and hurl some deadly curse at him. His mistress, he thought, was safe; she was buckra, white, and above the black man's evil. Yet he never once thought of leaving her alone; he wished she were away, but so long as she chose to stay he would remain with her. From her presence, too, he drew a certain courage. He felt that she was not afraid, and a feeling of pride possessed him—his young mistress could look calmly down upon a scene which even the principal actors regarded with secret awe.

He ventured a little information.

"Missis?"

"Yes?"

"Dat man is Paul Bogle, de father of de gal you speak about tonight, an' who always come to Aspley. He is a powerful man."

"And the old woman, Charles, who is she?"

"One Modder Bicknell, ma'am, a bad ole ooman. I hear she kill plenty of people wid wickedness—wid obeah, ma'am. She put ghost upon dem."

"She looks capable of anything," muttered Joyce to herself; then bent forward a little to hear what the woman had begun to say.

The crone was speaking now; she had quickened her pace and was whirling about swiftly, both arms raised high above her head. The chant had died away to a low hum; the strained attitudes of the people showed they were listening intently. Joyce heard the sounds that came from the woman; gibberish, it seemed, an incoherent meaningless spluttering from foaming lips. "She is going to have a fit,' thought Joyce, with a shiver of disgust.

"What is she saying?" she whispered to Charles.

"I doan't know, missis; she talkin' in de unknown tongue: de Spirit is talkin' through her."

Still the stream of meaningless sounds poured out of the woman's foaming mouth, and still she whirled round the circle. Then the peninsula-like cloud which had been threatening the moon detached itself from the parent mass and drifted towards the now dimmed, half-enshrouded orb. The woman stood stock-still and darted one arm toward it: "A sign!" she screamed, "de answer of de Spirit!"

Every face was turned upwards. Frantic eyes gazed upon what seemed to be a struggle between the light and the darkness above. "The answer is coming!" thundered Paul Bogle. "We will know tonight whether black or white will win!"

Steadily the cloud moved forward, and after it came creeping the dense black mass that now covered half the sky. At this moment the moon struggled out from beneath the veils of vapour that had dimmed it. Serenely it shone, as though conscious of its triumph. A groan burst from Paul Bogle and was echoed by hundreds of the expectant crowd.

But still they stared, and inch by inch the darkness drew towards the light. Joyce, too. Infected by the spirit of the people, watched the scene with intensest interest. At last the cloud touched the edge of the moon, a moment after it had swept over most of it. Darker and darker grew the night, swiftly the light departed. Soon it was all gone, and gloom profound had swallowed trees and hills. Only where the fires burned brightly at the bottom of the gorge could any object be distinctly seen.

There had been silence during the engulphing of the moon. Now there arose a wild cry of triumph, and high above it rang the voice of Paul Bogle—"A sign, the Spirit give us a sign!" Once again the chant rose, its measure beating quick and fierce upon the air. "Come, Charles," gasped Joyce, "I have stayed here long enough."

Carefully she backed her horse; then Charles begged her to dismount, took the horse by the bit, and led it round some trees and into the path again. Joyce mounted, and Charles, springing upon his horse, took the lead. In a short space of time they came to the broader way. The lad knew every inch of it, and took her safely to the open road.

Could Joyce have seen her face at that moment, she would have been startled by its pallor. She was shivering, nervous tremors ran through her; bitterly she blamed herself for having gone to Stony Gut, and, once there, for having stayed so long. What did that fiendish woman mean? What was the sign for which the man had waited and prayed? So the fears her aunt had expressed when she saw those mountain fires at Denbigh were not unfounded after all; a crisis threatened, and Paul Bogle and his kind believed they had received a sign from God, a promise of victory. She thought it must be very late; her aunt would be thinking that some accident had befallen her. She went as quickly as she dared. Charles now galloping by her side. He too was thinking, for he understood much that he had seen.

A few drops of rain fell, then the lightning flashed awfully, lighting up the surrounding country with terrible vividness. The road lay straight before her; another awful flash, and she saw a man riding at full speed towards them. "Dick, O Dick!" she cried, for in that instant she had recognised the rider. She pulled at her horse, calling out to Charles to stop. Her cousin had seen her too, though his horse had carried him past her. He was soon at her side, Charles falling to the rear once more.

"Joyce, what has happened? What is the matter? What kept you? Did not Charles warn you about the rain?"

He spoke hurriedly, labouring under great excitement. He had to shout his words amidst the crashing of thunder.

"Dick, I should not have stayed out so long; I know that it was foolish of me. But I went on to Stony Gut, and I saw—O, it is too dreadful!" She broke off sharply, fighting desperately the hysterical wave that surged through her. He knew that she was saying something, but heard no words.

They rode hard, and it was a stern race between them and the rain. But the horses were good, and the lightning, though terrible to face, yet helped to light them on their way. The heavy drops continued to fall, but the downpour only came after they had safely arrived at Aspley. "Thank God!" exclaimed Dick, as they entered the house, and heard the swift rush of the rain behind them.

All that night, until about three o'clock in the morning, the rain continued to fall. At five the next morning Mrs. Carlton and her niece were up and dressed; and sitting in the lighted dining room Joyce told her cousin all that she had heard and seen the night before.

"We can only watch them," said Dick. "I will write to the Governor about this." He looked care-worn and thoughtful.

The morning broke gloomily; no sun; only a dreary canopy of leaden sky, with black clouds driving across it.

Wrapped in waterproofs, they took their places in the buggy and started upon their tedious journey. As they went on they passed by groups of peasants. Joyce observed that many of these were clothed in white, and that their heads were bound up with white cloth. "They are some of those I saw last night," she said, and shuddered in a spasm of fear.

BOOK II

I

A Meeting of Heroes

When the West Indian hurricane is approaching the atmosphere gives warning. For days the heat is intense; there is a brooding stillness in the upper regions of the air; the sky is a dull grey canopy, a lifeless, neutral pall. Then black masses of cloud riven by livid lightnings come hurrying from the direction where the wild winds are raging scores of miles away; great sudden puffs of breeze sweep over the sea, lashing the surface of the water to angry hissing waves, striking the land with savage fury and bending and tossing the heavy branches of the trees with irresistible might. These are but indications of the coming destruction. Soon the storm itself, speeding fast upon the heels of its couriers, bursts upon the terror-stricken islands in a deluge of rain, and roars and rages as it passes onward to northern climes. In a few hours it has come and gone. But in its wake is desolation; behind it is visible evidence of its terrific strength.

So too, before the bursting of the storm of human rage and passion, the wild expression of hate and anger and madness, there are signs and warnings which the clear-sighted may plainly read. In the month of October, 1865, such signs were not lacking; from one end of Jamaica to the other there was restlessness, uneasiness, a presentiment of approaching disaster. The wise knew that the people were discontented, and acknowledged to themselves that behind all the exaggeration of the agitators there was truth enough to occasion searchings of heart, questionings of conscience. The poverty was intense, the ex-slave owner stubbornly withheld the land from the people, in the petty courts the peasant had little hope of justice, and thousands felt that only through a crisis could reform be effected. And yet, with a strange fatuity, most of those who felt uneasy in their hearts refused openly to believe that all would not be well.

Mr. Gordon had sent his emissaries throughout the country, and north and south and east and west sedition had been preached. And now from mouth to mouth passed that famous word of the arch-agitator—"the axe is laid to the root of the tree." When would the tree fall, and, after that, what? Bogle had his answer ready. From Heaven he had received a sign.

In the towns the agitators were busy, and conspicuous among them stood one man. That man was Mr. Mace, journalist, politician and taxpayer, and strong advocate of constitutional agitation. Mr. Mace was now writing as violently as he thought compatible with personal safety. Which means that he was attacking the Governor and Government with every form of vituperation he could command.

Mr. Mace's office was situated in one of the lanes of the city, and the warmest admirer of that gentleman could not contend that the exterior of the building was at all impressive. The place, a single-storey structure, had once been a shop where groceries were retailed; as a shop it had not succeeded in attracting customers, and had been abandoned by occupant after occupant in despair. For long intervals it remained without a tenant, and its owner had never seen the wisdom of painting or repairing it, as it did not seem likely that the rent received would ever repay any expenditure made in giving to it a presentable appearance. Then Mr. Mace, one day searching for a place where he might, metaphorically, lay his weary editorial head, heard of this untenanted shop and offered to take it over. Its owner closed with him at once, and in this unprepossessing office it was that some very pungent editorials were written, and political conferences frequently held. These conferences were sometimes enlivened by little feasts, the result of subscriptions raised on the spot and expended with a good deal of deliberation and judiciousness.

The office had a centre door and two shuttered windows on each side of this door; you walked into it from the lane, no step intervening. Once inside the office, you were not filled with admiration for its appointments, however highly you might think of the genius of the editor. It was dirty, littered, and furnished with but a rickety dealboard table, a bench without a back placed against one of the walls, and three or four yellowish chairs with their seats half gone. Behind this office, in a little room in a yard which was inhabited by some of the workers of the city, was the printing press, a small machine worked by hand, bought on credit some time before, and even then reputed to be but third-hand. In this room also were three compositors' cases containing a small quantity of type and some of the appliances used in the printing offices of that time.

Mr. Mace's organ appeared weekly; this, he said, gave his readers an opportunity of thinking over for six days the views which he expressed upon current events.

This morning, Mr. Mace, Mr. Robson, and four other gentlemen sat in the office commenting on the progress of the campaign which had been inaugurated by Mr. Gordon on the same night that Paul Bogle had perceived the sign from Heaven. Mr. Mace sat in front of the table, which he called his desk. The other chairs and the bench were occupied by his friends, who were not unaccustomed to physical discomfort. Mr. Mace was looking over a placard spread out before him; he was reading it with great deliberation and evident enjoyment.

"This will fix hem," he observed slowly, when he had ended his reading; "this is the very thing. Some of those fellows in St. Thomas must have jumped when they read this. You want to hear it?"

"Yes, make us hear it," said Mr. Robson "though I know all about it already. Mr. Gordon show it to me before him send it to Morant Bay."

"I have not perused its contents hither-to," said a tall, dark, clean-shaven man, addressed as Mr. Bolt, who emphasised every word he uttered, and spoke with grave deliberation. He was a constant contributor to the paper edited by Mace, and was regarded in certain quarters as a leader of thought. He surpassed Mr. Mace in the careful selection of his words. With him it was habitual; with the editor it was only occasional.

"Listen, then," said Mr. Mace; "it's worth hearing." His auditors assumed attitudes indicating the greatest attention; Mr. Mace cleared his throat once or twice and began.

The placard set forth that public meetings were to be held all over the island for the purpose of protesting against the wicked misrepresentations made against the people by the Governor and his supporters. It called upon the starving and naked people to come forth and make their voices heard; it implored them to reveal their true condition, their helplessness, and then to call upon heaven to witness and have mercy

Sentence by sentence was rolled out by Mr. Mace with every appropriate rhetorical gesture he could command. When he came to the words, "Let not a crafty jesuitical priesthood deceive you. Prepare for your duty. Remember the destitution in the midst of your families, and your forlorn condition"—when he declaimed these words his audience sprang to their feet and cheered. Much encouraged, he read on to the end; when he had ended he leaned back in his chair with a sigh of satisfaction.

"Now, gentlemen," he asked, "what do you think of that as a little fire on their tails?"

"It is fire," said Mr. Robson, "fire an' brimstone. They see now that they can't do what they please when we open cur mouth to talk. I hear they are all afraid already. You goin' down to Morant Bay tomorrow?"

"No," replied Mr. Mace. "My duty keeps me pinned to the point of action. From here I address the people and bring to their keen understanding a sense of the existing conditions that exist. That is purely constitutional." As usual with the editor, after he had balanced himself for some time on the dizzy heights of the Queen's English, he immediately dropped to the colloquial. "Not me, me brother," he added, "I don't want policeman to put hand 'pon me. Coward man keep sound bones, an' my bones don't too strong already. You goin', Robson?"

"Why should I go if you 'fraid to go?" was the not unreasonable reply of Mr. Robson.

"In consideration," said Mr. Bolt, "in consideration of the famous speeches which Mr. Robson delivered what time he spoke in defence of the public rights and liberties to extensive audiences of his fellowmen, I think his presence at Morant Bay, now that Bogle is preparing a striking demonstration there—and subsequently at other meetings henceforward to be held—his presence. I say, would be a distinct assistance to those who shall make the welkin ring."

Mr. Bolt was here referring to two speeches Mr. Robson had recently made at public meetings, when, carried away by the enthusiasm of the moment, he had uttered sentiments which were distinctly dangerous. He had been much praised for them, but hated to hear his conduct alluded to. For his wife had warned him that "he had better mind the prison," and now he never saw a policeman but he trembled, fearing lest the officer might have on his person a warrant for his arrest.

"Look here, Mr. Bolt," he said frankly, "If I had known there was any newspaper reporter at de meetings the other day, I wouldn't have said a word. It is a good thing them didn't report what we say, an', to tell you the God's truth, I don't want to hear anything more about de speech I make. I don't remember I said all the things everybody say I say, an' I will deny it if the Government prosecute me. You can go to St. Thomas if you like. Robson staying at home."

"But, Mr. Robson," remonstrated Mr. Bolt, "would you now relinquish your principles because of a sordid fear of consequences? Is this the time to falter? 'Breathes there a man with soul so dead, who never to himself has said, this is my own, my native land?' I feel the sentiment of disappointment in you. I regret to confess it, but confess it I must."

Mr. Bolt shook his head sadly, and shifted in his seat. Mr. Robson snorted contemptuously.

"That is what you and Mace is always saying," he barked. "Why don't you an' Mace go to these meetings an' talk? Why you leave everything to Robson? When I heard that the Government send a man-o'-war round the island the other day, how you think I feel? I see every word I say in Kingston and Spanish Town dance before my eye like fire, an' me wife say: 'them coming for you now, sure.' I couldn't sleep for a week, an' I wouldn't leave me house to let anybody see me. But you was all right. Mace write all de time, an' he is safe. It is only poor Robson they would hold, an' what am I getting more than anybody else? If I can get anything out of politics, it is good. But what I to get?"

"You have nothing to lose, so long as you are constitutional," observed Mr. Mace sagaciously. "We are working for a great end."

"What is that end?" demanded Robson; "I doan't see it now. We been talkin' and writing all this time, an' the Government don't make a move. They don't even say to me: 'dog, here is a job.' What is the use of it? Not a man work harder than me all this time for my country, an' I know that if anything happen I am the first man the Government is goin' to hold. An' you want me to go to Morant Bay? What for? To tie meself up more? If you can tell me what is going to come out of all this constitutional whatever you call it, I will listen. But I do enough already, an' am not doing no more."

"What are we striving for, gentlemen?" asked Mr. Bolt after a long silence. "What are our aims?" The question was intended as mere rhetoric, but Robson took it seriously.

"What we striving for? If you don't know, why you ask me? I don't know any more than you."

"Is it not to reform the country?" asked Mr. Bolt with a sweeping gesture.

"Of course," murmured two or three of his auditors, who were very pleased to have their motives explained to them. To reform the country might mean anything, but one was not called upon to go into particulars.

"Very well, then. Our aim is high. We follow a great leader. Be just and fear not, I say; then if thou fall'st thou fall'st a blessed martyr. What more could you ask?"

"I have a wife and three children," said Mr. Robson, "an' I don't want to fall at all. Why am I to be a blessed martyr, Mr. Bolt? I tell you I couldn't sleep for a week after I hear about that man-o'-war, an' every time I see a policeman me blood run cold. Things is coming to blood now. If Mr. Gordon want to go on, he can go on; he know what he is doin'. But I hear about some funny things in St. Thomas, an' I know that the people down there is not making fun. Mr. Gordon say them don't mean any harm, an won't do anything that is not lawful, but I don't sure about that. Bowie was here last night; he come to my house, an' tell me that the people swear them wont stand any more foolishness an' that them is going to act now. I tell him, 'All right. Bowie, but mind you'self,' and me wife call me when he went away an' ask me if I think my neck stronger than anybody else's neck, so that the rope that hang them wont hang me too. I like the words you read out to me just now; they are strong. But I not goin' down to any Morant Bay to speak. I done wid politics for the present. I will give somebody else a chance now."

That Robson the fearless speaker, Robson the man who held that he had been basely treated, Robson the leonine (up to recently), should suggest all sorts of vague fears, and show a decided inclination to back out of anything like active participation in the crusade now proceeding so vigorously—this was a terrible fact to face. Every man felt uneasy. They glanced at each other with enquiring eyes; they too had heard rumours that seemed to threaten developments of a more serious nature than any that had yet taken place. They argued that they could in no way be held responsible for anything that might happen. They confined themselves to denunciation, claiming the right of free speech to which, as British subjects, they were entitled. But Robson's wife had perceived that he might not be held blameless should disturbances occur, and Robson had now formally declared his intention of keeping out of harm's way, for some time at least.

Mr. Robson resumed. "Mace say he is not going to St. Thomas, for he have to stay here an' write. You going, Mr. Bolt?"

"Gladly would I go," replied that gentleman. "No dread of personal consequences would ever keep me back from the scene of duty when my country calls with thunderous declamation. But health, the state of my health, forbids. My medical physician has warned me against all excesses; I must be careful. My regrets are deep, but necessity is the mother of—" he stopped, realising that the saying, though perhaps never more correctly applied than in this instance, would not appropriately express his excuse. "Necessity knows no law," he concluded lamely, correcting his quotation.

Mr. Robson glanced enquiringly at the other men; each one gave some reason for remaining in Kingston, for not identifying himself with the forthcoming demonstrations in Morant Bay.

Mr. Mace grew thoughtful, "I must take care," he remarked, "that nobody outside of ourselves know that I printed these placards, and none of you must say a word about them, you hear?"

They all promised.

"Mr. Gordon is a host in himself," he went on, endeavouring to express admiration in tones of ecstacy, "an' there is plenty of people down there that will speak an' act. After all, it is their meeting, an' they must come forward in their own individuality. We have done our share. We have confined ourselves to constitutional agitation. They can never say that a single one of us had anything to do with any trouble, and I don't believe any trouble is going to occur. Remember, gentlemen, we all say that we don't know about any trouble; we have nothing to do with it: don't I right?"

"Now you talkin' sense!" exclaimed Robson, "an' if Mr. Gordon know what I know, him wouldn't go near St. Thomas. Shall I drop him a hint?"

"No; better not say anything to him," said Mace, "he would only think we backing out an' leaving him in the lurch. He is a member of the House of Assembly; them can't do him anything. It is we that them would want to touch."

"Besides," said Mr. Bolt, "he would wrong us if he thought we were leaving him to pursue alone his perpendicular course. We stand by him still, unto the end. We but say, let us look before we leap, and keep quiet in the meantime; in that there is no unfaithfulness. We shall be at our posts, ready to don our armour, when the time arrives."

The expression on Mr. Robson's face suggested that he had put off his armour and was not inclined to gird it on again in a hurry; but he said nothing. A few days would prove whether the Government and the white men, so strangely silent up to now, would bow to the will of the people as expressed by Paul Bogle. Mr. Bolt suggested that the Government would be compelled to yield, though he did not explain to what or to whom. But Robson had been a policeman, and something, almost instinct, warned him that the silence of the Government was no sign of cowardice.

There was not much conversation after this. These were the men who had been in the van of the agitation, and now that they knew that some blow was to be struck, that something definite was to be put to the touch, they were seized with an apprehension which mastered their minds in spite of themselves.

The trial of strength was approaching. Some of those who had provoked it were frightened in advance.

II

JOYCE GIVES HER ANSWER

The cane, planted in May, and watered by the rains which had fallen at intervals, was luxuriant; it stretched away on every side like a sea of soft light green, the sharp spear-like leaves waving gently in the sunlight and glistening with dew. The hills in the distance were still wreathed with mist, the whole landscape glowed in the living light of the morning. Dick's pulses throbbed with the joy of life. Joyce was back and it was good to be alive.

It was still early morning, and together they were riding through the estate. He had arrived from Westmoreland during the previous day, and in the evening his mother and Joyce had joined him, as had been arranged beforehand. They were to stay at Aspley till December, and then go back to Denbigh, which, being but a few miles from Kingston, was a convenient home and place of re-union during the Christmas season. From now on to December would be a very busy time at Aspley, for the cane was ripening and the crop had to be harvested and turned into sugar. Luck was with Dick, for the parish of St. Thomas had had a fair amount of rain, even while the skies had remained hard and bright over other parts of the island. He was in high spirits. Everything seemed to be going well.

"Aspley looks lovely this morning," he said with pride, as his eye ranged over the wide expanse of the estate. "We shall employ hundreds of extra labourers this crop; that is, of course—"

"You mean, if they will work?" asked Joyce.

"Yes. Some evil spirit seems to have taken possession of the people here. That revival meeting you witnessed has had its effect. I shall have hard work in disciplining them into regular labour, I fear."

"And you don't think they will do anything worse than grumble and shirk? You remember what I told you about Paul Bogle's 'sign from heaven,' don't you?"

"Perfectly," laughed Dick, "and at the time it frightened me. But, you see, the people here are always having signs from heaven, of one sort or another. Their reception of such signs is apt to be startling to a stranger; but you get used to it after a while."

"But Bogle spoke of the blacks defeating the whites."

"He expressed, I suppose, what he and others have been wishing for years."

"And you are not at all anxious?"

"I wont say that. Sometimes I am, distinctly. But what are we to do? We can't fly from rumours and sour looks. We cannot proclaim martial law on suspicion. I heard in Westmoreland that they were expecting an outbreak there in August. The month passed quite peacefully. There is uneasiness everywhere, but nothing more. The best thing we can do. I think, is to go on with our work and take no notice of what the peasants say. All the same, we must keep our eyes open, of course."

Joyce was silent for a space; then she said—

"I am wondering now if I should have written to mother about that revival meeting I saw at Stony Gut."

"You wrote about it? And what does your mother say?"

"Both she and father are awfully frightened. They want me to go home at once. I got their letter only three days ago; mother is in a terrible state of anxiety."

"And what are you going to do?"

"Obey, of course, sir, as a dutiful daughter should," she answered gaily, though the gaiety was not spontaneous. "I have said nothing to Aunt Gertrude about this yet. I thought I would tell you first."

On the brightest of West Indian days, when no clouds are visible in the sky, you will sometimes notice suddenly a dimming of the brightness, a sort of darkening of the sun. Instead of splendour there is instant gloom, and yet the sky itself is unobscured. Glance at the sun, and the cause becomes evident; that luminary's fierce heat has generated the gauzy films of vapour that now float lightly over its shining surface. The appearance of the earth is changed for a moment, and sensitive human beings are touched to melancholy: they feel the influence of that momentary dimming of the light. Joyce's last word took the brightness out of Dick's heart, and dimmed for him the splendour of the morning. If she went now she might not return for years. He knew her people. And he—he would have to continue to take part in the eternal trivialities of a narrow, circumscribed society, an alien in spirit and in thought.

"When do you think of going?" he asked at length, quietly.

"As soon as I can; they urge that upon me."

"Very well. I will follow you soon."

"You, Dick?" There was surprise in her voice, but there was also a note of gladness. "You will go home on a visit?"

"Not on a visit, but for good. Mother will be glad to leave this country, and I can persuade my father to go with us. Our properties can be well enough looked after by attorneys. We wont be the first Jamaica proprietors to shake the dust of the colony off our feet; nor the last."

Yet as he spoke he glanced with regret around him. He had loved his work.

He continued gravely. "There is really nothing to keep me here if you go; I should be unhappy here. And perhaps, the fears of your people apart, it would be cruel to ask you to remain. You would weary of it, as I have often done."

She tested him. "You have your work here, Dick, and you and your father were born here. You are one of the few men who think kindly of the peasants."

"I am selfish enough to think of myself first. And if you go I go."

"And if I returned?"

"Oh! But would you? Would you come back to this country? Remain here, live here? His eyes questioned hers; he hung upon her answer.

She held down her head, blushing. She answered softly: "I think I could, Dick—with you."

She was all rosy, a shy delicious feeling of happiness fluttering in her breast. She had answered at last, answered after a long waiting; and she knew now that this was the answer she had always intended to give, the surrender which was love's willing sacrifice of self. They rode slowly on, in silence, for a space.

"And so you would have followed me?" she said, knowing that he would and yet wishing to hear the avowal from his own lips again. "And suppose you had followed but in vain?"

"I should still have been content to be near you, dear. But there was always something that told me that our lives would move together as one; a sort of instinct. I knew it years ago at home; the conviction never left me. And so, even though we were thousands of miles apart, and years went by before we saw one another. I could wait. But for that conviction I should not have remained out here."

"You—you will tell Aunt Gertrude?" she asked.

"Let us both tell her," he suggested, and she consented with a blush.

As they neared the Great House they saw a woman walking quickly up the path from the gate that led towards it.

"Surely I know that young woman," said Joyce; "I seem to recognise her."

"It is Rachael Bogle," Dick answered; "the girl who came to warn us of her father's threat. I hope she suffered nothing for that."

"I like her," Joyce remarked; "she has been here to see me before."

They were now very near to Rachael, who had turned, and, perceiving them, was awaiting their approach. She scanned their faces keenly, smiling brightly in recognition of Joyce.

"Good morning, Rachael; are you going up to the Great House?" Joyce asked.

"Yes, Miss Graham. I heard last night you was come, so I call here this morning on me way to Morant Bay."

"I am glad to see you. Don't go away; I will come down in a few minutes," Joyce said.

Rachael fell behind the horses. She saw the two ride up to the house, dismount, and run up the steps. She watched them intently, with a slightly troubled expression in her eyes. When they had disappeared behind the great mahogany doors, she slowly and thoughtfully walked round to the rear of the Great House.

Flushing pink, her heart beating with excitement, Joyce went with Dick through the house to the room where Mrs. Carlton was usually found at this hour of the day. She wondered how Dick would break the news, what he would say. . . Mrs. Carlton heard them coming, looked up from the writing in which she was engaged at that moment, and glanced swiftly from one to the other of them. Then, before Dick could say a word, she rose, bent forward, and kissed Joyce with motherly tenderness. "I have always wished for this, my dear," she murmured.

III

RACHAEL'S REFUAL

When Joyce had taken off her riding habit, she ran downstairs and found Rachael waiting for her in a room which Mrs. Carlton kept as a sort of minor storehouse, and in which the tenants and other callers of that sort were usually received. It was furnished with a table and some chairs. Joyce bade Rachael take one of the chairs, she herself sitting down in another. Rachael immediately began the conversation.

"I come here the same morning you leave, Miss Graham, an' I hear you was gone. I thought you was gone for ever, but they say you was coming back, so I expect you, and I came today."

"I am glad you have," said Joyce; "I want to talk to you about yourself. Since I saw you last, Rachael, I have been to your village."

"My village, Miss Graham? Stony Gut? But I didn't hear you go there. . . nobody say anything about it." Rachael looked puzzled.

"I don't think they knew anything about it, and I would not mention it to anyone but you. You look a good girl, Rachael, and I am certain you have nothing to do with those of your people who are ill-disposed. Do you remember a great revival dance they had up at Stony Gut on the night before I left Aspley?"

Rachael looked at her questioner with frightened eyes.

"How you know what them have?" she asked quickly; then added: "But they all talk, and one of them must be tell you."

"I was there," said Joyce quickly.

"You there. Miss Graham? But no; because you couldn't be there; them would have seen you. How could you be there?"

"I went there, Rachael, not knowing what I would see. I was on horseback amongst the trees, and I saw and heard a good deal of what went on. There was an old woman who was dancing, and a man, your father, I believe, who said something about the blacks conquering the whites. I didn't see you among them. I am glad to say. Couldn't you warn your father that we know about these meetings? Isn't it a pity that he should try and stir up the people to do mischief?"

Joyce watched Rachael closely to see the effect of her words upon her. As she spoke on. Rachael's countenance assumed an immobile expression, and when she ceased the girl answered nothing. Joyce felt disappointed.

"It is, of course, your own business", she resumed; "but I think I should tell you that the Government knows all about what went on at Stony Gut that night. I couldn't keep it a secret, you see, and I had no wish to do so. But it would be a pity if there should be any trouble, Rachael, for your father might be concerned in it."

Rachael fixed her eyes on the ground, as if thinking. When she lifted them, she looked frankly at Joyce and spoke without reserve.

"I have nothing to do wid it. Miss Graham. My father know what him is doing and"—there was a touch of defiance in her voice—"he is not afraid. He not breaking any law."

"Perhaps not yet," said Joyce; "but he might do so at any time. Well, I have warned you, Rachael, for you are a decent girl, and we have not forgotten how you tried to help us when your father threatened to interfere with our labourers."

"It was Raines, not me father," asserted Rachael positively. "Me father is only standing up for the people of his own colour."

"But he need not be threatening to murder the white people of the parish at the same time," said Joyce, smiling in sympathy with the girl's loyal defence of her father. "I am sure I have never done the peasants here anything, and Mr. Carlton has been kind to them."

"Oh yes; he is a kind gentleman," said Rachael enthusiastically, "and you are kind too; John Roberts tell everybody how you help him the day his son dead, an' how you make Mr. Carlton give him a job. Kill you? An' kill Mr. Carlton? God forbid, Miss Joyce! Why you think them would ever do that? Them don't mean that!"

"I am very pleased to hear you say so," laughed Joyce, much amused by Rachael's enthusiasm. "You, at any rate, I am sure, will have nothing to do with it. I am going away—"

Rachael seemed suddenly fired with excitement. "You going to England, quite away to England?" she asked, and waited breathlessly for the answer.

"Yes," said Joyce; "I—"

"And you' cousin, Miss Graham: he is goin' to go on look after the property? he is going to stop here?"

"Yes; why?" Joyce was a little surprised at the interest which Rachael apparently took in the movements of herself and Dick.

"Nothing," answered Rachael; then feeling that the reply was hardly sufficient, she added: "I was wondering if Mr. Carlton was goin' wid you, for some of the people about here not pleased with him." The explanation was somewhat haltingly given, but Joyce did not notice that. Rachael hurried on, as if eager to change the conversation.

"You remember that man that wanted was to show you the way to Jigger-foot Market the day I say I would go wid you, Miss Graham?"

"Yes, I think so."

"Well, that is the man that want to talk to me,—and who hate Mr. Carlton; an' he get Bowie to persuade me father that I ought to be friends with him, an' Bowie try to make me agree, but I wouldn't have anything to do with a man like Raines."

"He wants you to talk to him? But what has that got to do with Mr. Carlton?"

"Nothing," replied Rachael, confused; "only I know Raines is a bad man, and Mr. Carlton better look out."

"I don't think Mr. Carlton is likely to mind if this man, Raines, dislikes him, Rachael;" said Joyce indifferently. "But you seem to be afraid of Raines. There is no harm in his wanting to talk to you."

"You don't understand," said Rachael, with a half-smile and a significant look, which was lost upon Joyce.

"I told you I was going to England," Joyce went on, intent upon a plan she had formed. "I shall have to take a maid with me, but Maria will not do. I have been thinking of offering to take you, Rachael. Would you like to go with me?"

"Wid you, Miss Joyce? To England?" Rachael had sprung to her feet.

"Yes, I should like to take you with me, if your father would allow you to go. Do you think he would?"

"He couldn't hinder me if I want to go," replied Rachael defiantly. "What a nice place England must be! I hear everybody there is white. Is it true, Miss Joyce?"

"Perfectly true," laughed Joyce.

"England!" Rachael sat down to consider the proposition. She was turning it over in her mind. There was a struggle going on within her, the reason of which Joyce could not guess. "I would like to go," she said at length, "but—"

"But what?"

"I can't go."

She looked on the ground as she answered, as if to conceal something in her eyes.

"Very well, Rachael," said Joyce; "but you seem to have decided very hastily."

"Dat is true, Miss Graham, but I can't go. I thank you all the same. England!" The struggle, plainly, was renewed in her mind.

She changed the conversation suddenly.

"You know what people was sayin' up here, Miss Joyce?" she asked.

"No, what was it?"

"I will tell you if you wont vex. They saying that you are going to marry your cousin, but I didn't believe it, an' I know now it isn't true."

Joyce froze instantly. She thought Rachael was forgetting herself. "What the people here talk about does not interest me," she answered; then it occurred to her that their guess had been sure and shrewd. She forgave Rachael at once, but rose, not wishing to be asked further possibly awkward questions, or to hear anything more about what the people of the neighbourhood were saying of herself and Dick. The girl rose too.

"You don't vex wid me because I tell you what I hear Miss Joyce?" she asked plaintively.

"No, Rachael," Joyce answered, laughing; "but you should take care what you say sometimes."

"All right, I will. Good-bye, Miss Joyce."

There was a half puzzled, half amused expression on Joyce's face as she watched Rachael marching off with easy springing strides. "I'm afraid I shall never understand these people," she thought.

Rachael also was thinking.

"She vexed because I tell her what people saying, an' because it isn't true," she muttered as she walked swiftly towards the gate. "I know it wasn't true. Perhaps she have a intended in England." It pleased Rachael to think this; it was a theory she had formed some time before. "Raines," she cried aloud, "who is he—de ugly bumptious savage! I would like to go to England, but if I go I can't be here, an' I prefer to be here. . . I wonder when she going? It must be soon, very soon. . ."

And all the way to the town of Morant Bay, whither she was bound, she kept on asking herself that question, and assuring herself that Joyce Graham's departure would be soon.

IV

Bogle's Ultimatum

Paul Bogle had his spies and his emissaries everywhere. Since the night of the great meeting he had grown bolder in his operations, had extended his influence far and wide over the parish, and had made tolerably certain that in the event of a rising practically every district of St. Thomas would rally to his side. He was now contemplating a personal visit to the neighbouring Maroon settlement, for, the purpose of sounding and influencing the Maroons.

Of Raines he did not feel sure; he disliked Raines, but felt that he could not do without the aid of his people. He doubted if Raines seriously intended marriage with Rachael; the Maroon never faced that question if he could avoid it. And Bogle, anxious not to quarrel with the man before he could do so to advantage, never pressed him on the point. There was a secret antagonism, ready to flame into open hostilities, between the two men. But it suited both to pretend to be on friendly terms, though the patience of Raines had been worn to a frazzle by the long weeks of bootless waiting.

On the morning that Rachael called at Aspley, and even while she was on her way to Morant Bay, a spy of Bogle's hastened to Stony Gut to inform the General, as Bogle was now called, that Rachael had visited the estate and had been speaking with Mr. Carlton and his cousin. It happened that Bowie was with Bogle when the bearer of these tidings arrived, and Bowie was not slow to turn the moment to advantage. He pointed out that it was only the day before that Mr. Carlton had returned, and that already Bogle's daughter had begun to haunt the estate.

"Which is not decent," said Bowie, whose idea of decency evidently was an illicit relationship between the Maroon and Rachael, in the general interests of a massacre.

"But she go to see Miss Graham, Bowie," urged Paul Bogle, anxious to show that he was not being flagrantly disobeyed, and eager to find an excuse for his only child.

"That's a good blind," said Mr. Bowie judicially; "but who it is going to deceive besides you? Not me. Not Raines. In fact, Raines say him is tired of you an' Rachael already. He told me so last night, when he hear that Carlton come back."

Bogle scowled heavily. "Raines say he tired of me?" he growled. "Raines forget himself! Who is begging him to help me, Bowie?"

For answer, Bowie shrugged his shoulders with the air of a man who is tired of arguing, and walked away, leaving Paul Bogle to his own thoughts.

They were not pleasant. In spite of his brave words, Bogle felt that he could ill afford to offend the Maroon just then. The next few days would decide much in the parish; at the least he must secure the neutrality of the Maroons. He did not want to sacrifice Rachael, but he could not abandon his ambition to drive the white men out of Jamaica, which, with characteristic shortness of view, he identified with the parish of St. Thomas. He could always look after Rachael, he thought, and when he had struck his blow, and won, Raines would discover that Paul Bogle was not a man to be treated indifferently.

Night had fallen when Rachael returned to Stony Gut. She found her father in the hut looking moody and thoughtful, and she knew from experience that in that temper it was dangerous to cross him. She had her dinner in silence and was about to leave the hut, when Bogle remarked with ominous calmness: "I have something partikular to cay to you, Rachael."

This brought her to a standstill at once. She guessed what he intended to speak to her about; he had mentioned it often before. There was something in her father's manner tonight, however, that warned her that a desperate struggle of her will with his was coming. She had been expecting this for some time, and had made up her mind as to her course.

"Two months ago," said Paul Bogle gravely, "I told you not to go to Aspley any more. You disobey me an' go there today. Don't you know those white people would murder me if them could?"

Rachael made no reply.

"Your name is mixed up wid Mr. Carlton. Everybody talking about you an' him. You forget your colour? Don't you always hear me say, 'colour for colour?'"

Still she said nothing.

Her silence irritated him. He glared at her, raising his voice.

"White people side with white people. Why can't black people do de same? Why them prefer to be treated like a dog by a white man? And

H.G. DE LISSER

you, my daughter—you worse than any, for you go yourself to look for a man who never move his foot to look for you?"

The taunt spurred Rachael to a rejoinder.

"But what Mr. Carlton do you, sah, that you should hate him an' curse him?" she asked sharply. "Who tell you I going to him? Why you persecute me like this, every day, every night, till I can't get no peace?"

"You are not to ask me any question!" rapped out Bogle peremptorily. "What I do is well done. I have my mission to perform."

"But what call I have with you' mission?" demanded Rachael, whose resemblance to her father, now that her blood was up, was striking. "I have nothing to do wid it. All I say is, leave me alone. It is not you that is interfering wid me, it is Raines. Why you want to treat me bad for a lying Maroon?"

Bogle was glad that she had mentioned Raines. That gave him the opening he was feeling for. He mastered his anger and spoke kindly enough.

"Mr. Raines is a very nice young man. Rachael, an' you not treating him as you should. Him ask me for you, quite straightforward an' honourable, which he couldn't do otherwise, seeing as you are Paul Bogle's daughter. I tell Bowie that, takin' it all into consideration, I have no objection; but he tell me that you don't give Raines good words, an' so I say I would speak to you meself. Why you don't give him good words?"

"Because I don't like him."

"That is not a good reason. Why you don't like him? Nothing is de matter wid him, an' he have plenty of property up at Hayfield."

"If him was covered wid gold from head to foot. it wouldn't make any difference to me. I don't like him, an' he know it; yet he is followin' me up an' won't give me no peace."

"But that is how a man go on when he wants to marry a female."

"But him don't want to married to me; he is only saying so. If him want to married, why don't him say he will do it now?"

"Well, he have to make preparation, for him can't get up an' married right away."

"Make him wait, then. Why him should get what him want, an' I don't get what I want? Who is he so? If I was to go to him as he want me to do, you think him would care about you? Raines not helpin' anybody but himself; him is only tryin' to fool you, but he can't fool me. You ask him if him will get married now, an' hear what he will say. And you, sah—you better mind yourself with him, or he will get you into trouble!"

This was open defiance; it was more, it was obvious contempt for Paul Bogle's judgment. His own daughter was daring to warn him! Was it the suspicion that she might after all be right, that Raines might be making a mere catspaw of him, which made Bogle's blood boil to hear her words?

"You are common," he stormed at her; "an' you get your commonness from you' brown mother, for you don't get it from me. You sambo slut! it is a white man you want, eh?"

She answered him with spirit, galled by his insults—

"A white man is better than a black man, an' you know it!"

"Arrrr!" he roared. "Is that how you speak to me? You don't afraid I box you to de ground?"

"You can't kill me, sah, for de law make for woman as well as for man, an' it is white people who make the law!"

"You tell me that? You tell me about white people law! You think I afraid of the white man an' his law? You will see tonight, you ungrateful wretch!"

With a shout he sprang towards her, and Rachael made a dash towards the door. But he was quicker. He caught her by the arm, swung her round, his right hand descending heavily upon her head. The girl screamed with fright and terror, and again he raised his arm to strike. But his terrified wife, fearing that her husband in his rage might not stop short of murder, threw herself upon him, clutching at his hands. "Paul!" she panted, "Paul! Mr. Gordon might ride up at any moment, an' what would him say if him hear a scandal in you' house!"

The talisman worked. Bogle knew that Mr. Gordon's movements were uncertain, and that once before he had appeared at Stony Gut when he was believed to be fifty miles away. It would not do for Mr. Gordon to come upon him beating his daughter He flung Rachael from him, fighting with his desire to thrash her into instant obedience. The girl, frightened but not subdued, huddled in a corner of the room, sobbing with rage and hate.

"Go," he said to her, after a minute's pause, during which his fierce breathing and her sobs were the only sounds to be heard. "Go outside, or I may injure you. But understand: jump high or low, you will take Raines de Maroon, an' if you love this Carlton, you will help him better by leaving him alone?"

Rachael dragged herself up from the floor, and without a word went out. The die was cast. She dried her eyes when in the open air, arranged her clothes, and composed her features. Then she deliberately turned and walked in the direction of Bowie's hut, which was situated farther to the north, a half a mile away. That Raines was staying there she knew; and she hoped to meet him.

When she reached the hut she sauntered slowly past it, and, as she had expected, was seen by some of Mr. Bowie's children, who were seated in the open air telling one another stories. They called to her and she went up to them, explaining that she was taking a walk. Hearing a strange voice, Mr. Bowie came out to see who the stranger might be, and, recognising Rachael, invited her inside.

"I just taking a walk, Mr. Bowie," she replied, "I can't stop tonight. I goin' back home now."

Raines came out when he heard her name called, and she bade him good evening. "You might stop a little, and keep us company?" be suggested; but again she refused.

"I will walk a little way wid you, then," he said, and stepped back into the hut for his hat. She offered no objection, as he had thought she would. When he came out she bade the children and Mr. Bowie good night and went off with her companion, leaving Bowie puzzled to explain this sudden change of attitude on her part. But as Mr. Bowie ranked all women with donkeys, mules and other such animals, regarding them as made for the convenience of man, he was persuaded that it was as useless to try to fathom the reason of a woman's actions as to fathom the reason of a mule's. "This female," he soliloquised, "is always forming like she hate Raines, an' tonight she take her own fool an' come an' look for him." He laughed contemptuously and returned to his hut.

Meanwhile Raines and Rachael walked on, she setting the pace by walking rapidly. She was going home, and seemed anxious to get there as soon as she could.

"I thought you was going to refuse me to come with you," was her companion's first remark when they were out of Mr. Bowie's hearing.

"It don't matter to me if you come."

"You mean you neither vex nor please?"

"Yes."

"Then you don't love me any more now than before?"

"Why you ask, when you know I don't?"

"But you' father give me his consent to married you."

"His consent is not my consent. If it is sufficient, why you don't married him?"

"You think you can get a better husband than me?"

"You have no intentions to get married, an' you know it. I tell you so long ago."

"But you' father is satisfied with what arrangements I make."

"I am not satisfied, an' I tell me father so already."

"Oh, you been talkin' about me?"

"Yes; an' I tell him I don't want you."

"Oh, oh! An' what he say?"

"What could him say? I am me own woman. Him can't force me to do what I refuse to do. I tell him straight out, just like I tellin' you now."

"An' it is because you wanted to tell me this that you come to Bowie's house tonight?"

"Yes."

Her rapid, walking had brought them to where the huts were situated near to one another. If she raised her voice it could be heard by others besides her companion. She had him at a disadvantage; he knew it, and remained quite calm.

"I see," he said, after a moment's silence "You goin' to Carlton."

"I tell you more than once before that you not to call him Carlton. Him is not Carlton for you. You an' him is not companion."

His eyes shone dangerously. "I call him what I choose to call him," he replied. "You tryin' to make him take you to himself, an' him is not even lookin' on you."

"What you know about it?"

"Oh! So you an' him is friends already?"

"That is not your business?"

"No? Dat remains to be seen. But perhaps you don't know him is going to married his cousin? How long he will keep you when she know about you?"

"Him not goin' to marry her; she goin' away shortly."

"Who tell you that?"

"She herself. If I want I can go wid her, but I staying here."

"To stay wid Carlton?"

"I not answering any more questions."

They were near her father's hut now, and she slackened her pace. She did not want Raines to go in with her. He would not have heeded her wishes had he wanted to go in, but he did not. He fixed his half-closed eyes upon her with a curious smile. His smile irritated her; she hated to be mocked at. And she wanted to wound him. She spoke deliberately.

"When I was at Aspley two months ago," she said, "I tell Mr. Carlton how you follow me up an' threaten me, an' how you threaten him. Him laugh at what you say about him, an' he say him will flog you if you ever rude to him, an' that if you ever do me anything I must come straight to him, an' he will teach you that de law is stronger than any Maroon."

This last shaft flew home; Raines started and uttered an imprecation. She moved swiftly away from him.

He precipitated himself forward, then checked the movement. "Don't run," he called out, "I just want to say something to you. I not coming any further."

She stopped, thinking that there was already a safe distance between herself and him, and wondering if his voice had been heard by her father.

"All I want to say to you is 'go on.' I can wait till my time come. Go to your white man till Raines is ready for him an' you." He turned and walked away; then halted and called out softly: "You better begin to say you' prayers from tonight."

A scornful laugh was his answer.

"You laugh now, but you will cry blood some day." was his muttered comment.

V

Solway's Temptation

Mr. Solway was smoking moodily in his room; it was night and nearly eleven o'clock, but he was not inclined to sleep.

Something had occurred to ruffle a temper never very placid at any time. He had learnt in the morning of Joyce's return to Aspley; he had wondered, on hearing the news, if he would be able to see her shortly, and had made up his mind to force the opportunity. In the afternoon, while talking with his uncle, a mounted messenger with a letter for Mr. Burton had arrived from Aspley. The man had other letters for planters living within a radius of ten miles. There was none for Mr. Solway.

Mr. Burton had opened his letter and read it quickly, glancing up at his nephew with a puzzled look when he had made himself acquainted with its contents. He might have said nothing, but Solway had seen his glance, and surmised that there was something concerning him in the older man's mind.

"What is it?" he asked bluntly. "Anything affecting me?"

"No;" said Mr. Burton slowly; "there is probably a similar invitation for you, but the man has not delivered it."

"You are invited to Aspley? Something special?"

"A dinner party. Mrs. Carlton is back, and she invites me to go and see them. . . They never came to see us when they were here last. . ."

"Thanks to Mr. Dick. And now they don't invite me—thanks also to him. I am not good enough, I suppose."

"Have you and Dick quarrelled?" asked his uncle quickly.

"Have I and that man ever agreed? I do not get on well with prigs and sneaks, and he is both, as I have told you before."

"I am sure he is not," retorted Mr. Burton warmly; "I have always found him a gentleman."

"And me a cad. Is that what you mean?"

"I mean that I wish you were on better terms with your own people in the neighbourhood, John. It is distressing to me in my old age, to find my sole relative an object of dislike to the Carltons. What did Dick and you quarrel about?"

"I am not in the habit of answering questions about my personal affairs," returned Solway insolently.

"I am afraid your personal affairs are not very creditable," said Mr. Burton bitterly.

"But my personal efforts at Cranebrook have resulted in saving the estate, at any rate; but for them, you might have had to be humble to people who are now ready to have you in their houses, though they shy at me."

Mr. Burton winced at these words; they had a sting in them. It was quite true that, but for his nephew's management during the last ten years, he might have been a bankrupt. He rose and left the room without another word. During the rest of the day the two men carefully avoided meeting one another.

And now Mr. Solway was moodily ruminating upon this quarrel and its cause. He felt keenly the slight of the Aspley folk; he was probably the only planter in the neighbourhood who had not been invited to their dinner. And he did not like to be reminded that Cranebrook was not his. He had no fear that it would not be his eventually; but in the meantime he was, after all, only something like an overseer. And Mr. Burton would go to Aspley, thus acquiescing in the insult that had been offered to him, and Joyce would know that there must be cause for his ostracism, since his own uncle remained on friendly terms with those who did not wish him to cross the threshold of their door. The more he thought upon all this, the more bitter grew his anger. It was while he was a prey to this evil mood that a male servant came to tell him that Raines the Maroon desired to see him then, if he might.

"Send him up," said Mr. Solway sharply, and Raines was admitted.

"Well, what brings you here at this time of night?" demanded Mr. Solway, "I haven't seen you for some days."

"Sorry to trouble you, Squire, but I goin' back to Maroon Town, and wanted to tell you first," the man replied.

"You mean that you are deserting this neighbourhood?"

Raines nodded affirmation.

"What is the reason?"

"Rachael Bogle hurt my feelings tonight worse than before, Squire. She tell me that Mr. Carlton threaten to flog me; so now I leaving Stony Gut for good."

"Afraid of Mr. Carlton's horsewhip?" asked Mr. Solway contemptuously.

The Maroon's face twitched, but he did not answer the question. Instead of that he said quietly: "Squire, day-after-tomorrow Paul Bogle going to Morant Bay—to the court house."

"Well?"

"He is goin' with a hundred men."

"You mean," said Solway slowly, fixing his eyes on Raines, "you mean that Bogle is going to Morant Bay to make a riot?"

"Yes; and after that—"

"And after that?"

"Bogle will send far an' near through St. Thomas to call up his people. He will march through de island, if the Government don't prevent him. He will kill every white man, every fair-skinned man, in Jamaica. Everything is arranged. It will be colour for colour, an' blood for blood!"

"My God! And you; you are going to warn the Maroons? The Government must know of this at once, Raines! You must put off your visit to your people, and go with me tomorrow to the Governor. Do you hear? I have already too long neglected to take this matter in hand."

Raines smiled a bitter, twisted smile.

"An' all that the Governor will do is to send some soldiers to Morant Bay, and Bogle will swear I am lying," he said.

"But we shall prevent a rebellion, man; don't you see that? We shall prevent bloodshed," urged Solway.

"Why should I prevent it, Squire—too soon? After they begin—yes. But not before."

"You savage beast!" stormed Solway; "do you want these negroes to massacre white people and burn our properties?"

"No, Squire; them wont have time to do that. The Maroons will come down too quick. But them may burn one property. An' if Paul Bogle kill one white man—" And Raines paused to note the effect of his evil suggestion.

Solway started. He was never quite certain how much this Maroon knew about him. It was quite possible that some one may have seen him meet Joyce Graham on the open road and have told Raines of it; you could never know who was spying upon you in the surrounding woods and cane-fields.

He thought the Maroon a fool to tell him of Bogle's intention if he wished for no interference. For now he must take steps to avert the threatened peril, and that within a day. He hated Dick Carlton, but he

H.G. DE LISSER

would never be a party to his murder by negroes. That such a suggestion had been made to him by the Maroon turned him hot with anger.

"Stay here tonight," he commanded; "I shall want you tomorrow morning."

"All right, Squire," replied Raines submissively, and turned as if to leave the room. At the door he paused.

"I pass through Aspley tonight on me way here," he said, casually as it were, "an' the people there tell me that de Great House going to give a big dinner."

Mr. Solway was suddenly reminded that he was not good enough to be invited to this dinner. And yet he was perhaps the only man who could prevent Aspley from being burnt to the ground. Curse their insolence! he thought swiftly, stung to anger again; were it not for Joyce Graham it would be a grim revenge to leave Bogle to wreck his vengeance on the Carltons. Why indeed should he hinder it? They were white, yes, but were they treating him like a white man? "These niggers about here say 'colour for colour,' but, by God, my own people treat me like a nigger," he reflected bitterly.

Colour for colour. He had heard that expression more than once of late. But did the white men always stand by those of their own colour? Did the black men? They were all a miserable, self-seeking, mangy, wretched crowd. A lesson taught with blood and fire might do them good: nothing else would. But that he must not permit; his every instinct was against it.

He knew why Raines wanted the uprising to take place. Let Bogle strike one blow and a wave of terror would sweep through the entire country. There would arise a wild imperative cry for reprisals; Maroons and regular troops would pour into Stony Gut, and Rachael and her father would be at the mercy of the Maroon. But Raines also hated Dick Carlton and would have him injured or dead. Would he, Solway, knowing that Raines was the instigator of the attack upon Dick, keep silent as to the Maroon's complicity? That was what Raines was now seeking to know. If Mr. Solway decided to side with his own people, the Maroon might have to answer some ugly questions, or even to defend him self against the serious charge of murder. Raines's course of conduct would ultimately be decided by what Mr. Solway said. And Solway knew it.

"What are you waiting there for?" he growled at Raines, who was still standing with his hand on the door.

"I always tell you what I hear, Squire," answered Raines, humbly enough. "They saying at Aspley that Miss Graham going back to England—her maid, Maria, tell the rest of de servants. An' they say—but perhaps you don't want to hear, Squire?"

"Well, out with it, and clear off!"

"That Mr. Carlton going to marry her."

"Go, damn you!" thundered Solway; and Raines left the room quickly with a crooked smile upon his face.

VI

DISILLUSION

Very early on the following morning, while Stony Gut was still wrapped in slumber and stertorous. Rachael stole silently out of her father's hut and took the path leading to Aspley. Her face wore a set, determined expression, the expression of one who has resolved upon some momentous step. She took nothing with her, never cast a backward glance at the village she was leaving. She walked quite leisurely, knowing that she had plenty of time; she seemed careless whether she was being spied upon or not.

As she went along the narrow path, the same by which Joyce had gone to Stony Gut on the night of the revival dance, the sunlight came pouring through the woods and all the birds awoke. Patches of light appeared on the ground; looking upwards she could discern the pale blue sky, while the multitudinous leaves of the trees around her glistened in the brightening day. She caught idly at wild orchids that swung downwards on long slender tendrils; with unconscious coquetry she gathered some of these flowers and pinned them to her breast.

Soon she was on the mainroad that ran by Aspley.

The brightness of the morning affected her spirits cheerfully; her thoughts were of the pleasantest. She was bidding goodbye to Stony Gut forever; now she could with good reason claim the protection which the master of Aspley had offered her many weeks before. How she had wished for this opportunity! Now it had come, and she could rejoice in it; now she would be free from persecution; and though she would be reviled by her people, that could hurt her not at all. She hummed the air of a song as she went on, and so taken up by her own thoughts was she that she did not hear, until he was passing by her, a horseman who was going her way. She looked up and recognised Mr. Solway.

He glanced at her more curiously than usual; she noticed his look and tossed her head as if resenting it. They were not a furlong from Aspley's gate.

Mr. Solway rode by slowly without a word, then suddenly turned his head and asked:

"Where are you going to?"

The question sounded like a command to answer, and she answered at once:

"To Aspley, Squire."

"To whom?"

But he could not surprise her into a rejoinder once more; she merely stared back at him and walked slow-footed. She observed that his face was drawn and pale, his eyes bloodshot and swollen, the eyes of a man who had not slept. He did not repeat his question, but laughed bitterly and continued on his way. Rachael wondered why he laughed, and why he had wanted to know whom she was going to Aspley to see.

When she reached the estate the workers were already about their business. She thought she would wait until Dick came out; she did not care to go up to the house and ask for him, as that would attract too much attention and she might have to speak to him before others. She wanted to tell her story to him alone.

She pretended that she had come to see some of the people she knew on the estate, and with these she remained, listening with indifference to all the news they had to tell, until she thought it was likely that Dick had left the Great House. Then she casually enquired of her friends where "the busha" usually went in the morning. They told her where he was likely to be found just then; and a few minutes after she set out for the place indicated, a cane field some distance away.

She had nearly reached this field when she caught sight of a lady on horseback going at a canter over the common and towards the gate by which she had entered a little while before. She recognised Miss Graham; Joyce too perceived the girl and wondered what she was doing at Aspley so early in the morning. Then Rachael came up to where Dick, with his overseer, was inspecting some calves. Within speaking distance of him she halted, then slowly resumed her walk. Thompson, the overseer, drew Dick's attention to her.

He beckoned to the girl. "You want me?" he asked.

She answered eagerly, "Yes, Mr. Carlton, I have something to say to you, but not here. I don't want nobody but you to hear what it is."

"Come along, then," said he, and walked his horse in the direction of the path which led from the Great House to the gate.

He paused when he came to a spot overshadowed by trees, and out of the hearing of anyone.

"You can tell me what is the matter now," he said, "nobody can overhear you here."

She plunged into her story with eagerness, narrating what had passed between her and her father, and between herself and Raines. She told him that she wanted to avoid the Maroon, who was dangerous, and to escape the constant persecution of her father. Mr. Carlton had promised to help her the other day; could he do so now?

Dick listened to her gravely. "But what can I do, Rachael?" he asked; "what do you want me to do?"

She felt a little disappointed at his question. She would have preferred him to suggest something; besides, hadn't she told him that it was on his account that they were watching her at Stony Gut?

"Why don't you accept Miss Graham's offer and go with her as her maid to England?" he went on, as she returned no answer. "Miss Graham is fond of you and would treat you kindly. And by the time you came back your father might be disposed to treat you again as he used to do."

"I don't want to go anywhere from here," she protested, "but p'rhaps you can give me an employment on the estate. I would like to stay here," she added looking him in the eyes with an expression the meaning of which was not dubious.

"They abuse me and watch me because I tell you anything I hear them say they want to do you," she continued rapidly. "Raines hate you because him know that—" she hung her head and hesitated. "Oh! don't you understand?" she burst forth with fierce energy; "don't you know?"

Dick was startled by this outburst; startled and bewildered. He understood now only too well, but thought it wisest to pretend that he did not. Here was a complication!

"I am very sorry that I am the cause of any unpleasantness between your family and yourself," he replied, evading her question; "but I suspected they would be angry when they found out that you had warned me about your father's intention to forbid my labourers to come back to work. Frankly, I think the best thing you could do would be to obey your father and allow him to act as he pleased towards me. He will not like me any the better, you know, if he believes that I have deliberately come between you and him."

"And what about Raines, Mr. Carlton? Didn't you say that if Raines trouble me, you would help me?"

"So I did, and so I will; but I don't think your father would force you to accept him if you remained determined not to. And look here, I may be able to help in this matter. Mr. Gordon is a friend of your father's, isn't he?"

"Yes."

"Well, I am on fairly good terms with Mr. Gordon just now; and when I next see him I could drop him a hint about Raines and you. That might help."

"You can do what you like, Mr. Carlton," replied Rachael sorrowfully, with something like a sob in her throat. "But after what you said, I did think that I could come here if them didn't treat me well at Stony Gut. But it is all right."

Her dejection, her words, the memory of his own promise, made him sick at heart. Eight weeks ago he had offered her an asylum at Aspley, and now that she had come to beg for it he was finding reasons for not redeeming his word. His real reason was of the best. Joyce and his mother would soon be leaving Aspley, and if Rachael were left on the estate the general impression would be that she had become his "housekeeper," a term employed to signify a far more intimate relationship. That she herself would have no objection to such an arrangement, which was rather too common to appear discreditable, he was only too well aware; she had just told him in almost so many words that she had fled from Stony Gut to him. What was he to do?

She stood there looking at him entreatingly, while he racked his brain for a way out of the difficulty. As both of them stood thus they heard the sound of a horse's hoofs, and caught a glimpse of Joyce as she rapidly rode up the long way that led to the house. In a minute she had disappeared from view. Mechanically Dick thought that her ride had been a very short one.

Then an idea occurred to him, "My mother will be going back to Kingston shortly, Rachael," he said, "and perhaps, if you care to go, she might take you with her. You could stay with her a little while at any rate, and afterwards we could see what might be done. In the meantime you can remain at Aspley; I will speak to my mother about it."

This arrangement was not quite satisfactory to Rachael, yet it was better than going back to Stony Gut. Instinctively she guessed that his objection to her remaining all the time at Aspley had something to do with his cousin. But Miss Graham was going away, going to far-off England, and Kingston was near. She could come back whenever she liked; in the interval she would be under his protection, and that meant a great deal.

"Go up to the house," he instructed her; "I shall be there before you." He rode back to where his men were working, and Rachael slowly moved away in the direction of the Great House.

So she had succeeded! She had now definitely cut herself off from all connection with her people, she reflected, and she must be careful to keep out of their way. Miss Graham was kindly disposed towards her and she could count upon her help; of Mrs. Carlton she stood in some awe; but she did not doubt that Mrs. Carlton's son would easily be able to have his way with that lady: in Rachael's view, Dick was little short of omnipotent. She began to calculate how short a time she could reasonably remain in Kingston with Mrs. Carlton before returning to Aspley. He would never turn her away then, she believed, and she would be vastly useful to him. She was strong, she could work, she would never allow him to be robbed, she would be able to warn him of any danger that might threaten him, and he would be grateful and would come to like her better than he seemed to do now. She thought him a little queer, for she had been admired often by many of the young white men of the parish. These she did not consider his equals; yet they were white men, and they would have been pleased had she noticed their compliments. But he, though she had come to him herself, had wanted to send her back, and even now she was only to stay a few days at Aspley. Miss Graham had something to do with his attitude, she felt certain. "P'raps," she reflected, "him is ashamed to like a girl like me because she is here. I am nobody an' she is a lady." The reflection stirred her heart to momentary bitterness.

When she got to the house, going round to the back entrance as usual, she saw Dick's horse tethered to a post and knew that he had arrived before her and was inside. She waited, talking to one or two of the servants whom she saw, and wondering how long it would be before he came out. After a few minutes' waiting she saw him come down the steps, his face grave and even sad.

Rachael looked at him in surprise, and of a sudden she realized that Aspley was to be no home for her. She became frightened; why, she did not know. When he beckoned to her to come to him, where the servants could not hear what he had to say, she went mechanically, with a quick beating, sinking heart.

"I am extremely sorry, Rachael," he began at once, "but it is impossible for you to stay at Aspley, and you cannot go to Kingston with my mother. If you want to go to Morant Bay, I can help you to do that, but that is about all I can do. I think you had better go back to your father, it will probably be the wisest course for you. Even if he threatens me in any way, don't let that trouble you. I agree with him that it would be best for you not to come to Aspley any more. It can do no good."

He broke off abruptly. He was aware that he had spoken with a bluntness that was almost brutal, and revolted at having to do so. But Rachael said nothing, uttered no appeal. The corners of her mouth drooped, the underlip trembled just a little. She understood perfectly all that his words signified. His people did not want her at Aspley; she was to come there no more. She was being driven away from the place, and this because they knew that she cared for him. She was nobody, and they were treating her as such. She turned and left him standing there, and went straight towards the gate.

When outside of the estate, and away from every eye, she sat down upon a bank, being at that moment conscious only of a feeling of intense humiliation and bitterness. She plucked at some grass growing near to her hand and began chewing it fiercely, while her body trembled all over with anger. They had driven her from Aspley as if she were of no account whatever, had treated her as they would one of their common labourers! And perhaps the servants would know of it, the servants who had always regarded her with a certain amount of respect because of her father. To be made a mock of, to be known to have gone to Aspley for protection and help and to have been driven away as an undesirable; to be talked of as a woman who had hung about Mr. Dick Carlton only to be told that he did not even want to see her on his estate—the thought cut her to the quick, and hot tears streamed from her eyes as she abandoned herself to the agony of shame that tore her through and through. She was done with them, done with them for ever. Her father was right; they were a proud overbearing lot, these white people, treating the natives as they would the dirt beneath their feet. But for how long would they be able to do so? She knew that something was being plotted against them, something that was talked about in whispers, something terrible, and for the first time she rejoiced in this knowledge. She ceased crying and pondered on the coming change which she had heard her father boast of; then, without knowing that she did so, she began to talk aloud to herself.

"Colour for colour; after all, me father is right. Them only want to make use of us; we are to work for them, an' them is to get all the benefit. Because we are black we don't count, an' because them is white them is to have everything an' to do what them like. Any black person that try to help a white one is a fool, as I find out today. We should stick to our own colour, an' have nothing to do wid them. They laughing at me now, an' talkin' about me, an' Miss Graham is heads up in the talk. It is she that put him against me, but she can wait an' see! Today is for her, but tomorrow may be for me!"

And now jealousy took possession of her, bitter consuming jealousy that turned her blood to gall. She was certain that Joyce had seen her when she was going to seek Dick Carlton, and had also seen her when she was talking to him, and she realised that if Joyce had been on her side Mrs. Carlton could not have withstood her son's desire that she should be allowed to remain at Aspley. Yes; it was Miss Graham who had objected; it was Miss Graham who had caused all her plans to go awry, all her hopes to be shattered. "Why she didn't stay where she come from?" she cried aloud. "Why she didn't drown in de ship when she was coming? I hate the very sight of her, wid her proud white face. She must be love him, an' want him for herself; dat is why she tell him to insult me out of the estate." And now she flung herself prone upon the bank and wept passionately.

If his cousin loved him, might not he love her in return? And if he did? . . . She beat upon the hard earth with her clenched fists in a paroxysm of despair. It came upon her that Dick must indeed love Joyce, otherwise he would not have agreed to send her away after having said he would let her stay at Aspley and would ask his mother to take her to Kingston. That was the explanation of his previous coldness and of his terrible hardness that morning. "She tell me a lie about him," sobbed Rachael, "she say she wasn't goin' to married him but was goin' away. An' now she want to take him away wid her."

After a while she grew calm again, and began to try to think. She could see no way out of the situation. She could not go back to Aspley. There was nothing to he gained by going to live in Morant Bay. She must return to Stony Gut; there was nothing else to do. Her mind ran upon Raines, and a feeling of detestation and disgust flooded her whole being. Whatever happened she would have nothing to do with him; she hated him, and she knew that he hated her also and would treat her ill if once she fell into his power. Would her father hear that she had been to Aspley that morning? The only danger was lest one of the labourers at Aspley should tell him she had been there; she would have to face that. But to go back to the village, when she had thought she had left it forever, was to drain the bitter cup of disappointment to the dregs.

Yet there was no other course to take. She rose, brushed her dress with her hands and turned her face in the direction of Stony Gut. Plunged into darkest despair but a little while before, she now began to imagine wistfully all sorts of hopeful contingencies as she walked homewards. She remembered she had not heard that Mr. Carlton, was going to England; and if he were going the news would have got about already. On the other hand Miss Graham was going, as every one now knew. When she had gone a dozen different things might happen; if she, Rachael, went to Aspley then, she would not be turned away. There was a little comfort in this speculation; besides, she possessed to the full the buoyant optimism of her race. So when she entered the village she was as calm as usual. If her face was pensive, no one noticed it. And no one asked her whither she had been.

VII

An Encounter

Not long after Rachael had taken the way that led back to Stony Gut, Dick Carlton rode out of Aspley in the direction of Morant Bay. He went slowly, his horse walking at a leisurely pace, and when he was about half a mile from the estate he pulled up, allowing the animal to crop the short grass that grew upon the edge of the road.

He was waiting, waiting patiently for some one. And yet there was nothing like patience in his look or in his attitude: he was livid with anger suppressed, and the tense grip of his fingers on the heavy whip he carried, the tense expression of his face as he waited, would have convinced any observant person that Dick Carlton's mission on the high road that morning was by no means a peaceful one.

One such observer there was Mr. Bowie, who happened to be on his way from Stony Gut to Morant Bay. Mr. Bowie had left the village some time after Rachael's silent flight, but had travelled by a different route. Coming upon Mr. Carlton on the high road, Mr. Bowie, who knew that it was not usual for white men to be found waiting as Dick was, and who at once noticed Dick's furious look, was filled with curiosity and straightway retired behind a tree to watch for what might happen. Thus hidden, he would be able to see and hear everything that passed; and he hoped he would not have long to wait.

Mr. Bowie had not taken up his position as a spy for more than an hour when he saw approaching in the distance, and coming straight towards Dick, a man on horseback whom in a minute he recognised as Mr. Solway. Dick perceived Solway also, and rode into the middle of the path with uplifted hand. Solway, perceiving who it was, and observing the signal, slowed his horse down to a trot, and then drew rein as he arrived in front of Dick. His coolness was admirable.

"May I enquire why you interrupt me on my way?" he asked with a sneer, as he stared at Dick in his most insolent manner.

"You know quite well," retorted the other, who also spoke coolly in spite of his anger; "but as you pretend ignorance I will tell you. This morning, on the pretence that you were going to Morant Bay, you waylaid Miss Graham on this road. You told her, or insinuated to her, things about me and an unfortunate girl which you must have known were lies, for I'scarcely think that you judge me by yourself—you must be aware that there can be nothing in this parish quite so low as you are. Your lies about me I do not mind: they are not likely to do any harm. Your baseness in mentioning to a lady a vile rumour which you yourself may have been the first to invent is unpardonable. You have no claim to be considered a gentleman, or a decent man even; and if you have been tolerated, it has only been for your uncle's sake. But now that you have shown yourself in your true colours, and have stooped lower than any negro labourer on your estate would have done—"

"You infernal hound!" roared Solway, his face darkened with passion, "I will make you eat your words!"

But Dick had already lifted his whip, and at a touch of his spur his horse sprang forward. The heavy whip slashed across Solway's face, and his horse, startled, shied violently across the road, dashing its rider against a tree and almost stunning him. Solway reeled, but managed, automatically, to retain a hold upon his reins; before he could rally his wits, however, Dick was again in front of him, and the whip was lashing and cutting at him, and his horse rearing and plunging. Had he not been taken at a disadvantage, he might have been more than a match for his opponent. As it was, he could make no fight and at the same time manage his horse. He was not the man to try to escape; at that moment he wanted, he panted, to kill; but a blow, aimed at him but falling on his horse's head instead, caused the frightened animal to shy again so violently that Solway completely lost his balance and fell heavily to the ground, where he lay stunned. Only then did Dick Carlton pause. A glance showed him that Solway was not severely injured, and, truth to say, he would not very much have cared if Solway had been. He looked contemptuously at the man stretched out on the ground, turned, and rode away.

Mr. Bowie saw it all, and at the instant his nimble mind took in the possibilities of money to be earned as a witness of an unprovoked and brutal assault. Then it occurred to him that no white man would bring another before the courts for an attack like this, as to do so would be to publish his humiliation broadcast. He was inclined to proceed on his journey to Morant Bay, leaving Mr. Solway to recover and help himself as best he could, when he remembered that Raines the Maroon was Mr. Solway's henchman. That determined him.

He ran over the spot where Solway lay, and saw that that gentleman was regaining consciousness. Mr. Solway raised himself on an elbow, looked around him with a dazed air, and immediately noticed Bowie. The latter held out a hand; Solway took it and rose to a standing posture with some difficulty. "Where is. . . where is that man who. . . where is Mr. Carlton?" he asked Bowie, pronouncing Dick's name with an effort.

"He run away after he assault you, Squire," Bowie answered. "He didn't wait at all."

"You were here when?" . . .

"Yes, Squire; I see everything."

The purple weal across Solway's face was not pleasant to look at, but even without it the expression on that face would have been horrible enough. Solway realised tha this man had witnessed the flogging he had received, the degradation to which he had been subjected. Even Bowie felt sorry he had admitted having been witness of the encounter between the two men.

"Catch my horse for me," said Solway. The animal had galloped off, but was now standing still not very far away.

Mr. Bowie obeyed, though at any other time he would have reminded Mr. Solway that he was not his servant.

When the horse was caught and led back, and Mr. Solway had remounted, he surprised the man by his next remark.

"You were going to Morant Bay to arrange for your riot tomorrow, weren't you?"

Bowie, too startled to lie, stared at his questioner open-mouthed. "You needn't deny it," said Mr. Solway; "I know all about it; you need not be afraid of me. On coming back from Morant Bay, call at Cranebrook to see me. You will find Raines there. Is that arranged?"

"Yes, Squire," answered Bowie submissively.

"And understand: not a word about this—this quarrel between me and that man who was here just now. If you talk about it I will have no further use for you. If you keep your mouth shut, it will be worth your while. Do you hear? It will be well worth your while. I want your help."

Bowie was overjoyed to learn that Mr. Solway wanted his assistance. He had often heard from Raines that Mr. Solway and Mr. Carlton were no friends, and he guessed that it was against Mr. Carlton that his services were to be employed. He was nothing loth. He promised to be silent.

"Very well then, I will see you later," said Solway, and rode slowly back to Cranebrook.

VIII

The Sounding of the Shells

Aspley Great House blazed with light, and from other Great Houses in the parish, within a radius of at least ten miles, had come a number of guests at Mrs. Carlton's invitation. There were some forty persons in all; and now a stranger could understand why in a Jamaica planter's house the dining room was the largest and best furnished apartment.

All the notable men in the parish were there; among them the Custos or Chief Magistrate of the parish. Dick's father had also come over from Denbigh. Mr. Burton, notwithstanding that his nephew had been ignored, had been one of the first guests to arrive. And when all who were expected were assembled in the drawing room, the tidings of Joyce's engagement went round and congratulations were showered upon her and Dick, she blushing, he looking decidedly uncomfortable.

Yet the gaiety of many of the guests was forced. As soon as these ceased laughing their faces became serious and set, and even when they sat down to dinner the shadow of some apprehension still rested upon them.

Old Mr. Carlton was puzzled. He saw that something was amiss, but could not imagine what it was. He hoped he would find out before he left Aspley for Denbigh, which he would do that night as soon as the guests had gone.

At first every one avoided the topic uppermost in every one's mind, entirely out of regard for Joyce. Her feelings as a stranger they considered, and her felicity as a newly-engaged girl they thought it their duty not to mar.

But the claret was plentiful, the whisky good, and the rum punch which the gentlemen had taken as an appetiser had not been devoid of an inspiriting influence on those who had liberally drunk of it. Then the dinner was considered excellent. Mrs. Carlton had provided with true Jamaica profusion, for even in a hospitable country the hospitality of Aspley had always been renowned. After soup there were birds roasted to a nicety, plump and toothsome, and black crabs, baked in their own shells and flavoured with native red pepper. These were delicacies; but as man was not made to dine on delicacies alone, the sideboards were laden with boiled hams, roast beef, turkeys, mutton, capons, ducks, and, as something to be regarded with an admiring eye, pigs jerked whole. Jerked pig was a Maroon invention; it was a sort of roast but nicer. Even at peril of indigestion it would be eaten at any hour of the night by the lovers of pig's flesh.

With such good cheer it was impossible for the guests to continue long depressed. Whatever the fear or the affliction, a good dinner appealed to the sympathies of the planter, and his mental processes or secret misgivings were not allowed to interfere with his meal: loss of appetite was not one of the ills from which he suffered. So as the dinner went on the talk became more animated, and at last one of the men, turning to Dick's father, observed that he supposed Mr. Carlton had heard the news. The old gentleman professed his ignorance of any particular news: his son had said nothing to him: was there anything the matter?

He was told, and now that the subject was broached every guest began to talk about it.

Two days before, Bogle and some of his friends had marched into Morant Bay, with a fife and drum band, expecting that a land case in which one of the people of Stony Gut was concerned would come on for hearing in the petty court of that town. During the earlier part of the day a boy was fined for assaulting a woman, and also ordered to pay the costs of the prosecution. Whereupon one of Bogle's followers called out to him not to pay the costs, and the magistrates immediately ordered the arrest of the man. But at a signal from Paul Bogle the offender was rescued and taken outside, and when the police attempted to apprehend the rescuers they were beaten off and ignominiously compelled to flee. Bogle and his men had then returned in triumph to Stony Gut, and on the following day some native policemen had been sent with a warrant to effect the arrest of himself and his aiders and abettors. The policemen had been set upon, beaten, then made to swear that they "would leave the whites and cleave to the blacks." "And," added Mr. Carlton's informant, "Bogle sent to tell the magistrates that they could expect him tomorrow, and could take him in the town of Morant Bay, if they dared."

"This means trouble," said another of the guests. "We have been taking the insolence of these people too calmly, and now they are beginning to threaten. What may not happen tomorrow?"

"Nothing that will alarm anyone," said the Custos of the parish, who had overheard the last speaker. "Since you are so apprehensive, it may ease your mind to know that I wrote today to the Governor to tell him of Bogle's stupid threat, and ask him to send us some soldiers. And I will have the volunteers called out tomorrow, and all the members of the vestry will go to town armed. Really, I think I am taking too many precautions: I am asking myself whether I too am nervous! But nothing has been neglected, you see."

The Custos had spoken loudly on purpose, and the tenour of his remarks was repeated by those who had heard them to those who had not. The effect was magical. In his hands was the authority for maintaining order in over two hundred square miles of country, and his personal courage was taken for granted. His confidence inspired the others, as he intended it should. The ladies recovered their spirits and the talk turned to other subjects. Genuine laughter was now heard. The Custos presently addressed himself to Joyce, who was sitting where he could easily speak to her.

"I hear you are leaving the island next week Miss Graham; it is not for long, I hope?"

"I think not," said Joyce; "I expect to return early next year; I have come to love our beautiful island."

"Yes, you would miss our sunshine in England; and everything is looking bright and cheerful now. This is a wonderful country. We have had bad times of late, but now, for some time on, you will find that we shall have little to complain of. We recover from our reverses very rapidly here. Do you intend to live in Jamaica?"

"Yes," Joyce replied. "I have become quite a colonist now."

"That's right! On what date do you sail?"

"The fifteenth."

"This is not a bad month to travel in, there are no hurricanes moving about the sea just now. You know, we have a saying out here about our hurricane season: 'July, stand by; August, hold fast; September, remember; October, all over.' There have been hurricanes in October, though. I trust you will not even be seasick."

"Thank you," laughed Joyce. "Hurricanes are almost as dangerous on land as at sea, aren't they? I have heard so."

"Rather! They are terrible. Hundreds of lives are sometimes lost in one of them; they are what we have most to fear in Jamaica. Take away our hurricanes and our droughts and we should go on our way rejoicing."

Above the hubbub of conversation and laughter, the clatter of knives and forks upon earthenware, rose suddenly a bellowing, booming sound. As it broke upon the ear the guests started, and some of them anxiously glanced at one another. Again the sound came bellowing through the night, and once again it was repeated. It seemed quite near. The servants in the room looked at each other with frightened faces. "What is that?" cried a dozen voices at once.

"Some one is blowing a shell near here," said Mr. Burton after a few moments, when the bellowing noise had completely ceased. "What can it mean?"

"It is a signal," said the man to whom the Custos had mentioned the arrangements he had made to check Paul Bogle.

"A signal? For what?" asked several men at once.

"A call, perhaps I should have said. It sounded so, didn't it?"

"It did," said Mr. Burton. "But who can be calling, and whom is he calling?"

"I heard that same sound last night ten miles from here. I guessed what it was immediately. It may herald a hurricane worse than any we have ever known in Jamaica." The speaker addressed himself directly to the Custos, and looked at him with serious eyes.

The Custos returned his look smiling.

"It may and it may not," he replied; "I prefer to think that it means nothing more than some fellow summoning his friends. A week ago I was told that there were secret nightly gatherings near my house. I heard that the men of the district were being called together by the blowing of a horn. I thought it my duty to make enquiries, and I found that a big dance was held three times a week in the neighbourhood, and that the horn was used to summon the dancers. Churches use a bell, you know, and the effect is not generally startling."

His cheery assurance, obviously assumed as it now was, had not the same effect as his speech earlier in the evening. The laughter died away, the talk was not so animated as it had been before. The dinner ended as it had begun, gloomily.

Shortly after dinner the guests began to leave. Dark clouds gathering to the east seemed to threaten a downpour later on, and this was a good excuse for those who were too troubled to pretend any longer to be gay. Dick seized an opportunity of taking the Custos aside for a moment. "Tell me frankly," he said, "do you fear any outbreak tomorrow?"

"Not the slightest, my dear Dick," replied the other man assertively; "and if any did occur the volunteers and the magistrates could deal with it. And I have sent for soldiers, as you must have heard me say at dinner."

"Well, my case is this, Custos. I have promised to drive my father to Kingston tonight. Tomorrow he and I have to meet two men from Spanish Town on business—we are selling some property. But I am wondering if I should leave my mother and cousin. If Paul Bogle—"

"Dick," interrupted the Custos, "have you ever seen these negroes with guns?"

"No; I don't think they have many."

"Quite so. But we have. See? Now, even if you remained here, what could one man do against them if they got out of hand? I promise you, however, that they won't be permitted to get out of hand!"

He shook hands warmly with Dick and went to bid the other members of the family good night.

Mr. Burton was the last of the guests to take his leave. He had lingered to add another congratulation to the many he had offered; he was sincerely fond of Joyce, and showed that he was.

"I will come and see you the first day you are back at Aspley," he said, as he bade her goodbye. And remember to tell your mother that I said you are very much like her, only prettier. Don't blush; I am old enough now to say what I think. God bless you, my dear girl, and bring you safely back to us."

His buggy rolled away, and he turned and waved her a last farewell.

Soon after Mr. Burton had gone, Dick and his father set out on the tedious night drive to Kingston, some forty miles away. His mother and Joyce had shown no fear whatever at being left alone; if they had, Dick would have insisted on remaining. But the Custos half reassured him, and he was quite satisfied that his own tenants were loyal: he knew they could be trusted. Nevertheless, as the horses trotted over the rough road that led to Kingston, Dick's mind ran persistently on Stony Gut. The echoes of that weird bellowing call still rang in his ears; the certainty that it had a sinister meaning haunted his mind. What were they doing at Stony Gut now? Since he had sent Rachael away from Aspley he had had no news of Paul Bogle. He had not seen Rachael since; she had gone in silence, and the silence had remained unbroken. Could she have told him anything? He was more than usually thoughtful tonight; in his heart there was unrest. It was true that he would be away from Aspley for two days at the most; it was true that the Chief Magistrate was responsible and considered a reliable man. Yet Dick knew that no one was more bitterly hated by the peasants in St. Thomas than this naturalised German, Baron Von Kettleholdt, and so he wished he could have learnt something about Paul Bogle's intentions. For though every alarm had hitherto passed away with no serious consequences, still no one could say that no real danger was threatening the land.

Rachael might have told him. She, even if away from the village, might have found means to keep in communication with it. Yet he could not have acted otherwise than he had done towards the girl, though he still deeply regretted the hard and seemingly unfeeling part he had been called upon to play. He distinctly recalled Rachael's piteous face, and another scene rose before him: the offended look of Joyce when he had suggested that Rachael should stay at Aspley, and the frightened remonstrance of his mother. Afterwards he had learnt from his mother what had happened; how Solway had met Joyce and suggested as plainly as he dared that her cousin was Rachael's lover, and how Joyce had left Mr. Solway without a word and had ridden back to Aspley. There had been no estrangement between himself and Joyce; yet he guessed that she was no longer inclined to think kindly of Rachael. Solway's poisonous insinuations had not altogether been devoid of effect.

The fireflies were dancing, were flashing their green and golden light among the trees and bushes on each side of the road. The two men heard the rushing of some river as they passed over the wooden bridge spanning it. Without quite knowing that they did so, both Dick and his father listened for signals, for calls such as they had heard that night. But no sound save those made by running water or by the frogs come to their ears; the country was silent. Could their eyes have pierced through darkness and distance at that moment, could they have seen the village of Stony Gut just then, all their questions, asked of themselves in doubt and wonder and vague speculation, would have been answered once and for all. For even while their minds ran upon Paul Bogle an ominous ceremony was taking place at Stony Gut.

The village was alive with men and women. These had been coming in since eight o'clock, and more were coming still. Already there were fully two thousand people gathered in the clearing in front of the chapel, where torches tied to sticks stuck in the ground gave off a garish light. Amongst the murmuring crowd could be seen men with horns and shells slung at their side, and every man carried some weapon, a cutlass, a scythe attached to a pole, or a club. The guns were very few, and old for the most part; but the long sword-like cutlasses looked ugly in the hands that grasped them, and on the faces of the assembled multitude there was a look of settled determination. Some of the men, divided into companies of fifty, were being put through a rude sort of drill, others were taking a pledge, administered by Paul Bogle, who, all gravity, swore them to fidelity and secrecy with tremendous oaths, and threatened with awful torments all those who should break away from him. Near him, surveying the people with impish glee, was the old obeah woman whose wild ravings Joyce had overheard on the memorable night of "the sign."

From the door of her father's hut Rachael watched the scene with straining eyes. More than once that day she had heard her father mutter that the time had come; and she knew now that this great gathering meant bloodshed and war.

IX

How Tidings Come

Ten days had elapsed since Mr. Robson, Mr. Mace, Mr. Bolt, with their friends, had met at the office of the journalist to discuss the political situation. During the interval nothing of importance had happened to any of these three gentlemen. No policeman had appeared with a warrant for Mr. Robson's arrest. Mr. Mace had taken new courage; even Mr. Bolt had recovered from his sudden and mysterious indisposition. They had seen one another frequently within the last few days, being possessed of abundant leisure. This morning, October 11th to be precise, they assembled themselves together as usual, and then it was that Mr. Mace surprised his friends with news of a distinctly exciting character. It was nothing less than the story of Paul Bogle's recent exploits, of which something was said in our last chapter. A correspondent of Mr. Mace's paper had sent the news by special messenger; it had arrived this morning. The politicians were immediately fired with excitement. These events, they decided, must be discussed with Mr. Gordon. They hurried to his office in the business section of the city. He was not there. His clerk suggested the Tabernacle, Mr. Gordon's meeting house. To the Tabernacle, accordingly, went Mr. Robson and the others.

Arrived there, they entered the meeting room and found, not Mr. Gordon, but a gentleman whom they did not know. Mr. Gordon's caretaker told them in a whisper that this gentleman had come in about five minutes before and was waiting to see Mr. Gordon. The three men eyed the stranger curiously, sat down, and then opened a conversation for the purpose of impressing him with a sense of their unlimited importance and astonishing intelligence.

They mentioned, casually as it were, the news they had received that morning from Morant Bay, and were gratified to observe that the gentleman (who, they agreed in their minds, looked like "a pure white man") gazed at them with more than ordinary attention.

"Them wont do him anything," said Mr. Robson cheerfully, referring to Paul Bogle; "them is too cowardly. Paul teach them a good lesson.

Him can't talk or write like us, for him haven't our education; but if it come to stick an' fist, he is there!"

"The utmost punishment the magistrates could inflict upon him," commented Mr. Bolt, "is the infliction of a fine. They will be afraid to proceed to extremities, no matter how impressive the promptings of their oppressive inclinations. Bogle has shown determination of spirit, and his promptitude of action, combined with the devotion of the populace who rally to his call, will have surprised the tyrannous plantocracy, and will have warned them not to proceed too far. If they fine him he will pay the fine: it will be a bagatelle. But he will not be daunted. He will continue his horizontal march towards the establishment of a new era, we assisting him in Kingston with pen and tongue. He will submerge them into acquiescence, for he has shown that he has the people behind him in solid phalanx."

Mr. Robson gazed at his friend admiringly. The latter's use of geometrical terms in ordinary conversation always seemed to Robson to indicate a powerful mind. Unhappily, it only awakened envy in the breast of Mr. Mace.

"They are acting as they ought to act," agreed Mr. Mace. "They are acting splendiferously." He brought out this word as a sort of trump against the "horizontal" of Mr. Bolt. There was defiance in his voice.

The latter graciously nodded. "Yes, that is the way to act if they mean business," he observed. "If you are going to perform an incident, do so with comprehensiveness. Let the other side see that you are not fooling, that you strike the iron while it is incandescent." Mr. Bolt was determined not to be outdone in the matter of polysyllables.

At this stage it occurred to Mr. Robson that a little prudence might not be out of place. After all, the stranger was a white man, and might be an enemy. "We don't even know Paul Bogle," he remarked, addressing no one in particular. "We never go to Morant Bay. We don't write him a single word, and, to tell de trute, I would never put pen to paper about de Government, for them might get hold of it one day. Paul Bogle is workin' all by himself."

"I put pen to paper, and so does Mr. Bolt," observed Mr. Mace loftily. "We are not afraid of our actions, seeing that they are all constitutional."

The door opened and Mr. Gordon came into the room. He was looking careworn and depressed, thinner than when we last saw him and obviously unwell. He coughed as he entered. "Mr. Carlton!" he exclaimed, looking surprised to see Dick in the same room with three of his henchmen. "Is there any news from your parish? Or perhaps you have come to see me about the money for the boilers? I am sorry, but—"

"I came to Kingston this morning," said Dick, "and hurried here to see you as soon as I could. Never mind the money now, Mr. Gordon; my purpose here is more important than that. Do you know if any serious disturbance threatens in my parish?"

"I?" cried Gordon; "how should I know? You have just come from St. Thomas, Mr. Carlton. I must ask you how you left the parish."

"I wish I really knew," said Dick bitterly. "Perhaps I should not have left it last night. But your friends here evidently have news if you have not."

"That is so," agreed Mr. Mace. "Information of an important character has been transmitted to me by special despatch. This is its purport." With due regard to rhetorical effect he told of Bogle's defiance of the St. Thomas magistracy.

Gordon listened with great attention, but to the surprise of his followers manifested no pleasure in the news. "I heard as I came in," he said, when Mr. Mace ceased, "that a boy from St. Thomas has been here this morning enquiring for me; perhaps he was sent to tell me about the row. I will wait till he comes. I am sorry this thing happened, though; it will give the Custos and the rest an opportunity to wreak their hatred for me on Paul Bogle and his friends."

"Mr. Gordon," said Robson solemnly; "you know how I always agree wid you. But this time I are obliged to part company wid what you say. They can't do Paul Bogle a single thing, for him have the whole parish behind him. He show himself a man, an' you would be wrong to discourage him."

"Maybe you are right," returned Gordon wearily; "but I am so broken down in health that I should like a little peace just now. I must write to Bogle and tell him not to go any further with this matter. He must depend upon the arm of the Lord more than upon his own strength."

Something like contempt was visible on the faces of his auditors as they heard his words. A derisive exclamation escaped Mr. Robson's lips.

They had no time to comment on what Mr. Gordon said, however, for at that moment the caretaker opened the door and told his employer that the boy who had been asking for him that morning had returned. The boy, he said, had a letter which he had been instructed to deliver to Mr. Gordon himself.

"Excuse me," said Gordon to his guests, and went outside. He came back almost immediately with the letter in his hand, and sat down to read it.

A groan burst from him as his eyes glanced over the first few lines, and then his whole body was agitated violently. A film passed over his eyes as he raised them from the letter and gazed speechless at the three men who looked at him with fear and wonder. Never had they seen him in such an awful state of terror, and so contagious was the emotion he displayed that they too began to tremble as if they had an ague fit. Dick went white. What did this agitation mean?

"My God!" exclaimed Mace, "what is it?"

With a shaking hand Mr. Gordon passed him Bogle's letter, which Mace eagerly seized and commenced to read aloud.

"The iron bar is at last broken in this parish," he read, "which all is left now is to put our shoulders to the wheel. The oppression has been long, but God will give us the victory, for we try to serve Him, and we must work out our own salvation and strike for our freedom. Every man is prepare and take oath to be slave no longer, and by the time this letter reach your hands we will all be in Morant Bay to sweep away all the fetters them put upon us. We have cutlass and stick, and we don't fraid for gun; we will drive them all out of the parish which belong to the people. Who to dead will dead, and the Maroon at Hayfield will join us if we want help. Pray that God will give us strength to do the work He call us to do."

A deathly silence ensued when Mace ceased reading. A peculiar ashy hue spread over the faces of the politicians, and their lips twisted convulsively. There was a roaring in Mr. Robson's ears and an awful drumming in his heart. He and Bolt and Mace experienced a feeling of physical nausea, and none could sufficiently control his tongue to speak.

It was Gordon who broke the silence.

"Poor Bogle; poor fellows; and God help me now, for all the blame will be put on me!"

"But why?" said Mace, speaking with an effort, his own voice sounding strange to him. "You are not there, and you don't know anything about it. Perhaps nothing will happen. Bogle don't say what him is going to do."

"No; dat is true," stammered Robson, whose hands trembled so that it seemed as if he had lost all power of control over them. "Bogle may not do anything; don't them have police and volunteers?"

"They will blame me for it?" repeated Gordon mechanically; "they will say I stirred up all the trouble; they have been saying it for a long time. They hate me, and now they will take their revenge."

"But what you do?" asked Mace. "You don't do much more than we, and—"

"We have done nothing," cried Mr. Bolt, speaking for the first time. "I have nothing to do with Bogle; I have never beheld him. I, I, I—" he broke off suddenly, his voice falling him.

"What you fear, Mr. Gordon?" asked Robson faintly.

"Bogle's letter speaks for itself, Robson. By this time he must be at Morant Bay; he is going there to fight. They can have no force to stand up against his; they will be beaten and slaughtered: Bogle says so."

"He will kill them?"

"Yes, I know Bogle's temper is ungovernable when once aroused: may God appease it!"

"God?" broke in Dick indignantly. He rose, towering over Gordon. "You cannot divest yourself of responsibility in this matter, Mr. Gordon! You dare not shirk your duty in this matter! Listen to me. The magistrates know that Bogle was contemplating some fool's act, and the volunteers were called out. They have sent to the Government for soldiers. But some harm may be done unless these people are appealed to by someone who has influence with them. Will you come with me, to St. Thomas, Mr. Gordon? We may be in time to prevent mischief."

His anger, his earnestness, impressed his hearers, and especially Robson. They trembled as they heard his words, and particularly when he mentioned soldiers Soldiers! That meant shooting. And Mr. Gordon himself was terrified!

But if Bogle could be stopped all might yet be well. Robson, as an old policeman, knew what effect prompt action had upon a mob and all his old respect for the white man's energy in moments of emergency came suddenly back to him. Had a Police Inspector entered the room just then, Robson's hand would have flown to the salute. Had the officer called him to attention, he would have obeyed. The agitator had disappeared. The old sergeant of police, ready to look up to his superior officers, ready to do what he was told, ready even to face an armed mob if courageously led, and to fight with his disciplined comrades against men of his own race—that was Robson now. He bent over to Gordon.

"Mr. Gordon, couldn't you send and tell the Governor? That would show you don't approve of violence."

"Mr. Carlton says that the Governor knows of it already, Robson, and in any case he would accept no warning from me."

"Then do what Mr. Carlton tell you, and go wid him to Morant Bay."

There was sense in this advice; but Mr. Gordon shook his head dejectedly.

"If Bogle was in earnest, the worst must be over by now," he groaned. "Poor people! No. The only thing we can do now is to keep quiet. God may have averted the danger at the last moment; all things are possible to Him. We had better part now, and say nothing at all. Answer no questions, and have no conferences. We are guiltless of any evil intentions." A wave of pessimism swept over him: "I will bid you good-bye at once, for I do not think that any of you will ever see me again," he muttered brokenly.

"You may well say that!" exclaimed Dick passionately. "This riot or rebellion can be traced to your influence. And now, when you might do something to prevent it going further you talk in cant phrases. I will go alone to Morant Bay, Mr. Gordon; but you will not escape if any harm has come to the white people there."

He rushed out of the room, leaving the agitators trembling and Mr. Gordon sitting as one stupified. Mr. Gordon's last words rang like a prophesy of woe in the ears of the men. Everything that they had said or written would be brought against them; they too would be victims; Mr. Gordon clearly had no hope that he would escape.

Had Mr. Robson attempted to stand just then, it is certain he would have collapsed in a heap to the floor. It was cruel that just when he had begun to believe himself immune from danger it should become so awfully imminent, so dreadfully certain. He could not think, he could only feel; and again that terrible nausea attacked him and he retched slightly.

"What are we to do?" whispered Mr. Mace.

Mr. Gordon shook his head hopelessly. "They will be harder on me than on anybody else; you haven't so much to fear as I. I can give you no advice; I don't know what to do myself."

A ray of hope pierced through the thick gloom that had settled over the three men; Mr. Gordon had now said that they had less to fear than he. So their case was not so desperate as his; that was one comfort. Mr. Bolt glanced towards the door. It plainly was not advisable for him to remain much longer in Mr. Gordon's company. A similar thought crept into the minds of his companions. The rats know when to leave the sinking ship.

They filed out quietly, and left him there. Once in the open they glanced round apprehensively, half expecting to see policemen advancing to arrest them.

"We better not walk together," whispered Robson; "them may suspect something."

The others readily agreed. Without even saying good-bye, each man hurried off in a different direction, endeavouring to look calm and unconcerned, in spite of shaking limbs and a strong inclination to break into a run. Every eye that fell upon them caused them to start. Never, they thought, had so many persons stared so curiously at them, they were being watched by everyone. The city was full of spies. Home was their goal, and each man, when he reached that sanctuary, professed to be ill and incontinently took to his bed.

Gordon remained alone. After the departure of the men he had turned to his desk, his head sinking down upon it, his soul a prey to despair. He could not think; all that he could realise was a vivid, lurid picture of what might at that moment be proceeding at Morant Bay, and the vision made him shudder. For hours the stricken agitator remained thus, and when it drew towards six o'clock, and it was already growing dark, he left the Tabernacle, casting upon it a long, lingering look, as though he expected he never would see it again.

All that night, as he lay awake, he imagined flames rising all over the unhappy parish of St. Thomas, and the dread spectre of a gallows loomed before his staring eyes.

X

Bogle Goes to Morant Bay

The town of Morant Bay was built on an elevated slip of land that faced the sea. The main road along the southern coast of the island ran through it; behind it the ground rose gradually into hills and mountains. It was a rather primitive place, consisting mainly of a few small shops and houses belonging to a lower middle-class order of people: the two most conspicuous buildings it possessed were the court house and the Anglican church, and it was in the court house that, today, October 11th, 1865, the Vestry was to meet.

This building was of brick-and-wood, two storeys high; the second storey was reached by two flights of stone steps leading up to a flag-stone platform over which a portico was built. On this platform the doors opened. Underneath the steps was the entrance to the ground floor, and on this floor were the public offices of the parish. The court room was on the second storey: this room was also used as the Vestry Hall. Adjoining the court house, on its western side, stood a smaller structure utilised as a school house.

It was about noon. In front of the court house was a large open space, and there it was that the volunteers called out by the Custos were stationed. Presently the members of the Vestry began to make their appearance, but without arms of any sort. They had brought guns with them to town; but these had been left at several houses in the town, the gentlemen feeling at the last moment that to go to a meeting of the civic authorities with weapons would be unworthy of their courage and damaging to their prestige.

Most of them nodded to the volunteer captain as they passed him, and more than one glanced quickly about them as they climbed the steps leading to the Vestry Hall. There was nothing in the aspect of the few townspeople who lingered in the square to give rise to any feeling of apprehension.

The meeting was called to order.

The Custos glanced enquiringly at the vestrymen. "Shall we begin now?" he asked.

They nodded acquiescence, and then commenced the usual debates over matters of trivial moment. The arguments were long, the details seemed unending, and as the time slipped by some of the men would sometimes catch themselves listening intently for some sound from the outside instead of to what the particular speaker was saying or the clerk was reading to them.

The tension became painful, but not a man would move. Everything that had to be done would be done that day; and though some could not check the rapid beating of their hearts they strove to display no sign of secret misgiving.

Outside, in the town, all was peaceful and still. The idlers who had been attracted by the volunteers had wandered off long ago, the volunteers were lounging on the court house steps. Thus three hours passed, and now the business of the meeting was drawing to an end at last.

The chairman looked at his watch, then glanced round the table.

"We shall soon be through now, gentlemen," he remarked, "there's very little left to do. I am glad we have been allowed to get through our work uninterrupted."

Another quarter of an hour past; then he turned to the clerk.

"Anything more today?"

"No, sir, that is about all."

"Very well; we can have some refreshments now."

"Thank God!" broke from one of the vestrymen involuntarily.

The incongruity of the exclamation caused every man in the room to burst into laughing. But one might have detected in the ring of their laughter an expression of relief.

All at once it ceased. Every man there seemed to catch and hold his breath, and the face of the Custos paled perceptibly. The rapid beat of a horse's hoofs came sharply to their ears, the notes of a bugle rang out piercing and clear, the voice of the volunteer captain was heard shouting a swift command. Above his call rose wildly another voice—

"The rebels are coming—they are upon you!"

"My son's voice!" exclaimed an aged clergyman who had been gathering up his papers. "God have mercy!"

The other men started to their feet: their faces had grown pale, their hands were clenched. "It is not possible," cried the Custos, "they would never dare."

"It is true," said Mr. Burton, who was one of those present, "Listen."

A distant roar seemed to fill the town, the sound of a great crowd shouting. It increased in volume every moment. Already some of the listeners could distinguish the words that were being shouted—"Colour for colour, blood for blood!"

Moved by a common impulse every man rushed to the porch and looked out upon the square.

A vast concourse of people was slowly advancing towards the court house. As the Custos and the Vestrymen showed themselves, the vanguard of the mob raised a terrible shout that chilled the blood in the veins of the little group that stared at the scene before them. Menacing hands stabbed the air as they pointed at the Custos, conspicuous at that moment as he stood in front of his companions and watched the wild, gesticulating, raving multitude. Pale as death, with a tightening about his heart which seemed to presage some dreadful calamity, he stood there waiting. The mob hurled curses at him. His gaze wavered for a moment, but with an effort he recovered himself.

Before the court house steps the volunteers stood drawn up two deep. They were mainly white and mixed-blood men; among them Dick's overseer, who had only that morning been summoned to take his place in the ranks. The volunteer captain kept his eye on the Custos, awaiting his instructions. The latter stared steadily at the advancing crowd, drew a handkerchief out of his pocket and waved it, at the same time calling out, "peace, peace!"

"War!" was the answer thundered back; "No peace; we want war."

The crowd halted now, and the Custos's eyes searched the foremost ranks of it for Paul Bogle. He soon perceived him. That leader was standing in front of his followers, a rifle in his hand, his head swathed in a red turban, his bloodshot eyes rolling fiercely. The Custos waved his handkerchief towards him, "Peace, Bogle, peace!" he implored.

Bogle laughed savagely: "It is war how," he cried with a wild gesture: "Colour for colour and blood for blood!"

Face to face with that raging crowd, now not more than thirty yards from them, the little band of volunteers looked pathetically helpless in spite of their guns. Amongst the mob there were women as well as men, women who seemed wilder and fiercer than the men, and who screamed and danced in an ecstacy of fury as they spun round and round, tossing their skirts above their heads. The men were armed with heavy cutlasses, a few carried guns, and the look on their faces showed that no appeal could move them now.

But once again the Custos made an effort to persuade them.

"Bogle!" he called out, "Bogle!"

Paul Bogle threw up his hand. This was the signal for which his people were waiting. They surged forward. As they did so the volunteers fell back.

The supreme moment had arrived. With a groan the Custos opened the Riot Act and began to read it.

A shower of stones from the women rattled against the steps of the court house and fell thick and fast upon the volunteers. Crimson streaks appeared on the faces of some of them. The mob howled with delight. Then, high above the tumult, the voice of the Custos was heard shouting, "fire!"

The guns spoke, seven or eight of the insurgents threw up their arms and pitched forward; the mob hurled itself upon the volunteers and a hand to hand combat commenced.

The unequal struggle lasted for less than a minute. The volunteers, having no time to reload, were completely at the mercy of their foes. Some of them were beaten to the ground, the others turned and fled into the lower storey of the court house for shelter, and prepared to defend themselves. "Follow them!" commanded Paul Bogle, but two or three shots checked the ardour of the crowd. Upstairs, the Custos and vestrymen had already retired inside and shut the doors. But the besieged men were now separated, and those above had no arms.

The volunteer captain grasped the danger of this situation and proposed to his men that they should make an effort to join the Custos. They agreed, and, making a desperate sally, rushed out of their shelter and up the court house steps. A few shots were fired at them, and a volley of stones, but they escaped unhurt. The doors upstairs were quickly thrown open and the volunteers dashed into the room. And now they were all together, a forlorn band, while the crowd outside, feeling sure that the imprisoned men could not escape, raged round the building and shouted imprecations at its long-hated foes.

The Custos looked around him; many of the men were wounded and in the faces of all could be read the despair of their hearts. The rebels still kept firing at the court house, and their fire was returned by the volunteers, sometimes with deadly effect. But each man had only a few rounds of ammunition left: in a little time weapons would be of no use to them.

"What shall we do?" cried the Custos. "Great God, are we to be murdered as if we were wild beasts! Mr. Price, will you not speak to them? Perhaps they will listen to you." This man was the only black member of the Vestry.

Mr. Price shook his head sadly.

"It would be no use, Custos; they are my own people, but they hate me almost as much as they hate you. I know my last day has come."

"Very well," returned the other despairingly; "I will speak to them again. Open the door."

"Are you mad?" shouted the others; "they will fire at you the moment you show yourself."

"Open the door," he repeated.

"We can keep those brutes off," said two of the volunteers; "we will fire if they make a movement to come within gunshot. You can open the door if the Custos wants to speak to them."

One leaf of the door was cautiously opened, and, the muzzles of two guns showing on each side of him, the Custos stepped to the threshold. His face quivered as he heard the savage scream that greeted his appearance. "How they hate me," he thought; "what have I done to make them hate me like this!"

He made signs that he wished to speak to the people, and the shouting subsided. He began to speak; his voice was hoarse, every line of his face was set hard; but the words came forth distinctly and reached the ears of those for whom they were intended.

"It is I you seem to be most angry with; I hear you cursing my name. I am not conscious of having done you any wrong; I have never sought to injure you purposely. I do not deserve your hate; I—"

But the insurgents greeted his speech with yells and a shower of stones. Two shots were fired at him, then he was pulled back into the room by his comrades, and the door was slammed and barricaded once more.

"We must remain here until morning," he said. "If my letter to the Governor reached him in time, troops must now be on the way to this town."

"We may be able to keep them off till then," said Mr. Burton, "If they don't attempt to rush the building. But if they do we are lost. I wonder what they are doing now."

They still heard the shouting, and now there was a distinct cheer, as if the mob were rejoicing over some achievement.

H.G. DE LISSER

"What can it be?" the Custos muttered.

He had not long to wait for an answer.

"Look!" exclaimed Mr. Burton suddenly seizing him by the arm. "they have set the building on fire!"

It was only too true. The school house to the west of the court house was burning fiercely, and the strong westerly wind that was blowing had swept the flames towards the roof of the latter building, which had already ignited. The besieged men looked on horror struck. The roof blackened, then broke into glaring cracks; flaming shingles began to fall into the room. It was clear that to remain there much longer would mean for them all a hideous death.

A hurried conference was held. There was only one thing to do, and that was decided upon. The tables and benches with which the door was barricaded were hastily removed; the door was thrown open and the men rushed out. The mob, not counting upon such a move, had withdrawn some distance away from the burning buildings; this gave the fugitives a chance. They dashed towards the back of the court house, where stood one or two houses and the ruins of an old fort; they reached these in the nick of time, their pursuers yelling at their heels. Once again they prepared to defend themselves.

Darkness was coming on, and under its shelter they might yet escape. So they hoped; but Bogle, drunk with blood and fury, and transformed now out of all semblance to a human being, had no intention of sparing his enemies. The firing recommenced, and Bogle's voice was heard shouting out a command: "Bring fire an' burn them out; don't let one of them escape!" A few minutes later a dense volume of smoke rising from the rear of the building in which the fugitives had taken refuge showed that this order had been obeyed.

And now, exposed as they were in front to the fire from the besiegers' guns, and with the flames rapidly approaching from behind, the doomed men began to fall. A couple of volunteers replied to the insurgents' fire, but ammunition was running low: clearly there was nothing for it but to make another rush into the open. Along the beach below grew clusters of thorny penguin and some stunted shrubbery; they might scatter amongst these and hide until help should come. It was a forlorn hope, but the only one left to them. "Are you ready?" the Custos asked.

"Before we go," said one of the two clergymen who had that day attended the Vestry, "let us ask our Heavenly Father to forgive us our sins and give us strength to bear what is to come." He knelt as he spoke, and the others knelt with him. One or two shots fell amongst them and part of the roof crashed down amidst a shower of sparks and blazing embers. Then they rose, clasped one another by the hand and rushed forth, scrambling down a sloping bank towards the beach. The mob cheered wildly and followed.

Paul Bogle saw the flight and the pursuit. The fight was over. And while the smoke from the flaming buildings hung over the town and the hunted men sought for safety wherever it might be found, Bogle's voice rose triumphantly above the shouting of his followers as he proclaimed himself the victor in that day's dreadful struggle. God had sent him to do the work, he thundered, and had aided him in the work. The prophecy was fulfilled, the day of oppression was over; now he was master, now would he clear the country of the hated white man.

"Victory!" shouted Bogle again and again, "Victory!" . . .

Fifty miles away the Governor of the colony was pacing to and fro like a caged lion, his hands tightly clenched, his lips set. Now and again he would look out of the window of his house in the direction of St. Thomas, as if he would pierce through the darkness and see what was happening there. One question obsessed his mind. Would the relief he had sent arrive in time? Could it arrive in time?

XI

Rachael's Warning

When Dick rushed out of Mr. Gordon's Tabernacle, one purpose was uppermost in his mind. He was tired, he had been travelling all the previous night, but now he was returning to Aspley as quickly as horses could carry him: not one moment was to be lost.

A word to his father, and he had started on his journey. Bitterly he blamed himself for having come on to Kingston; for now he knew, as he might have guessed before, that Bogle was bent on an expedition that only a miracle could prevent from having a bloody issue. He did not spare his horses. He was travelling against time. But the roads were bad, the heat was intense, and often he groaned as the hours passed and his progress appeared so slow.

When about ten miles from Morant Bay he changed horses, obtaining a pair of young mountain ponies with plenty of dash and go in them. While these were being harnessed he made some casual enquiries about the peasants of the neighbourhood, but heard only the same sort of stories he had been hearing for some months. No one had heard of any riot in the town. It was now nearly five o'clock, and he reflected that if trouble of a serious character had occurred in the earlier part of the day the news would already be known in this section of the parish. He drove on somewhat easier in his mind.

Soon he was but two miles from the town, with the sea on his right hand, and to his left high ground, thick woods and pasture lands. For over an hour, he had seen no human being; but now, not far in front, were two persons standing in the middle of the road and apparently waving to him: an uncommon occurrence. One, he saw, was a woman, the other a man; his heart beat quickly as he recognised Rachael Bogle and John Roberts.

Rachael quickly ran up to the buggy as he brought his horses to a standstill.

"Stop!" she panted, "turn back, Mr. Carlton; turn and drive right back to Kingston: it is war in de town!"

"Good God! you don't mean to say?—"

"Yes; me father come down this morning, and them is fighting now. It was John Roberts tell me this morning that you gone to Kingston an'

I run out here to see if I could meet you. Nobody know I come. Turn back at once, for God's sake, or them will kill you as them killing the rest."

"Tell me, Rachael," said Dick hoarsely: "have they beaten the volunteers?"

"Yes; De town is full of them; nobody can escape. It is useless your goin' on."

"Do you know if they intend to attack Aspley? But of course they will if they get the upper hand at Morant Bay—! I must go on at once!"

"You know what you doin', Mr. Carlton?" cried Rachael, horrified: "Jesus! Them will chop you to pieces!"

"I must take my chance of that."

He waved her aside and lifted his whip. As he did so there was a crashing in the thicket to the left, followed by a scream from Rachael. He glanced in the direction whence came the noise, and caught a glimpse of a fierce evil face, furious with hatred; the next instant a huge stone came whizzing through the air, smashing his hat and striking him just above the temple. He fell back as if shot, jerking the reins as he did so, and the startled horses darted off at a wild gallop towards the town. Rachael screamed and ran forward as if to drag the buggy back. The effort was futile. Then she turned with fury upon Dick's assailant.

"Still tryin' to help your white man," snarled Raines; "but dis time you don't succeed. Him gone to hell now!"

"You beast, you wretch!" raved the girl, "if I had a gun in me hand I would shoot you. But I will live to see de day when them will hang you for what you just do. You murderer! You watch me, an' you follow me to kill Mr. Carlton; but your day will come!"

"You' father's day will come long before mine, me good woman," Raines sneered at her. "Yes, I did watch you, for I know you, but when you call me murderer, what you call you' father? What he doing now?" He moved towards her, hate blazing from his eyes. She stooped swiftly and picked up a stone.

"If you come one step nearer, I dash out your brains'" she swore, and flung the missle at him. It struck him in the face and the blood started. "I will settle you today," he hissed; "I have let you off too long!"

But John Roberts, though he feared the Maroon, would not stand by and see Rachael Bogle ill-treated. He threw himself between them. "Stop, Mr. Raines," he called out, "you can't teck an' advantage of Miss Bogle like dat."

Raines saw that he would be at a disadvantage in fighting two persons at once. He glared at them both, then with one band wiped away some of the blood that trickled from his wound, and looked at it.

"You draw me blood," he said at length to Rachael, showing her his ensanguined hand. "You draw me blood for Carlton, same way as you tell me one night that him would flog me like a dog. He don't do it yet, an him will never do it, for you know where he gone to now. I finish wid him now, but I don't wid you yet. Wait till you see you' father upon a gallows an' ask him how he like it! As for you—you can wait."

He was gloating over the girl's misery as he spoke, and looking at his own blood as it the sight of it delighted him. "Wait till you see me again," was his last word, and walked off in the direction whence Dick had come.

Rachael gave no heed to his threats.

She was sobbing, sobbing with wild abandonment. Then she threw herself by the roadside and screamed as if in torture.

John Roberts went up to her.

"Miss Rachael," he implored, "doan't cry so. P'raps Mr. Carlton doan't dead, an' may get away. Come, let we go after him."

He helped her up and forced her to accompany him.

"But even if he don't dead he may try to go to Aspley an' may meet some of de people who will kill him," Rachael gasped out. "Them will go to Aspley too."

To this Roberts made no reply, thinking Rachael's words very likely to prove true. But her mention of Aspley caused him to remember one of the ladies there. He trudged on in silence for some part of the way.

They came to a trail leading into the woods, and Roberts paused. "Miss Rachael," he said hesitatingly, "you t'ink you can go on alone?"

"But why you leavin' me?" she asked; "where you goin'?"

"To Aspley. Miss Graham was very kind to me when Mr. Solway turn me away, an' I gwine to tell her to hide."

Into Rachael's mind rushed the recollection of the last time she had been to Aspley. Her father was master of the parish now; the lives of the white people in it were at his mercy. Miss Graham, who had treated her harshly, who had caused her to be turned away from Aspley as if she had been a pest, who loved young Mr. Carlton—why should Miss Graham be helped and spared? She could stop Roberts from going, or, if he would not be prevented, could warn her father of his intention in time.

"Why you want to help Miss Graham more dan anybody else?" she asked the man, frowning slightly.

"She very kind to me, Miss Rachael, an' you you'self used to say she was kind to you."

Rachael remembered. Yes; Miss Graham had treated her very kindly once—before she knew. And she had liked Miss Graham too. Joyce's face, as it looked on the day when she asked Rachael if she would like to see the white people of the parish murdered, rose clear and distinct to Rachael's mental vision now.

And another picture came before her. She saw the crowd howling and cursing before the court house, heard the shots, and imagined the awful end of the unfortunate men imprisoned there. The rebels would burn Aspley as they had burnt the court house; they would murder Miss Graham like that. . .

She covered her eyes with her hands.

"Go on," she said to Roberts, and there they parted.

Her way lay straight before her. She walked and ran, hoping that Dick might have fallen out of the buggy; for then, if he were not dead, she might save him yet. She uttered a cry when, at last, she spied the buggy at a standstill in the distance. Running up to it, she perceived that the frightened horses had dashed into some trees by the roadside and that one of them was down and bleeding. But Dick Carlton was not there.

Where was he? It was growing dark; unless he was near she could not hope to find him. She called his name loudly several times, and listened intently for an answering cry. None came to her. But of one thing at least she was certain: he was not dead, for if any of the people had come upon him and attacked him they would have left his body on the road. He must have escaped, she thought, and the darkness would shield him unless he had pushed on towards the town. She was near the town now; she would hurry on to see if he were there; if he were not she would come this way again tomorrow and search for him, should she escape her father's eye. She gave one last call, then walked rapidly away. He was not dead, she kept repeating to herself; he could not be dead. And he would know that it was she who had warned him, who had saved his life.

H.G. DE LISSER

XII

THE ATTACK ON ASPLEY

After leaving Rachael John Roberts pushed on to Aspley, choosing the by-paths instead of the main road, as he did not wish to meet any of the people who might form part of the following of Paul Bogle. When he reached Aspley he found that place in a state of confusion, for news had already arrived of the march of Bogle from Stony Gut, and some of the Aspley labourers had gone with him. No one had been at work, and the tenants, fearing Bogle's people, were uncertain whether they should remain where they were or take to flight. There was no one to give orders. At any moment a panic might occur.

Roberts pushed on to the Great House, and there he asked for Miss Graham. She was in the little storeroom downstairs, with Mrs. Carlton. He walked boldly in, all ceremony being set aside just then. He told them just what had happened, expressing his hope and opinion that the young master had escaped in spite of Raines; then he pointed out to them plainly that Aspley might at any moment be attacked.

All the blood left Joyce's cheeks when she heard of the attack made upon Dick and of the awful risk he ran in the midst of that blood-thirsty crowd, if indeed he had escaped. Mrs. Carlton moaned and hid her face in her hands. She feared the worst. Dick was probably murdered, and her husband was far away. For the space of a minute she was terror-stricken and helpless, stunned by the blow which had fallen upon her with such terrific force. Then pride came to her aid, and she recovered her self-possession.

Some arrangements had to be made for the safety of Joyce and herself: it was dangerous to sit there and hopelessly bewail their misfortunes.

"I have been through something like this before, dear," she said sadly to her niece, "and I know what it is. We can fly to no house near here, for they will all be attacked and destroyed. Aspley is the strongest place in the neighbourhood."

"Let us go upstairs," she continued, rising to lead the way. "We must lock and bar the doors and windows. Roberts, can you use a gun?"

"I t'ink so, ma'am," answered John Roberts, dubiously.

"Charles can; Mr. Carlton taught him. Charles!"

The lad, who was within hearing, hurried into the room at his mistress's call. Mrs. Carlton mentioned where Dick's rifles were kept, and Charles hurried away and quickly brought two of them, with a quantity of ammunition. Then some house servants came in, trembling and frightened, looking to their mistress for protection, and the little party proceeded upstairs.

Roberts and Charles next went round and made every window and door secure, and soon the house was like a fortress shrouded in darkness. Only one candle was kept burning in the drawing room, and no gleam from it could find its way outside through those thick walls and heavily shuttered windows. A light shower of rain began to fall just then; the night indeed threatened to be showery. Nine persons in all were sheltered in that house. Two of these were white women who knew that their lives depended on the bravery and devotion of two black men.

The servants huddled in a corner of the room; the ladies sat on a sofa side by side, trembling, terror-stricken, wondering what horror was to come. The men, their rifles loaded, stood in the front-piazza waiting until the inevitable attack should begin. Now and again they muttered a few words, but for the most part they waited in silence.

Thus upwards of two hours passed, and they seemed ages. The suspense was well-nigh unendurable, though the anxious women knew that every hour they gained was precious. Presently Charles stole into the drawing room and up to Mrs. Carlton. "I t'ink I hear dem, missis," he whispered, "Dem coming now."

Every one in the room rose and followed the lad to the window near which he and his companion had been standing. He had unbolted the shutter and thrown up the sash, opening the former but an inch or two so that he might hear what passed without. The only risk he ran was if a bullet should find its way through the aperture, a not very probable contingency. "Dem wont come too near," Charles explained to Mrs. Carlton, "after I shoot one or two."

Yes, they were coming; there could now be no doubt of that. They were singing as they marched, singing triumphantly; and someone amongst them was beating loudly on a drum. The ladies and servants listened with throbbing hearts. Charles thrust the muzzle of his gun through the partly-opened window.

The attacking crowd halted, and voices were heard raised in an altercation. "Them gone already," cried someone, whose voice Charles recognised as that of one of the Aspley tenants. "Them run away 'bout two hours ago. It's no use goin' to de house." Other voices were heard eagerly corroborating this statement.

"You lie!" shouted a man in threatening tones; "you lie; an' if I catch any of you tryin' to help de white people I will kill you like I kill dem."

"Dat is Mr. Bowie voice!" exclaimed John Roberts, and the crowd came on again.

It was not very large—some fifty persons altogether. Its leader, Bowie, halted in front of the Great House and surveyed it. The thick walls, the heavily-shuttered windows, seemed to frown defiance at him. He knew how strong the place was, and now it was silent and in darkness, forbidding in appearance and grim.

"Who is in there?" he bawled: "who over is in there, you better come out an' surrender to Colonel Bowie, or it will be de worse fo' you!"

No answer was returned.

"Do you hear me, you people?" called out Bowie once more. "Doan't make me come in an' take you out, or you will sorry you put me to dat trouble. De country belong to we now, you know, an' we can do what we like wid you." Still there was no answer.

Colonel Bowie lost his temper. "De damn white woman think them can treat we as them like?" he roared. "Teach dem a lesson. Fire at the damn place!" Two guns went off, and two bullets flattened themselves against the walls. The attacking party cheered. "Kill de white brutes!" shouted a voice, and again the guns went off.

Then everybody commenced to speak at once Bowie roared out orders; other orders were screamed forth by other men; some members of the crowd rushed up the steps to the front door and hurled their bodies against it; then there was a cry—"bring an axe an' let us chop down de door."

A scream escaped one of the terror-stricken domestics as she heard these words, and someone outside caught the sound.

"Them is in there," this man cried, "I hear one of them scream. Bring de axe, bring de axe!" And two or three men sped away to get an axe.

Then Charles quietly pushed back the leaf of the shutter which opened towards the step, and leaned out of the window. In that posture he could aim at the portico with ease, nor did he need to see it; the noise that came from it was a sufficient guide for his purpose. His movement was quick but not hurried. He pointed the gun, pulled the trigger, and the detonation was immediately followed by a wild scream and a precipitate flight of the crowd down the steps. He drew back swiftly, seized the gun Roberts held and fired that also. Then he banged the shutter to and crouched beneath the window sill.

An answering volley broke from the guns below, accompanied by curses; but those who fired and those who cursed had withdrawn so far that the shots did no more damage than the curses. A man had been killed, as the cries of the people below showed clearly, and the effect of that one death, and of the silence with which Bowie's threats had been received, had, apparently, a dampening effect upon the insurgents' ardour. They had come prepared for an easy victory and up to now had been repulsed with loss.

The noise below ceased suddenly; evidently some sort of council of war was being held. Those in the house could hear no word of it at first, but as the discussion grew more vehement the talkers raised their voices, and then something of what they said was audible.

It seemed as if some person had arrived and now was arguing with an assumption of authority.

Bowie was urging that the house should be set on fire! "Set fire two or three places at one time, back an' front together, an' burn them out," he urged; but a voice remonstrated.

"No! I will not have the place destroyed!"

It was not a negro's voice. Roberts, as he heard it, started and looked puzzled. To Mrs. Carlton it sounded familiar.

There was another argument below, and they could hear Bowie say angrily: "I am giving order here; an' if we don't burn them out, what we to do?"

After this, the talking again became confused; then, to the surprise of the besieged party, the crowd seemed to be giving up the attack.

Joyce turned enquiring eyes to her aunt: Mrs. Carlton shook her head doubtfully. "I can't guess what they are going to do, dear; but the house won't burn tonight. It is drizzling now."

"Them seem to gone, missis," said Charles; "an' it raining harder now."

"And by morning the soldiers should be here," said Mrs. Carlton to Joyce.

Another hour of that nerve-racking vigil passed. The window through which Charles had fired had been partly thrown open again, and by this window stood the lad, listening, and hearing only the steady patter of the rain upon the roof and ground and trees. They lighted a candle in the piazza, and waited.

What was that? Was it the sound of horses moving slowly? Mrs. Carlton thought she heard it. Other noises were perceptible also, faintly perceptible, but no voices could be heard. Charles divined what was taking place. "Them surrounding de house, missis, but dat wont help them!"

An explosion which shook the Great House as though an earthquake had caused the solid earth to rock and tremble startled the servants into violent shrieks. Mrs. Carlton wildly clasped Joyce to her, and the two women moaned with horror as they realised that there was no defence against this form of attack. Another explosion, and a wild triumphant yell rang through the darkness. Roberts' teeth chattered with fright. Charles looked at his gun doubtfully.

There was a trampling of feet on the stairs, in the dining room—and then the rebels rushed in upon Roberts and Charles. The latter fired, but a sweeping blow from a cutlass almost severed his head from his body, and the poor fellow, faithful to the last, fell almost at the feet of the young mistress whom he had always regarded as his especial charge. Roberts crouched on the ground unresistingly, and was contemptuously kicked. A tall black man sprang in front of Joyce and Mrs. Carlton and waved the others off. He beckoned to Bowie and whispered something in his ear.

"You must come quiet, Mrs. Carlton, you and you' niece," said that worthy. "We not doing you nothing if you don't make a resistance. One of them servants can come with you."

The man who had whispered to him went up to the frightened domestics. "One of you get up at once and help your mistress out," he ordered.

Joyce's maid, Maria, obeyed mechanically. There was another whispered conference between the man and Bowie. Bowie gave the order to Maria now. "Get some fresh clothes for you' missis, for we goin' away from here at once." He turned to his followers. "Search de house an' take what you like," he said, "but don't stay long."

The men scattered noisily, kicking out of their way the chairs and wantonly overturning the tables. They roughly commanded the servants to show them where the liquors were kept; and while they were collecting bottles of rum and wine and whiskey, and smashing everything they could not take with them, Maria came back with a bundle of clothes, and Bowie and the other man motioned the ladies and the servant to follow them. They went downstairs and to the back of the house, and here they saw that the big door and part of the wall had been blown away. There was a smell of gunpowder in the humid air.

A waggon covered with tarpaulin, to which a pair of mules were harnessed, was drawn up at the door. Evidently everything had been arranged to take them away. Their lives, then, were to be spared, for the present at least. But spared for what?

In spite of their terror and misery, pride sustained Joyce and Mrs. Carlton now. They did not wish to be touched by any of these men, so they mounted into the waggon hastily and unaided. They found a mattress in the waggon. Then Bowie told Maria to get in with the ladies, and the maid obeyed. A blast from his shell summoned his followers from their drink and their work of destruction; Bowie and the tall man jumped on horses that were waiting for them, and presently the procession started. Bowie rode before the waggon, the other man rode behind, the rest of the rebels walked in a disorderly, noisy fashion. Already they were half drunk, and the two ladies, as they heard their drunken shouts, knew that even their leaders might not be able to restrain these men.

XIII

What Became of Dick

As Rachael surmised, Dick had escaped, though by a narrow shave. His heavy felt hat had deadened the force of the blow which Raines had hoped would kill him; but he had been stunned, and there was a nasty wound above his temple. The horses had galloped wildly away, never slackening their speed until they dashed into the trees amongst which Rachael found them, and the violent collision and the plunging of the animals had shaken Dick back to consciousness again. His head was throbbing and racking with pain; every object danced before him; the light trap swayed from side to side and threatened momently to overturn. Dazed though he was, he understood his danger. He half climbed, half threw himself out of the buggy, and scrambled out of the reach of the horses' legs; then he remembered what was going on ahead of him, and realised with an anguished heart that there was little chance of his getting to Aspley in time.

He must wait until it was night, and then see if by some means or other he could reach the estate. He got up and tried to walk, but staggered; there were terrible pains in his head and it was still bleeding. He bound up the wound with his handherchief and hurriedly looked round for some place of concealment. The wood to the left of the road was the most obvious place, but it was damp. On the beach to the right grew penguin and stunted bushes, amongst which one might hide, and the beach itself was firm enough to walk upon. He made his choice and crossed the road; then, knowing that if he stood upright he might be seen by people going to the town or coming from it, he went down on his hands and knees and crawled along, keeping behind the bushes whenever he could. His idea was to get as close to Morant Bay as possible, and to learn for himself what had happened there. Even now he hoped that the volunteers and vestrymen had been able to hold their own, or that Bogle, even if victorious, had stopped short of actual murder.

By the time Rachael arrived at the spot where his buggy had been wrecked he was out of the reach of her voice. Not long after that, for she walked much more quickly than he could go, she passed him on her way to the town, though neither knew it. He was very near to her then, lying behind a cluster of penguin, exhausted by loss of blood and by the efforts he had made to crawl so far. It was dark by this. That someone was passing he knew, for he heard the sound of footsteps. He was thinking of Joyce and his mother, and Rachael was thinking of him.

Little by little, pausing to rest and to gather strength every now and then, he neared the town. Presently he heard the sound of a gun, and stopped dead, wondering if his friends were still holding their own. After a while another shot was fired, then another. "It sounds more like an execution than a fight." he groaned.

He went on more carefully now, holding in check his impulse to rise and rush into the town and face whatever fate might be in store for him. He was mad with anger and a desire to strike at those who were threatening all that was dear to him; he ground his teeth at the thought that he was creeping along like a coward while a rebel gang was murdering his friends.

He could hear the shouting of the rebels now. A red glare somewhere in front of him proclaimed that some place was on fire; many persons were passing in groups along the road talking excitedly, singing ribald songs, or laughing wildly. He was very close to the ruined fort; he began wondering whether he would be able to escape the eyes of the people who might be scattered along the waterfront of the town, and then strike out for Aspley. The endeavour seemed hopeless, but he calculated that the men must have rifled all the shops and would soon give themselves over to feasting and drinking and carousing. Then might come his opportunity.

Cautiously, foot by foot, he crept forward. He felt weak and weary; only his will, exerted to the utmost, compelled him to persist. Now he was opposite to the old walls of the fort; his knees were stiff, his hands bruised and sore, and at any moment he might be discovered. He halted to take breath, and just then he heard a moan.

He listened intently; the sound was repeated, and he dragged himself towards the spot from which it came.

The noise he made, slight though it was, was heard. A man's voice, weak and tremulous, spoke: "I am almost finished by now; why not leave me to die in peace?"

He quickened his movements and found himself crawling amongst penguin, the sharp edges of which cut his hands. Then he felt something soft, and whispered: "who are you?"

A groan answered him, then the man spoke: "Burton," he said.

"Burton! This is Dick Carlton. Are you seriously injured?"

"I am dying, Dick; it's all over with me now," Mr. Burton gasped out. "I was shot twice. They have killed the Custos and some of the others. I don't know what has become of the rest. They must be near here." This was said with many pauses and gasps, in a hoarse whisper, and the voice broke into a sob.

"Can I help you in any way?" whispered Dick, though he felt that his offer was hopeless; "what can we do?"

"I am past help, and if they see you, you will be murdered like the rest of us. Oh, the brutes, the brutes! what a day this has been, what a day!"

Dick crouched there, feeling that he could not desert his dying friend, yet torn with anxiety as to the fate of his women folk at Aspley. Shrieks of laughter and loud shouts still came from the town, but he judged from the lessening noise that the greater part of the people were leaving. For where? He knew only too well the answer to that question.

"Mr. Burton," he whispered again, but this time there was no reply. He felt for Burton's hand and lifted it; it was stiff and heavy. Then he cried like a child, bitter tears of rage and grief, and again began to imagine fearful things, things that to think of almost drove him mad.

Was the entire country in rebellion? Were all the white people being massacred, had hell broken loose at last? And Joyce and his mother up at Aspley alone, or perhaps being done to death in the house—if indeed worse had not befallen them!

Once more he set out on his journey, but his exhausted body would not answer to the driving impulse of his will. He crept but a few paces forward, then fell prone to the earth in a dead faint.

When he recovered consciousness the dawn was breaking. Along the rim of the eastern horizon the sea was glittering in a golden light. Shafts of fire came shooting up into the sky, which from dull grey changed swiftly to opal, then flushed into wonderful amethystine and azure hues. A gentle breeze blew over the surface of the sea, stirring it into ripples. The sun surged upwards with blinding effulgence, its level ardent rays lighting up the whole country and revealing in all their hideous detail the wreck and ruin wrought by the rioters a few short hours before. Where the shore shelved down to the sea the pellucid water was streaked with colour, purple and pink and blue, and under it the white sand gleamed, and curious little crabs crawled and scurried over the rocks that cropped up here and there close to the beach. After the dark rain-threatening night a glorious morn had come. But the town woke up to terror, and the dawning brought despair to the hearts of hundreds of men and women who during the night had fled for refuge among the woods and rocks.

Dick staggered to his feet, knowing that concealment was out of the question now. He glanced sadly at Mr. Burton's body, then walked slowly on; there were corpses here and there, but out of the bushes came creeping two or three wounded men who had hidden themselves in the dark as he had done.

The townspeople were up and about, and the wounded men were seen immediately. But the insurgents had gone, save a score or two of them; these scowled at the wretched fugitives but made no movement to molest them. They were gazed at curiously by some women, and even sympathetically; to one of these Dick called, but she shook her head and glanced hastily at the strange men who had evidently been left behind by Paul Bogle as a sort of garrison.

He must get a horse at any cost and escape from the town. The rebels had evidently had enough of killing for the present, but later on the few of them that were there would be reinforced by others, who might urge them to mischief. In the meantime he might be able to bargain with these men, and perhaps learn from them whether Aspley had been attacked last night or not.

He went up to them, and asked them if he could hire a horse. A man who appeared to be their leader shook his head in the negative. Would they tell him if any attempt had been made to attack the estates in the neighbourhood of the town? No, they would not. He left them then and went back to the beach, where he saw a coloured man whom he knew; the man was wounded and was bargaining with a boat man to take him off in his boat; he recognised Dick and invited him to go into the boat with him. But Dick refused. "I must get to Aspley," he said, and then the man told him that the rebels must have reached Aspley long ago.

He sat down on a log by the beach, burying his face in his hands. All that he could dare hope now was that the tenants at Aspley had befriended his people and aided them to escape. The house was probably destroyed and the estate ruined, but that did not matter if only the women had escaped. But if they had escaped, how long could they remain in safety with bands of the insurgents scouring the country and with the white men flying in terror for their lives? He groaned, and once again gave way to utter despair.

Over the sea came the deep roar of a cannon. Starting up Dick saw a steamer in the distance heading towards the shore. Everyone else in the town had heard the sound; in an instant the beach was alive with people all gazing intently at the ship which momently drew nearer. A flash, another roar, and the cry went up in the town that a man-of-war had arrived. Then the vessel was seen to come to a stop in the open roadstead, and one, two, three boats dropped from her side into the water. Panic seized the handful of insurgents who had gathered on the beach, and now every man and woman there was talking and gesticulating, and pointing to the boats which, propelled by strong arms, came darting through the water like things endowed with life. The crowd around Dick was thinning rapidly; Bogle's garrison were fleeing as fast as their limbs would go. Straight towards the beach flew the boats, each crowded with black soldiers and with marines; and other boats were now seen skimming over the water, the oars flashing in the brilliant morning light. The first boat grounded, the men leaped ashore, and a young lieutenant came hurrying up to where the wounded men were grouped.

He saluted. "Not quite too late, I hope?" were his first words; then glancing at the haggard, blood-stained men before him he added sadly: "it looks so."

By this his men were falling into line; in another five minutes the sun was beating down upon the fixed bayonets of the troops, and the townspeople were gazing with awe at the stern faces of the officers who gave directions and seemed to have eyes for no one. Dick approached one of these, the chief, and explained to him the situation in the parish: there were probably women and children farther on who needed help; he mentioned Aspley.

He offered himself as guide, if he could obtain a horse.

"Very well," said the captain briefly; "I will send twenty-five men to search your neighbourhood." He called to a young officer.

"This gentleman will be your guide," he said to him; "you will rescue all the women and children you can and obtain conveyances for them. Bring them here. If you meet any of the rebels, and it is not convenient to make them prisoners, shoot them."

His subordinate saluted and hurried away to fulfil his orders.

Dick went with him.

It was John Roberts who related to Dick and the officer what had occurred: Roberts who had remained all the night at Aspley hoping for the master's return. The rebels had had a long start; no one knew in what direction they had gone. "I must follow them," said Dick; "but the officer looked at his pale drawn face, and shook his head.

"I must go back to the town for orders," he said sympathetically; "and you must come with me: you can hardly stand."

"And leave my mother and cousin in the hands of those brutes?" cried Dick.

"Soldiers and Maroons will be scouring this parish in every direction within the next few hours. From what your man has said, it does not seem that any immediate danger threatens your people. You must go back with me."

Dick would have protested, but his wound, and forty-eight hours of fasting, had sapped his strength. He reeled, overcome with weakness and misery. The officer bade Roberts harness Dick's horse to a buggy, and in this he placed the young man, ordering Roberts to drive.

Then they returned to Morant Bay.

XIV

"Colour for Colour"

The interior of the waggon was not uncomfortable. The ladies could sit up if they liked; the tarpaulin prevented the rain from penetrating; yet they were prisoners and ignorant of their destination, ignorant of their fate, and fearing the worst. They heard the jabbering and singing of the disorderly gang that was leading them away; there were insolent shouts and boastful assertions in plenty. Nevertheless they were not molested; and after the lapse of an hour, passed in silence and agony of mind, Mrs. Carlton and Joyce began to converse in whispers.

Mrs. Carlton's memory went back to the uprising she had known in the days of her youth, when there was short shrift allowed to those who fell into the hands of the rebellious slaves. These rebels were no better than those slaves: why then had they not been murdered? It was easy to see that preparations had been carefully made to bring them away from Aspley; the waggon showed that, and the objection that had been made to the suggested burning down of the Great House. And the voice, the voice which they had heard protesting against the firing of the house? Mrs. Carlton was sure that she knew it. There was some mystery here.

All during the night they travelled, the rain drizzling almost incessantly. As they went on they caught at intervals the sound of distant shouting, which their own captors answered triumphantly. The whole countryside was awake that night. Rapine and ruin were having their way; there was nothing to check the rebels, nothing to disturb their feeling of security, their certainty that the country was in their hands at last. Had they indeed gained the upper hand? the older woman asked herself; was this colony to become what Hayti was? And Dick?—was he dead? And Joyce and herself. . . ?

A sort of torpor stole over them as the morning dawned: a torpor born of weariness and despair. They were roused with a start. The waggon had stopped, and Bowie had come up to it and was telling Maria that they might alight for a few minutes if they wished; and have something to eat. He added that it was useless for them to attempt an escape, which indeed they already knew.

They alighted from the waggon, and found that they were alone. But they could hear the men talking among the trees nearby, and preparing breakfast. Maria got them some water in a tin can lent to her by one of these men, and they made some sort of toilet. Then the girl brought them some coffee in a can, some bread, and a tin of meat which had been stolen out of the store room at Aspley. They managed to swallow a little of the coffee, but could not eat.

The halt lasted for close upon an hour. Just before they started off, they heard the rebels arranging their plans. The main body proposed to leave them there: they were going to attack an estate in the neighbourhood. Ten men were to accompany them, with Bowie and his tall, silent friend. Mrs. Carlton sent Maria to ask whither they were being taken. Bowie laughed and rudely said they need not trouble about that. They caught again the sound of the voice that had puzzled Mrs. Carlton the night before: it was lifted in rebuke of Bowie's rudeness, and it seemed to them that Bowie was answering angrily.

"Joyce," whispered Mrs. Carlton, so that Maria might not hear: "did you hear the man who was speaking to Bowie just now?"

Joyce nodded yes.

"Whose voice was his like, do you think?"

Her niece hesitated a moment, then said. "Mr. Solway's; but this man is black."

"It is easy to blacken one's face and hands. . . Dick horse-whipped him. . ."

"Then you think? . . ."

"He has allied himself with the rebels, in revenge. He was always worthless. I understand everything now, dear; the blowing up of the door, the waggon. These people would never have thought of such things.

"What can he mean to do with us, Aunt Gertrude?"

"God knows. He is keeping out of our way for the present. He doesn't know we have found him out; we had better not let him know. The Maroon who attacked Dick was his servant, Joyce."

They fell to silence then, each thinking. They were astonished at the discovery they had made, and Mrs. Carlton especially was horrified. Solway, a white man, a planter, allying himself with negro rebels! The thing was almost incredible. Perhaps he had planned Dick's murder: she knew his passionate disposition. To what further depths could he not now sink!

But to Joyce the discovery that Solway was leading the gang was a sort of relief. The awful, ultimate horror upon which her mind had dwelt with maddening intensity all through the night: surely that was impossible now. This desertion of the white man's cause was base enough, this leaguing with rebels; she felt contempt for the man, loathing, detestation. But for him, Aspley might have held out until assistance had arrived. But at the least he would save her from disgrace at the hands of the savages that were singing and shouting around her. Save her from them—but for what? Whither were she and her aunt being taken?

The tedious journey continued; the singing ceased. Some of the men were talking querulously now; the way was long, they grumbled; they were tired, they wanted to turn back; what was the meaning of this journey?

Some of them began to argue with Bowie. He assured them that they would reach that night the place to which they were bound, and that he was acting under special orders from Paul Bogle. This did not satisfy them. They were growing insubordinate.

"Who is dis man wid you, who don't say a word to we?" one of them demanded suspiciously, and Bowie evaded the question with a laugh. The man alluded to pretended as though he had not heard, but once again the query was put, and this time with angry insistence.

"Him is from St. James," Bowie now answered, having had time to invent a lie. "Him is from St. James, an' you better mind what you say about him. Him is a friend of de Maroons."

This silenced the insubordinate for a while, but they looked upon the mysterious stranger with no friendly eyes.

Mr. Solway, in the meantime, was controlling his temper with an effort. He knew that these rebels were dangerous, though they had not yet suspected who he was. Already he was not on the best terms with Bowie, whose designs he had checked more than once since the attack on Aspley had begun, and who refrained from breaking openly with him only because of his fear of Raines. Bowie distrusted him, and there was no knowing when his distrust, and the natural insolence of the man, would sweep away the restraints that hitherto had kept him faithful to his arrangement.

Solway had been thinking bitterly all during the night; and with the daylight, with every hour that passed, the situation in which he found himself was outlined clearly and still more clearly in his mind. He had begun to see himself as he was; something within his nature stirred and he was conscious of self-contempt.

He was disguised as a negro, was riding with these men as a companion, as a fellow rebel. He angrily repudiated the idea, but it persisted. He hated the men around him, hated the rebels, already he was burning with a desire to see vengeance taken on every one of them, a terrible punishment inflicted. Although he had not been in Morant Bay, he knew something of what had happened there, and guessed the rest. And he might have prevented it! That was the maddening thought, the cancer that festered in his brain. He had been in the secret, for Raines had told him of Paul Bogle's plans, and a word in time might have ruined the whole plot and might even have brought the conspirators to justice. And he had wanted to denouce Bogle to the Government; that morning when he had ridden out of Cranebrook hoping to meet Joyce he had made up his mind to warn the authorities. But he had wished first, as he put it, to expose Dick Carlton to the girl who thought too well of him; then had come Dick's insults and the flogging—a humiliation which had changed his hate for Dick into relentless fury. After that his whole being had been consumed with a wild mad passion for revenge.

Dick was dead; he felt certain of that; he knew that Raines was implacable. He felt no regret at the end of the man he had detested all his life; he wished it had been his hand that had struck Dick down. He dwelt upon this in an effort to prevent himself from thinking of the fate of the men at Morant Bay, his uncle amongst them; but this he could not do. He had quarrelled with his uncle. That last estrangement between them had endured. But the old man had been kind to him, had loved him; and now he was dead, hacked to pieces by murderous hands, and he, John Solway, might have saved him! He had not expected such an awful tragedy; had not imagined that the rebels would have been so successful; had hoped and believed that the magistrates would have escaped and that what would have been at most a mere riot would have been stamped out in time. Had Dick alone lost his life—it suddenly flashed through his mind that even so he would have been a murderer, accessory to a dastardly crime. He impatiently fought down the suggestion. But try how he would he could not veil the fact that his hatred of one man had made him an accessory to the murder of many. This was what his revenge had meant!

"Colour for colour!" That was the rallying cry of the rebels all over the parish today, perhaps all over the country. And he, when the crisis came, should have stood by the people of his own colour to the last. He had failed to do so. . . yet not altogether. His being here was proof of that: He was saving two white women. But for this effort of his they might have perished horribly.

This reflection salved his conscience for a while. He dwelt upon it. He had known that Aspley might be attacked, and Cranebrook also, but Raines had arranged with Bogle that Cranebrook should be left alone, and he himself had at almost the last moment planned with Bowie the rescue of Mrs. Carlton and her niece. He had not ventured to stipulate through Raines that Aspley as well as Cranebrook should be spared, though, hoping as he did that the rebels would not be allowed to go too far unchecked, he had constrained himself to believe that all the Great Houses would be able to withstand attack until armed help should come. He had remained at Crane brook while the rebels had marched on Morant Bay. One or two men whom he could trust had watched the road that led to Aspley; it was these who had informed him of Bowie's approach from Morant Bay. On the receipt of the news he had acted promptly. Hastily disguised, he had ridden at full speed to Aspley, and had arrived in time to prevent an attempt to burn, the house. He had bribed Bowie into his service on the day that Dick had flogged, him, with Bowie as a hidden witness. His influence with the man, and especially Bowie's fear of Raines, had been sufficient to compel the rebel to obey his orders especially as he himself had suggested the blowing up of Aspley's backdoor and had provided the means to do it. His object had been to rescue the women; day-break might have found a larger force of people gathered under Bowie, and then nothing could have saved the besieged.

Up to now he had succeeded. Had he, after all, done so badly? Would any warning from him to the Government have prevented the outbreak? Why blame himself when, no doubt, his way of acting had been the providential means of this rescue? "Perhaps I am the only man in this parish," he thought," who has been able to save a woman."

But he did not like the muttering of the men, and Bowie's attitude was not reassuring. The successful rebel was in many ways, subtle and obvious, a different man from the peasant farmer whom he had awed into respect even a few hours before Bowie spoke to him now as to an equal; there was a suggestion in his manner as though he knew he was master of the situation. Perhaps Bowie guessed that he could have no sympathy with those who were crying "colour for colour" and who had dipped their hands in the blood of his people.

His plan was a simple one. He was taking Mrs. Carlton and Joyce to Port Morant, where there might be a ship of some sort. There might be some white and mixed-blood people at that port, and these would be of assistance if Bowie and his men should revolt against him. As he had promised Bowie, he would pay these men liberally for the work they had done, though that would not prevent him from hunting them down as rebels afterwards. They imagined that Raines with his Maroons were with them! It would not be long before they discovered their mistake—curse them!

In the meantime he must hurry on; he could not arrive one moment too soon at Port Morant. Another whole night in the woods, and what might not happen?

Thus his thoughts; but ever the feeling grew that he was forever damned as a traitor.

A halt was made at sunset and some food prepared. The rebels drank more liquor, wasted time, refused at first to proceed. Bowie, affected too by drink, was distinctly surly now. He knew that his followers were eyeing Solway suspiciously, were aware that he was disguised; they had noticed that he kept himself from them as well as from the ladies when these left the waggon, and this behaviour angered them. Bowie feared for his authority and began to ask himself why he should any longer obey Mr. Solway's behests. On Solway trying to speak to him as they started once more, he bluntly refused to pay any attention.

But they made good progress, and Solway began to breathe more freely. Soon they were near to Port Morant, soon they would be within hailing distance of the town: the men knew it and began to talk about it. "Why you goin' to Port Morant. Mr. Bowie?" peremptorily asked one of them; "an' why these two white females is to drive in cart while we walk?" The man spoke in a loud tone, and evidently at the instigation of the others. The waggon-driver pulled up his mules at once. "Trouble begins here," muttered Solway, and felt for his revolver.

He moved to Bowie's side and whispered something. "Tell them you'self," retarted Bowie sharply. "I am no sarvant of yours."

Bowie's words were overheard by Mrs. Carlton and Joyce. They clung to one another, feeling that a crisis had come.

"Who is dis man, Mr. Bowie?" demanded the rebel who had asked that same question some hours earlier. Mr. Bowie's answer was a reckless laugh.

"We doan't understand all dis sort of dam foolishness," continued the speaker. "Port Morant is de worst place for we to go to, for we are not numerous, an' white people may be dere. An' why should we, teck dese females to Port Morant? Teck them out of de waggon an' make us see them. I know de young one; she pretty enough for me."

A ribald laugh welcomed his words, and the men began to move towards the waggon. Solway placed himself beside it. "Bowie," he called out, forgetting under the stress of the moment even to try to disguise his voice: "Bowie, I am depending upon you!"

"Stop!" shouted one of the men. "Dat is not a black man, though his face is black. I know it all de time! Who him is?"

"Him is a white man, a white man!" cried the others, certain now that some deception was being practised upon them. "Him is a white man trying to help de white females. Don't let them escape, don't let them escape! Colour for colour!" And as one man they surged forward.

"Colour for colour it is, them," shouted Solway desperately, carried away now with rage, bitterness, and a feeling of remorse that he had betrayed two women of his race into the hands of a drunken crew who might shame and murder them. "Colour for colour, and I am a white man! Off with you, quick! or I will send some of you to hell." He fired his revolver as he spoke.

But Bowie was not a coward. He rode straight at Solway and tried to throw him from his horse. The cutlasses of his men swung in the air, and sudden stabbing pains warned Solway that he was wounded. He went mad now; he was wildly aware that he was not only fighting for life, fighting to save Joyce and the mother of the man he had hated, but fighting also to avenge the murdered men in Morant Bay, upon whose horrible end he had not ceased to dwell.

"Colour for colour!" He would fight upon that cry. He emptied his revolver, not knowing if any of his assailants went down; he made his horse rear and plunge amongst them: they drew back in fright, but came on again with their wild cry of "Colour for colour! Blood for blood!"

He was down. The cutlasses flew high to finish him, when sharp and clear came a command through the sir—"Halt! The man who stirs is a dead man." With a yell of anger and surprise the rebels turned and made a dash towards the trees. "Fire!" rang out a voice, and two men fell. But Bowie and the rest were fleeing, and after them went a dozen soldiers, black men like the rebels but in the service of the Queen.

Out of the surrounding wood poured more soldiers, two or three with torches in their hands. A young officer was with them, and a tall, stern-looking, elderly man upon a horse, whose eyes flashed as he surveyed the scene by the light of the torches. Some of the soldiers had surrounded the waggon, a couple were bending over Solway. Amongst the former was the officer, and he had lifted the tarpaulin which covered the waggon. "Women!" he exclaimed, and turned towards the man on the horse. "There are two ladies here, sir, he explained, "the rebels must have been carrying them off."

"Ah!" exclaimed the latter. Then: "help them out!"

He glanced at the bodies lying on the ground. "Are they dead?" he asked.

"All but one, sir; he has been wounded by the others but is still alive."

A soldier held a torch low down, while the officer helped Mrs. Carlton and Joyce to the ground. The man on the horse dismounted and drew near to the ladies. But these were hurrying to the spot where Solway lay, his face bleeding profusely and showing white here and there where the black dye had been rubbed off." This man is disguised, Your Excellency," cried the lieutenant. "He seems to be a white man."

The Governor, for it was he, darted a sharp glance at the face of the dying man. The wish flashed through Solway's mind that he might die unknown, but he knew this could not be. If only he could hide the truth, could save his name from being known as that of a renegade, that of a traitor to his people! This was now the desire that possessed him, forced him to speech. He struggled to lift his head and a soldier raised it gently.

"I am a white man," he muttered weakly: "Solway of Cranebrook. I was trying to save the women. . . Stained my face. . . it was the only way."

His eyes sought those of Joyce, there was supplication in that wild, piteous look "I was trying to save you," he murmured and seemed to wait for her reply.

"I know," she answered, pitying, and covered her face with her hands. A look of gratitude flashed from his eyes.

"We must remove you to the town, poor fellow," said the Governor, and motioned some soldiers to take up the wounded man. He turned to the ladies. "I arrived at Port Morant an hour ago by steamer," he said quickly. "We heard the firing and hastened here. Not too late, I am glad to say."

H.G. DE LISSER

The soldiers bent over Solway to lift him; they heard him murmur something, then his head fell back.

"He has fainted," said the officer.

The Governor glanced downwards. "He is dead," he said quietly.

BOOK III

I

At Stony Gut

For days it had been raining all over the parish of St. Thomas, for days heavy black clouds had been driving across the sky, descending low at intervals to break into drenching rain. Every stream had become a river, soft earth had been transformed into mud, the foliage of the trees was heavy with moisture, and the constant dripping of water from the leaves might have been likened to bitter tears. The sun shone through the clouds but rarely, at night the stars were hidden; brilliant sunshine and soft radiance alike were blotted out. There was gloom and sadness everywhere.

Wherever one looked the same depressing prospect met the eye. Black and grey were now the dominant hues of the landscape: of the mountainside, of the earth and of the sky. The birds shrank for shelter in their nests, the insects hid beneath stones, or under the roots of trees and in holes in the ground, domestic animals herded under trees, hanging their heads, disconsolate, and men and women moved about with heaviness in their hearts. Draped in grey, with black clouds hurrying or brooding overhead, the country seemed as though it were in mourning. A deep and awful melancholy had settled down upon it, the melancholy of death. Where but two weeks before you would have heard the sound of human voices, were now desolation and silence. In village after village, once fully peopled, there was hardly now a human being to be found.

Such a deserted place was Stony Gut. Night had fallen, night which brought but a deeper darkness than had enveloped the Gut as with a shroud all during the sad and dreary day. A death-like stillness pervaded the village; every but save one was empty, and in that one a miserable tin lamp flickered and smoked. There were three persons in the hut, a boy, a very old woman and a young woman, and for more than an hour these had not exchanged a single word. The young woman was seated on a chair drawn close to a table, her arms were outstretched on the table, her head rested on it, face downwards. For a long while she had remained thus, not moving. The boy was seated on a box, his eyes fixed on the closed door as if he were expecting some one; the old woman was crouching on the floor, and she too was watching the door. Her gaze indicated impatience; her clawlike fingers moved incessantly, she seemed to be mumbling something to herself and she looked afraid. Presently she reached over towards the young woman and pulled at her skirt.

"Rachael, you hear dat?"

Rachael lifted her head wearily and listened: the boy had sprung up and had put his hand upon the latch of the door.

Distant, almost inaudible, the faint tooting of a horn came to them through the heavy silence of the night; the sound died away; then once again they heard it.

The old woman rose hastily, her face alive with fright.

"Dat is not him, Rachael. Paul Bogie would come quiet if him was comin' at all."

She hobbled to the door and opened it. The rain had ceased falling for some time, but the rivulets formed by it were still running noisily. She bent half-way out of the hut and listened, her heart in her ears. The tooting of the horn came to her much more distinctly now.

Mother Bicknell wheeled round with a rapidity remarkable for a woman of her age. She grasped Rachael by the arm and shook her. Rachael's head had again fallen downwards, as though she cared to hear and see nothing of what might pass.

"Rachael, Rachael," the old woman entreated. "come! It is de Maroon an' de sodjers. It is de Maroon horn we hear."

"Even suppose it is, where we to go to?" asked the girl, raising her head and looking at the old woman with spiritless eyes.

"We can hide in de bush near here till them all gone away. If we stay here dem will catch us."

"I been hiding long enough. I been hiding day after day, an' I am sick of it now. I don't do nothing an' I don't see why them should harm me. How long we to go on hiding, wid de rain wetting us day after day, an' sometimes not a bite to eat?"

The tooting of the horn was very insistent.

"Stay if you want to stay," rejoined Mother Bicknell; "I wi' hide. You' father not coming here tonight, an' if them catch me them wont spare me."

She stayed for no more words. Out of the hut she hurried, and the boy followed her, casting a glance of amazement at Rachael, who had again resumed her posture of utter abandonment. Mother Bicknell and he crept into a cane-field near at hand and hid among the canes. They hardly dared to breathe as they listened to the war horn of the Maroons proclaiming the approach of those dreaded auxiliaries of the Government.

Rachael heard it too, heard it distinctly, but her tired body and dazed, grief-stricken mind felt incapable of any further effort. It was difficult to recognise in her now the happy laughing girl of a few short months ago; she was thin, emaciated, and looked at every object with wandering, distraught eyes. Suffering was expressed in her every feature, her every movement.

After the fight at Morant Bay was over, on the day when the magistrates were murdered, she had been forced to go back to Stony Gut by Bogle. Early next morning she had been sent to a neighbouring village by her father to summon come men he wanted. She had performed this errand, and then had hurried back to Stony Gut. From there she had hoped to be able to go down to Morant Bay to look for Dick; but on her return to Stony Gut she had found the village in a state of confusion. News had come to Bogle that troops had arrived at Morant Bay, and though he had some five hundred men with him, and might be joined later on by several hundreds more, his followers began to waver. They had risen, had struck one blow, had indulged in a brief orgy of terror and blood. Then, swiftly, had come reaction and fear, and Bogie now found his authority slipping away. All were for abandoning Stony Gut as being much too near to Morant Bay, and Bogle was compelled to bow to their wishes. They were going farther north, and the women and children were also making the exodus. Rachael could do nothing save accompany her father.

After that they had been constantly on the move. The men began to desert, each one now eager to save himself by flight or surrender. The women went where they could. Bogle's victory had lasted for one day only; now he himself was a fugitive and a reward of four hundred pounds had been offered for his capture. Followed by a small number of men, he had parted from Rachael and his wife two days before, and Rachael had gone on to Jigger-foot Market. This village she had found deserted; but Mother Bicknell was still there. On Rachael's mentioning that she was going on to Stony Gut, the old woman, terrified at being left alone once more, had begged to be allowed to accompany her.

They had arrived that day, and later on the boy had appeared, having been sent by Paul Bogle to spy out the situation. Bogle would come on to Stony Gut that night if no danger threatened there; if there was any danger the boy should return to tell him what it was. Mother Bicknell was glad when she heard that Bogle was coming; she was afraid of loneliness. Rachael received the news with indifference; nothing seemed to interest her any more.

She felt that her father could not escape, and she saw that his family was ruined. She herself, although she knew she was guiltless of any punishable act, was a wanderer. Her strength had given out; she had not the endurance of the women who worked in the fields, and there were days on which she had starved. Not an hour had passed without her wondering whether Dick had escaped, whether he had managed to get away, or had been killed, like so many of the white men at Morant Bay. She had asked her father nothing, and those to whom she had spoken could tell her nothing. Perhaps he was dead; dead, although she had warned him and had tried to save him. They might know at Aspley, and her chief reason for returning to Stony Gut was that she might be able to walk over to Aspley and learn the news. There, too, she would be safe, for she knew many of the people at Aspley; and the tenants, as she had heard, had remained loyal, and therefore had nothing to fear.

Rachael wondered whether the ladies at Aspley had escaped. She hoped so. She had seen enough of murder and bloodshed to sicken her soul: she wondered how her father could have been so cruel, so terribly revengeful. But others, she had thought since that awful day at Morant Bay, others could be as cruel as he was; for the punishments of which she had heard were terrible. The white man was striking now, and striking with a merciless hand.

When Mother Bicknell, on hearing the horn of the Maroons, advised her to escape, she had already made up her mind to be a fugitive no longer. No one could say that she had done any wrong; they could not blame her for going where her father compelled her to go. Besides, she was too weary, too utterly broken to move. It seemed to her that for the past week, day by day, night after night, she had done nothing but skulk and crawl from one place to another, always half starved, always in dread of discovery. She had scarcely slept. Even if they put her in prison for being Paul Bogle's daughter, that could not be worse than the hardships she had for so long been obliged to endure.

Very loud and clear sounded the horn of the Maroons; they had entered the village now. Had the night been bright a strange sight would have stood revealed at that moment. Anyone looking towards the gorge where it narrowed would have seen emerging from it a mass of greenery, as though the trees had been endowed with movement and were marching on the village. As soon as the moving mass reached open ground, it dissolved into separate shadowy units, from amongst which came the sound that had sent Mother Bicknell in mad haste out of the hut.

The Maroons, faithful to their ancient treaty had come down from their mountain villages at the Government's first call, and now were marching upon Stony Gut in their war dress. Each man had covered himself with a profusion of creepers. If one had seen an army of these people in the woods, and at some distance away, one would have taken them for trees. Tonight they had come with a triumphant sounding of their war horns, for they expected to surprise no foe. They had come to destroy Stony Gut, and afterwards to push on in pursuit of Paul Bogle.

An exclamation of surprise escaped him Rachael had risen and was staring at the newcomers, whose forms and faces she could but indistinctly see. But the light in the room, faint though it was, revealed her to those who peered in at her. "It is Rachael Bogle," said the guide, "Paul Bogle's daughter."

She recognised the voice. It was that of the man who had caused Mr. Carlton's death, if he was dead—Raines the murderer.

II

Rachael's Reward

Raines' exclamation had a striking effect upon the two white men who stood outside. Both uttered something and pushed forward to look at Rachael. Raines turned to them: "It is she." he said, "same one. But I didn't expect to find her here tonight."

The two men stepped into the hut; one was evidently a military man, the other was dressed as a police officer. They gazed curiously and sternly at Rachael, who returned their look with a stare in which misery and helplessness were blended.

"Where is your father?" asked the police officer in a hard voice. She stammered forth her reply: she did not know.

"She not goin' to tell you de truth, Inspector. I tell you already what I see her do wid me own eyes; after that, what can you expect?" This said Raines in a hard, bitter voice.

"That is true enough," muttered the Inspector. "She is a rebel, the arch-rebel's daughter, and herself a murderess."

If Rachael had been astonished at the stern manner in which she had been addressed, she was now startled and amazed to hear herself spoken of as a murderess. She could not understand; they were making some mistake: she looked from one of them to the other, then her eyes met those of Raines. In his face she read malice and triumph; dazed as she was, and hardly able to think or feel, she perceived that he had hatched some devilish plot against her.

They gave her no time to speak. "Take her to some other hut till we have settled what is to be done," said the Inspector to Raines; and the Maroon caught her by the arm and hurried her away. Out of the hearing of the white men he whispered in her ear: "Didn't I tell you that Carlton couldn't help you? Where is he now? Dead; and you—you will hear about you' self before long."

She returned no answer. He took her to a hut nearby, thrust her inside, and set half a dozen Maroons to watch lest she should attempt to escape.

All the Maroon's bitter threats she remembered now. They hissed in her ears. She knew that they were flogging women in Morant Bay.

She had heard that one woman, identified as amongst the murderers of a vestryman, had been hanged. But she herself had taken no part in the attack on the court house; she had done nothing except try to save Mr. Carlton; surely they could not punish her for that! She crouched on the mud flood of the hut, where she had fallen, her knees drawn up and classed tightly by her hands. The unexpected charge had taken her completely by surprise. Her accusers had not even mentioned whom they thought she had murdered. She only knew that she was a prisoner, and that Raines, her enemy, had brought the soldiers and the white men to Stony Gut. What would they do to her?

She waited in a dull stupor of despair, and while she waited her case was discussed in her father's house.

"We cannot take that woman with us," said the Inspector, "we may have far to go and we start about daybreak. We can spare no men to send with her to Morant Bay. We had better try her here."

"But when?" asked his companion: "it wouldn't be legal, would it, to try her tonight?"

"This is martial law," said the Inspector, "and we cannot stick to civil rules and precedents. I have authority to try every rebel we capture; we will give her a fair trial, and it cannot matter whether we try her now or wait until late tomorrow morning."

As the Inspector said, the whole parish was under martial law, and many men had been hanged and shot after the briefest of trials. The order had gone forth that no one who had been directly concerned in the attack on the court house or the murder of any white man should receive mercy, and what these two men had heard about Rachael had already convinced them that she was a true child of her father, the chief author of the horrors at Morant Bay.

Nor did her appearance at all prepossess them in her favour. She who had prided herself upon her looks, upon her dress, upon her superiority to the other girls of the village, made no better show tonight than some common country drab. She had been found in the very heart of the rebels' country, at Stony Gut where Bogle had planned the rising and the massacre. She had denied all knowledge of her father's whereabouts. Raines the Maroon knew her, Raines, whose people had remained faithful to the Government, and who was even now on the track of Paul Bogle. Raines, they felt, was a straighforward, courageous man: they trusted him implicitly: he was a Maroon, and the praise of the Maroons was in everybody's mouth. Why should Raines have accused her wrongfully? What could he gain by speaking against a young woman who was just like most others in the parish, only, perhaps, more wicked and depraved? Raines had told them two days before that, he himself and one other man had seen her attempt to murder young Carlton. The latter had escaped but the woman's intention had been murder, and that under martial law, was a capital offence.

They would try her at once. They would hear what she had to say in her defence. They would confront her with their witnesses: she should have justice. More than justice she must not expect.

They had Rachael brought back into the room, now suddenly transformed into a court. The Maroons crowded at the doorway to gaze upon this strange trial; the white men were the judges; Raines and an ex-rebel were the witnesses for the prosecution. Raines told his story simply, and with every appearance of truthfulness. He was at Morant Bay, where he had witnessed the struggle between the people and the volunteers. As he was a black man, the rebels had not interfered with him, and while he was in the town he had noticed Rachael Bogle among the women who were throwing stones at the volunteers; she was near her father. He had lost sight of her, and later on had slipped away, his intention being to press on to Kingston to warn the General there. Rachael Bogle must have left the town before he did, for while on his way he saw her and a man in front of him. It was just then that Mr. Carlton of Aspley drove up in his buggy; and he saw the woman stoop, pick up a large stone, and throw it at Mr. Carlton. The stone struck the latter and he fell back, then the horses took fright and dashed away in the direction of the town.

Rachael was asked if she had any question to put to the witness. She could only stare at the man as if petrified.

The other witness was brought in, a wretched-looking creature whom Raines now took with him wherever he went. His life was in Raines's hands, and he knew it. Raines was aware that he had been a rebel.

He swore that he had been concealed in the woods by the roadside when Rachael and her companion had attacked young Mr. Carlton. He was so afraid that he had not dared to show himself till two rebels had passed. Afterwards Mr. Raines came up and he had joined him. That was all he had to say.

They asked Rachael what was her defence. She looked at them for a moment in silence, then fell into a fit of hysterical raving. It was Raines who had planned to murder Mr. Carlton, she shrieked, Raines who had sworn to injure him. If Mr. Carlton was not dead he himself would tell them this. She had tried to save him; but Raines hated her and this was his revenge. She called upon God to be her witness; she called down His malediction upon Raines. She ended abruptly, having exhausted herself in invective. Then a burst of passionate sobbing convulsed her frame.

The judges glanced at one another. How could they believe such a story? What semblance of truth did it have? She had appealed to Mr. Carlton's testimony; but they had heard nothing of him at Morant Bay. He may have gone on to Kingston; anyhow, he could not be called as a witness. Besides, the attempt of the woman to cast the crime upon Raines was too grotesque for anything. And what of the other witness who had corroborated the statement made by Raines?

Thus they deliberated, and to them the case seemed clear. It might be harsh to hang a woman, but women were hanged every year in the colony for murder, and this thing with which the rebel's daughter had been identified had been a massacre, a massacre of white men and a rebellion against the Government.

The Inspector pronounced the sentence. They had found her guilty; she was to be hanged in the morning. Two Maroons took her away.

At first she did not, could not understand the hideous thing that had been done to her, the still more hideous thing that was to follow. Her brain refused to grasp it. She had not been brought up a heathen; she had learnt when a child that God punished the wicked and helped and rewarded those who did right, and surely during the rebellion she had tried to do all the good that lay in her power. Would God desert her now? Would He suffer her to die an awful death, guiltless though she was?

She dwelt on her sentence, and the horror of it grew upon her. She thought of Dick: surely if he were alive and could guess her predicament he would hasten to save her—he who knew the truth. But he was dead or far away, and she was to die, to be hanged in the morning; Oh God, it could not be true, it could not be true! She sprang up with a shriek, then tottered and fell prone upon the earth-floor of the hut, and there lay silent and still. There was to be for her no reawakening to taste of the bitterness of death.

For when they came for her at break of day they found her unconscious; bodily weakness and privation and the brief overpowering terror of the night had done their work. She was alive, but unless they restored her to consciousness she would know nothing more, feel nothing more, on this earth. They told her case to the officers; the military man was emphatic in his order that the woman should suffer no unnecessary torture, and Raines and the Inspector perforce submitted. The soldier, accustomed though he was to seeing men die on a battlefield, was heart-sick of this work.

The blackness of the sky had faded into a dull grey; grey also were the cliffs that looked down upon Stony Gut, and grey mist shrouded the trees and rolled heavily through the gorge. Greyness everywhere, an unearthly, appolling hue. The sun was hidden as though it would not shine upon a scene which desolation, silence and the ashy pallor of death alone befitted. They lifted Rachael's body out of the hut when the order was given, and bore it to the gallows-tree. . .

She passed from her trance into the Valley of Shadows.

Heavy puffs of smoke began to rise slowly into the heavy air. From all the fragile structures around they came, the damp thatch burning badly in spite of the fire heaped up within the huts. Denser and denser became the smoke, then some shafts of flame darted upwards here and there, and the burning of Stony Gut began. The soldiers and Maroons watched the fires for a little while; then they cut down Rachael's body, which they had been commanded to bury decently. Their work in the village was done.

When the men had gone and the last echo of their tramp had died away, a boy with awestruck face crept out of a cane field not far from the tree which had served as Rachael's gallows. After him crawled an old woman. They had lain concealed all night, not daring to move lest the sentinels should hear them, and had momently expected discovery. They had seen something of what had taken place, and understood more. The old woman especially had understood, and when the soldiers had gone she told the boy that Raines had been the cause of Rachael's death.

The boy was famished; fear was written all over his face and peered eloquently out of his eyes. The old woman was now past fear, and her failing strength barely sufficed to bring her to the spot where Rachael's grave was dug. The boy looked at her doubtfully, then called to her. She mumbled something but made no movement. Then he turned and left her and sped away, to find Paul Bogle and tell him the news.

III

The Man Who Waited

The rains had ceased in St. Thomas, and once again the country was glowing in a warm and yellow light. The heavens shone out, a vast canopy of dazzling blue, across which shining, snow-white cloud-islands drifted, slight, unsubstantial, changing their shape at every moment, and sometimes melting into the atmosphere even while one gazed upon them. Grass and weeds and shrubs were growing luxuriantly; every tree was a wilderness leaves washed clean by the rain and refreshed by the moisture which they had drawn from earth and air. The ground was still damp and heavy; the mountain streams still rushed downwards, brawling their way to the rivers which they fed. But the birds and the creeping things of the forest knew that the rainy season was over, that the sun would lord it over hill and dale once more, that the woods would once again be alive with sound and colour, and that every plant of use to man and beast would give forth its increase bountifully, and give of its best.

There is no autumn in these tropics. The leaves do not fall, leaving each tree to stand, a dreary skeleton, looking as if the hand of death had touched it. Wet and dry: into these categories are the seasons divided; and after the heavy rains the earth puts on its brightest colours, the hills are then most beautiful, summer is at its bravest and its best. And now the burning, oppressive heat was passing away; already the breath of a cooler time was blowing sweetly across the land. Change was in the air, change welcome and grateful, and every living creature seemed to know it. After the parching heat of August and the drenching rains of October was coming a season of light refreshing showers and golden sunlight: a time of plenty and a time of peace.

A time of peace, for the insurrection was at an end. Two weeks ago and anarchy had reigned triumphant for a brief space over more than two hundred square miles of country. Two weeks ago, and white women and children had been hiding amongst woods and rocks, terrified, horror-struck, momently expecting death. For a few hours, for two days at the most, the rebels had been masters of the parish; then swiftly the scene had changed; with lightning-like rapidity the voice of authority had spoken, the hand of power had fallen, and every rebel and malcontent had learnt that what they had thought was the Government's weakness was only strength disguised.

Every white woman and child had escaped. Every leader of the rebels, save one, had been captured, and many had been executed. Law and order had been restored by methods which had sent a shudder throughout the entire island: the velvet glove had been flung away, and the iron hand, grim and terrible, had been striking down all opposition with merciless severity. The politicians who had called upon the people to show their strength were all in custody awaiting their trial. Tomorrow Mr. George William Gordon was to die. Bowie, who had been caught with arms in his hands, had pleaded guilty to the charge of insurrection and murder and had died defiant, cursing his captors. But Paul Bogle was still at large, and never would the Government rest satisfied until he had been despatched out of this world, his end to be henceforward a lesson and a warning to every would-be leader of rebellion. Five hundred men were on his track, and his capture could now be but a matter of time.

Precipitous mountains overhang a little valley in the north-eastern section of St. Thomas, and the way up these mountain sides is by narrow tracks which only the adventurous mountaineer will climb. These tracks lead up to woods of hardy trees which send their roots down into the loose limestone rocks, finding sustenance there, although there seems but little soil on that bare and sterile surface. In the depths of these woods a man might hide for a while, but there he would find no water save such as fell from the sky and settled in the crevices of the rock, and no food, save such as he might capture with his hands: wild birds and rats. Up there it would be cold at nights, and day and night it would be lonely. No sound would one hear save the chirping of the birds by day, and, at night, only those mysterious noises which the darkness brings, and which to a superstitious mind seem a prophesy of woe and doom.

In the valley below there were settlements, but these were all deserted now. They had belonged to a band of rebels whose houses had been given over to the flames: their owners were scattered about the country and the fields were left to the mercy of whoever might wish to take from them the provisions which grew there. Once or twice during the last few evenings they had been visited by a man who came down to them by one of the mountain tracks which we have mentioned; a man who crept furtively, pausing every now and then to listen and to peer about him, as though he suspected an enemy behind every bush or rock. When he reached the valley, he would gather what food he wanted, taking by prefernce ripe plantains and sugar cane, things that needed no cooking. He took only a small quantity at a time, so that no casual passer-by should notice that the fields were being disturbed when he had supplied himself, he climbea back up, up, up, hundreds of feet above; beyond the woods to which the tracks led, over bare rocks to still higher clumps of trees whither no paths could go.

Nearly a week he had been here. He had come by little known and circuitous ways to this part of the country, had travelled by night, and had avoided the presence of every human being, white or black. Concealed, he had witnessed the burning of the huts below. He knew that the soldiers down there, were searching for him, knew that a reward had been offered for his can ture, and realised, as indeed he could not but realise, that he could not hope to escape. He could not live for long like a wild beast, without even the companionship of other beasts. He was not afraid of men; but at night, when alone in the darkness, surrounded by the vast silence of the mountains and gazing at the distant overarching sky, he trembled as he thought of those whose deaths lay at his door and whose spirits might at that momont be around him. Physically, Paul Bogle was a brave man. But underneath the veneer of his religion lay deep the superstitions of the African savage. He heard the voices of ghosts in every wind that swept through the trees amongst which he lay concealed; he saw the eyes of ghosts in every star that shone down upon him; he perceived their movements in the rustling of every branch. He was haunted; haunted by his own fears. The utter loneliness of day and night, the knowledge of his certain, approaching doom, the sense of his utter failure, the realisation of his ruin: this, and the ghosts that had come to torment him, were slowly driving him mad.

Yet he waited and hid. He still had an object in life a purpose to which he clung desperately as a drowning man will cling to a tossing plank in the swinging circle of a desolate sea. There was one spot on the mountain-side where he had his lair, from which he could command a wide view of the surrounding country without being seen himself. Once since the burning of the huts he had seen a body of men come that way, and he knew that, like the former party, they were looking for him. They were Maroons, and they had searched in their fashion; they had spread out in a wide semi-circle, singly and in couples, each one armed with a gun, a cutlass and a knife, and each having a horn with which he could with a single blast summon his companions to his aid. Bogle's eye had searched amongst the nearest of them for a man he knew quite well, and whom he thought he could recognise even at some distance away. He had not seen that man, and after an hour or so the Maroons had gone away. But he knew that they or others would return shortly, and his hope was that Raines, the man for whom he waited, would be amongst those who should come to search for him again.

IV

FACE TO FACE

It was growing towards sunset one afternoon, when Paul Bogle, watching from his point of vantage above the valley, caught sight again of the human hounds upon his track. The light was still clear and every object below stood out distinctly. He saw the men halt at the entrance to the valley, and one man amongst them appeared to be giving them orders. Presently they dispersed, each going in a different direction, their leader alone making straight for the village which had furnished Bogle with food for some days. Bogle could not discern the face of this man, but something about his gait, and perhaps also something intuitional, warned him that this particular pursuer was he for whom he had been waiting. The greater portion of the reward for the capture of Paul Bogle would go to the man who actually found him: Bogle had heard as much. If he surrendered, his captor would be all the better pleased.

He began to crawl downwards. A bit of sugar cane was all he held in his hand; a child could not have been hurt by it. He had left his knife behind, and as, taking care he should not be seen, he crept and wriggled towards the village, he seemed no antagonist whom a well-armed man could have reason to fear. When he had reached the valley he crawled to the edge of a patch of cane and there lay on the ground. He began sucking loudly the bit of cane he held. He guessed that, judging by the route his pursuer had taken, it would not be many minutes before Raines would appear upon the scene.

He had not long to wait. Walking cautiously, with his gun firmly grasped in his right hand, came Raines. His eyes glanced from right to left as he came, and his head was thrust forward in an attitude of attention. Suddenly he heard the noise which Bogle made with his mouth, and immediately halted. With his left hand he raised his horn, ready to summon assistance. Before he could blow it he heard Paul Bogle's voice calling his name in supplication. He lowered his hand and saw a miserable object lying on the ground not forty paces from him.

"Raines, Mr. Raines," whined Bogle. "Thank God it is you. You an' me was always old friends, an' I know you will help me now. I am almost dead from starvation."

Raines looked at Bogle curiously, noticing that the man made no attempt to rise.

"Save me," implored Bogle pitiously. "I been hoping to meet somebody like you. If you don't help me it is all over wid me now."

Raines smiled and took a few steps forward.

"It is you, General Bogle?" he asked, using the title which had so delighted Bogle a few weeks before. "You are the last man I ever expect to see here. Don't you know de Government want to hang you?"

"Yes; I know it, Mr. Raines," answered Bogle humbly, "an' them will do it if you don't assist me. We used to be friends."

"So you didn't win, General," ginned Raines. "The white people get the better of you. How you let them do that?"

Bogle groaned, then sat up. Raines raised his gun.

But Bogle made no effort to stand. He turned towards Raines a face so pitiful, his body looked so weak and emaciated, that the Maroon needed no further glance to convince him that Bogle had suffered terrible privations since his abandonment of Stony Gut.

"Where is your gun?" asked Raines.

"I throw it away long ago," said Bogle truthfully.

"That was foolish," said Raines. "Suppose you did meet any soldier or Maroon?"

"I couldn't fight them." replied Bogle wearily. "All I been eating is cane an' banana. I lose me very knife."

"General, you hear that Rachael dead?"

"Dead? No! How?"

"Them hang her: so I hear. They say she kill Dick Carlton. I did always warn you dat she would get into trouble because of that young man. An' he don't dead at all, as it happen. So you lose everything, your daughter an' all, General."

Raines had drawn close to Bogle now, contempt exhibited in every line of his face. And indeed Bogle looked a depicable object, for he had hung down his head and was sobbing, his hand still grasping his bit of cane.

A horn blew somewhere to the south of them and was answered by another. The Maroons were reassembling.

"Come," said Raines to Bogle; "get up. I will see what I can do for you."

Bogle struggled to rise, and Raines held out his left hand to pull him up. Then, with the suddenness and swiftness of an earthquake, something happened. Bogle had darted upwards and flung himself upon the Maroon, fastening his teeth in the latter's face. Taken completely by surprise, Raines dropped his gun and grasped his assailant with his hands, emitting a terrific yell as he did so. In the silent valley his yell rang far, and the mountains took it up and echoed it wildly. It rang throughout the valley, a call to the Maroons, Raines knew they would hear it and prayed that they would arrive in time.

Bogle had almost bitten off the Maroon's nose, and his Lands were about the man's throat. They swayed desperately for an instant, then fell; but Bogle was uppermost. His big thumbs pressed hard against the windpipe of the Maroon; Raines thrust his hands upwards and beat at Bogle's face, then tried to roll him over. The Maroon's mouth was open, his tongue lolled out, his face was streaming blood. He remembered his knife, and tried to feel for it, but his position shifted incessantly and he could not grasp it. He tried to scream, but that awful grip on his throat did not relax for the tenth part of a second—Bogle was choking him to death. A black mist swam before his eyes, a terrible drumming was in his ears, his eyeballs were bursting from their sockets—God! he was dying! Then Bogle lifted his head and dashed it against the ground, once, twice and again, and Raines lay still. The rebel leader looked down upon him with the glare of a maniac. "You hang Rachael," he muttered, "an' now you know how hanging feel. I will die easier than you."

Horn answered horn as the Maroons came hurrying to the spot. There was a hubbub of voices calling to one another, voices exclaiming in amazement. Paul Bogle rose from over the prostrate, lifeless body of Raines, looked round, saw and picked up his bit of sugar cane, and awaited the Maroons who came rushing upon him. They covered him with their guns, but he did not stir. They grasped him roughly by the arms and bound him tight with ropes they carried, but he uttered no protest. They cursed him, some of them struck him; but all the strength, all the energy, all the fierceness of spirit for which he had been renowned had left him. He could hardly walk as they dragged him away. He did not even glance once at the body of Raines.

On the morrow when, an hour after the execution of his friend and leader Mr. Gordon, they led him to the gallows at Morant Bay, he died in silence. His gallows was the blackened stone-arch of the courthouse, under which the white men had made their last appeal to him for mercy—and made it in vain.

V

DENBIGH ONCE MORE

Four weeks had passed since the hanging of Paul Bogle, and Dick had now been a full week at Aspley making arrangements for the carrying on of the estate during his absence. He was going to England with Joyce, and his mother and father were going also. He had had to employ a new overseer, the old one having been one of the victims of the Morant Bay massacre. The new overseer was a man with a good reputation, and Dick was satisfied he could leave the property in his hands for the six months that he would be away from the island.

This evening he was expected back at Denbigh; indeed, he had been expected for some hours, and Joyce and his mother had begun to wonder what had delayed him so long. Old Mr. Carlton had come up a couple of hours before; he had been in the city all day, and now was waiting for his son on the front verandah of Denbigh, with his wife and niece. He looked much older than when we first saw him at Denbigh, less than a year ago. He had aged much in the last couple of months, and so had Mrs. Carlton, who looked frail and worn. Which was not to be wondered at, seeing that for some three weeks she had lain ill. those two nights in the damp woods of St. Thomas having had a severe effect upon her. Joyce too was looking pale and thin; the roses had all faded from her cheeks, nor did she smile so readily as before. Often had she thought of their flight from Aspley, of their suffering in the woods, of their fears for Dick, and of their reunion at Morant Bay when a warship from Port Morant, on which as refugees they journeyed to safety, had called at Morant Bay, and Dick had come on board to enquire if any news had been heard about them. Often and often did she dwell upon that meeting: she would never forget it. Often too did she think of Rachael and of the strange silence concerning her. She knew that Rachael's father was dead, but the girl herself had disappeared, and not even the people at Aspley could say what had become of her. She had saved Dick's life and then had gone—whither? No one knew.

She thought of Rachael kindly now, very kindly. She wanted to see Rachael again, to help her if she could; she knew that the girl was alone in the world, unbefriended: the very house she had lived in had been burnt to the ground. Search had been made for her, and enquiries: Dick had done his best. But John Roberts could find out nothing, and the people who had lived at Stony Gut and the neighbouring villages could only say that Rachael had parted from her father some days before his capture and had gone her own way. Sometimes Mrs. Carlton would also talk of Rachael; and perhaps Mrs. Carlton thought more about the girl than Joyce did. Mrs. Carlton never looked at Dick but she remembered that Rachael had saved his life.

Mr. Carlton had had a late dinner and was telling of his experience that day at the Kingston court house.

"I had quite forgotten the man," he was saying, "but I knew him when he was in the police force, and a very decent fellow he was. He remembered me all right, and of course I did my best for him. They gave him three weeks in gaol: the others got off. I am sure they deserved punishment far more than he did."

He was speaking of Robson. After having been kept in confinement for some time, Robson, Bolt and Mace had been brought to trial before a civil tribunal, and, luckily for them, at a time when passion had given place to reason, and a reaction had begun against the merciless punishments meted out under martial law. The men had done their best to induce gentlemen of good position to give evidence as to their personal character, and Mr. Carlton had gladly responded to Robson's appeal. The kind-hearted old gentleman had spoken so warmly in Robson's behalf, had protested so stoutly that he had never heard any evil of him, and had always regarded him as a respectable man, that Robson had escaped with a slight punishment. To the surprise of everyone, Messrs. Mace and Bolt got off scot-free, their defence being that they had only indulged in frank criticism of the Government and had not been accomplices of Mr. Gordon, nor even acquainted with Paul Bogle. Which last was true. The abusive articles they had written were not considered distinctly seditions by the court. But there were reputable men, white men, who had heard Mr. Robson speak, and the memory of these was of greater value than Mr. Robson's mere declarations of inoffensive intention. When Robson heard his sentence he thanked the judge for his clemency and protested aloud that he would never again interfere with politics. Mr. Mace and Mr. Bolt also left the court room in a chastened frame of mind. They had escaped imprisonment, but their dread and fear of the last few weeks had made an indelible impression upon them.

"It was amusing," Mr. Carlton went on, "to hear Robson. He raised his hands and wrung them as if he were taking leave of public life. The poor fellow looked like skeleton.

"He had a narrow shave," the old gentleman continued reflectively. "If he had been taken to Morant Bay, like Gordon, he might have been hanged."

"They have all had a lesson," said his wife. "We might have been murdered."

"Yes. Thank God, you escaped. But what changes have taken place, what changes! The House of Assembly is gone, the magistrates are all to go; everything, they say, is to be different from what it has been."

"And better, let us hope," said Joyce. "There has been any amount of bloodshed—on both sides: I shudder when I think of it. I wonder if it is true, what Mr. Gorden said the day he came to buy the boilers at Aspley. He was arguing with Dick: I heard him. His words have come back to me very often during the last few weeks."

"What was it he said?" Mr. Carlton asked.

"That there can be no remission of sins, save by the shedding of blood. It is a text, isn't it? It seems a hard saying, but these changes you speak of, changes in the Government, changes in the courts, changes everywhere—they are only coming now, after the shedding of blood."

"I don't mind what changes are coming," said Mrs. Carlton bitterly. "Our blood came very near to being shed, yet we have never been unjust to the people. If it were not for Joyce and Dick," she continued, addressing her husband, "I don't think I should ever want to come back to Jamaica after I got home."

Mr. Carlton glanced anxiously at her. He could not but remember that on several occasions during the last thirty years he had expressed a wish to leave the island forever; but now that he was going away, only for a time as he hoped, he did not want to be reminded of that wish. In spite of everything, his heart was still with the country where he had spent all his life.

"Joyce and Dick have made up their minds to come back," he said, "and I want to be near them. I think we should like to lay our bones where our children are, Gertrude."

The moon was rising over the crest of the eastern hills, round and beautiful, and a soft silver light pervaded the landscape. Very clearly could be seen the mountains upon which they gazed: they towered yonder, ineffably calm and peaceful. In the sky, scattered far apart, a few stars trembled. No threatening fires blazed tonight on the mountain sides, no grim portents of ruin and blood.

"I wish Dick would come," said Mrs. Carlton; "I am getting anxious about him."

"He is coming now," replied her husband: "I hear the buggy."

He went to meet his son; and when Dick came in Joyce noticed that he looked sad, so sad that she wondered what news he could have heard. Then she guessed. It must have something to do with Rachael.

He eat very little supper. When supper was over his mother, who also had noticed how grave he was, tactfully retained her husband in the dining room, while Dick went out with Joyce on the verandah. He had already explained why he was late. He had arrived in Kingston in the forenoon, but instead of coming straight on to Denbigh had gone over to Spanish Town to see Inspector Strachey. He did not say what he had wanted to see the Inspector about.

"You have heard something about Rachael, Dick?" whispered Joyce. "I guessed it the moment I saw you tonight."

"You guessed rightly, dear. I have heard something."

"Yes? And—?"

"Rachael is dead."

"Dead!"

"It is only too true. I heard that Inspector Strachey wanted to see me; in fact he wrote me to say so a couple of weeks ago, but did not mention what he wished to see me about. I can quite understand why he didn't. He would not want to write such a thing. The blame is partly his.

"He was in Kingston yesterday and was enquiring for me, very urgently. I knew he was in St. Thomas immediately after the rebellion, and it flashed across me that he might know something about the fate of Rachael He knew all about it."

"What was it?" asked Joyce, almost inaudibly.

He told her in brief, broken sentences, painful for him to utter, dreadful for her to hear. As he spoke, her head sank upon the railing of the verandah, her face covered by her hands. She was crying softly, crying in pity for the unfortunate girl whose brief life had ended in so dark a tragedy.

Dick laid his hand gently upon the pale golden hair of his bethrothed, soon now to be his wife. "Dearest," he whispered, and found no other word.

For a space there was silence. Then Joyce raised her head and with tear-dimmed eyes looked towards the east and thought of Stony Gut behind those mountains, where Rachael's body lay in an unknown, nameless grave.

"Poor Rachael," she murmured. . .

THE END

A Note About the Author

H.G. de Lisser (1878–1944) was a Jamaican journalist and novelist. Born in Falmouth, Jamaica, de Lisser was raised in a family of Afro-Jewish descent. At seventeen, he began working as a proofreader at the *Jamaica Daily Gleaner*, where his father was editor. By 1903, he earned the position of assistant editor and began writing several daily articles while working on the essays that would fill his first collection, *In Cuba and Jamaica* (1909). His debut novel *Jane's Career: A Story of Jamaica* (1913) has been recognized as the first West Indian novel to have a black character as its protagonist. In addition to his writing—he published several essay collections, novels, and plays throughout his career—de Lisser was an advocate for the Jamaican sugar Industry and a Companion of the Order of St. Michael and St. George.

A Note from the Publisher

Spanning many genres, from non-fiction essays to literature classics to children's books and lyric poetry, Mint Edition books showcase the master works of our time in a modern new package. The text is freshly typeset, is clean and easy to read, and features a new note about the author in each volume. Many books also include exclusive new introductory material. Every book boasts a striking new cover, which makes it as appropriate for collecting as it is for gift giving. Mint Edition books are only printed when a reader orders them, so natural resources are not wasted. We're proud that our books are never manufactured in excess and exist only in the exact quantity they need to be read and enjoyed.

bookfinity

Discover more of your favorite classics with Bookfinity™.

- Track your reading with custom book lists.
- Get great book recommendations for your personalized Reader Type.
- Add reviews for your favorite books.
- AND MUCH MORE!

Visit **bookfinity.com** and take the fun Reader Type quiz to get started.

Enjoy our classic and modern companion pairings!

Classic & Modern